DEMONS ARE A GHOUL'S BEST FRIEND

This Large Print Book carries the
Seal of Approval of N.A.V.H.

A GHOST HUNTER MYSTERY

DEMONS ARE A GHOUL'S BEST FRIEND

VICTORIA LAURIE

THORNDIKE PRESS

A part of Gale, Cengage Learning

Detroit • New York • San Francisco • New Haven, Conn • Waterville, Maine • London

LIBRARY OF CONGRESS CATALOGING-IN-PUBLICATION DATA

Laurie, Victoria.
    Demons are a ghoul's best friend : a ghost hunter mystery /
by Victoria Laurie.
    p. cm. — (Thorndike Press large print mystery)
    ISBN-13: 978-1-4104-0777-1 (alk. paper)
    ISBN-10: 1-4104-0777-2 (alk. paper)
    1. Psychics — Fiction. 2. Large type books. I. Title.
PS3612.A94423D46 2008
813'.6—dc22   2008011504

Published in 2008 by arrangement with NAL Signet, a member of Penguin Group (USA) Inc.

Printed in the United States of America
1 2 3 4 5 6 7 12 11 10 09 08

For Jim McCarthy,
my agent, muse, and friend

ACKNOWLEDGMENTS

I'm often asked where I get my ideas for story lines. Here is the tale of where this idea came from.

Picture it: Arlington, Massachusetts, late April of '06. It's a beautiful spring day, and I'm walking to the post office when a thought occurs to me. I reach for my cell phone and call my agent, Jim McCarthy. "Hey," I say when he answers the phone.

"What's up?"

"Just wanted to double-check when the outline for the M.J. sequel is due."

There is some tapping of keys in the background; then Jim says, "That would be tomorrow."

"Ah," I say. "Okay. Cool."

There is a pause, then: "Tell me you're almost done with it."

"I'm almost done with it."

"Really?"

"No. Haven't even started it."

7

There is a heavy sigh, followed by some thumping noises — I assume it's Jim knocking his head against his desk. "Okay," he says after a bit. "Tell me what it's about and I'll call your editor and tell her it's going to be late."

I stop at the curb and tap my finger against my chin. "Well," I say, trying to think fast. "There's this ghost. . . ."

"Uh-huh?" Jim says, scribbling notes in the background.

"And M.J. hunts it down and busts it. . . ."

Pause.

Pause.

Pause.

"You're kidding me," he says.

"It's a work in progress," I say brightly.

"Tell me you at least have *some* idea what this one's about!" he says, his voice panicky.

"I have some idea what this is about."

"Really?"

"No, Jim. No idea at all."

There is more sighing and more thumping. I imagine Jim is gonna have one hell of a headache later. Finally he says, "Okay, okay, okay. We can fix this. I've got this book at home. It's full of weird ghost stories about New York. I'll go home and read it, and maybe there will be an idea in there that you can use."

8

"Cool!"

"Promise me you'll go home and think of something on your end," he demands.

"I promise I'll go home and think of something on my end."

There is another pause. I think Jim wants to say, "Really?" again, but by this time he's caught on and doesn't ask. "Call you tomorrow," he says, and clicks off.

Fast-forward a few hours. I am "thinking" *really* hard in my comfy chair with a bowl of popcorn and the telly tuned to my favorite show. The phone rings. It's Jim. "What's up?" I ask, noting that the time is after eight.

"I'm reading this book," he says nervously.

"Uh-huh," I say, muting the TV.

"It's dark out."

"Yeah?"

"I'm all alone."

"Okay?"

"And I'm creeped out," he admits. I should have mentioned this earlier — Jim is a big wuss when it comes to things that go bump in the night.

"How can I help?"

"Listen to some of these stories so I don't have to keep reading this book!"

And so I did. I listened, and none of them impressed me very much until Jim mentioned a ghost that was rumored to haunt some remote wooded area in upstate New York. This ghost was said to wield an ax, and he liked to chase people through the woods with it.

From that story, this one was born. So if you read this novel and are happy with it, send a kind thought to Jim, who took one for the team and for me — otherwise, you might have ended up with some dull story about a girl ghost eating popcorn and watching the telly. ☺

Special thanks, adoration, and love go to the following people:

My fabulous editor, Kristen Weber, who is beginning to understand why they call me "Last-minute Laurie." My *amazing* agent and friend, Jim McCarthy, who gave me the gift of this story and all of Gilley Gillespie's best lines. My wonderful friends Karen Ditmars and Leanne Tierney, who gave me Teeko and her sister-in-law. My sistah, Sandy Upham, who gives me love, support, and encouragement and who is "livin' the dream!" with me every day. My fabulous brother and sister-in-law, Jon and Naoko Upham. My amazing aunties, Mary Jane Humphreys and Betty Laurie. My fantastic friends who read my stuff and are quick to pat me on the back: Tess Rodriguez, Nora Brosseau, Dell Chase, Suzanne Parsons,

Maureen Feebo, Debbie Huntley, Janice Murray (we're all pulling for you, J-Lo!), Molly Boyle (and her mum!), Jaa Nawtaisong, Silas and Nicole Hudson, Betty Stocking, and Pippa Terry. I couldn't do it without you guys, and I'm so grateful for each and every one of you.

Andrew had gone a little pale, a common reaction to my intuitive abilities. "He's really dead?" he asked me.

"Yes," I said, and reached up to squeeze his arm. "I feel he died shortly after he left home."

Andrew swayed slightly, and Steven jumped out of his seat. Pulling the chair out, he set Andrew down and handed him a glass of water. "Drink," he said firmly.

Andrew looked around, probably extremely self-conscious of where he was and what he was doing, but he took a small sip and thanked Steven. "My mother is going to freak," he said. "All these years she's held out hope that Richard was still alive."

There was a flurry of information going on in my head, and I had the distinct feeling that not only did Richard die shortly after he left home, but that he had been murdered. "Tell me about when he ran away," I said.

Andrew took another sip of water and said, "It was thirty years ago. I was seven and Richard was sixteen. He was my hero in a lot of ways. He had his own car, and he smoked pot, and he was supercool. And then one night he had a really bad fight with my dad and he left, just like that. No good-byes, no 'See ya later,' just gone."

CHAPTER 1

"He's late," snapped Gilley, my business partner and best friend, as he stared gloomily out the window. "I tip him generously every day, and this is the thanks I get?"

I looked away from the magazine article I was reading at my desk and glanced at my watch. It was two minutes past ten. "Wow," I said sarcastically. "He's two whole minutes late! My God, man! How *do* you hang on?"

Gil turned away from the window, his irritation with the deliveryman now focused on me. "M.J.," he growled. "I make one small request from this guy, and that is to deliver me a Diet Coke and a bagel with cream cheese every morning *by* ten a.m. Not around ten. Not after ten. Not somewhere in the vicinity of ten. By ten, as in *no later than . . .*"

I rolled my eyes and went back to reading the article. There was no use in trying to carry on a civil conversation with Gil until

13

he'd had a few sips of his Diet Coke. And there was also no use in offering some suggestions concerning the withdrawal he went through every time the delivery guy was late, like having a stockpile of Diet Coke in the closet or picking one up on his way to work in the morning. Nope, Gil liked his morning routine just the way it was, and that included the hissy fit he'd throw when his breakfast wasn't on time. It was my strong belief that Gilley hung on to this routine due to the fact that the delivery guy was a hottie. Didn't matter that he clearly wasn't gay; Gil liked to flirt with him anyway.

With another growl, Gil began to pace back and forth across my office, which was annoying, but there was no way I was going to say anything.

"Doc's a pretty boy!" squawked my African Gray parrot. "Doc's cuckoo for Cocoa Puffs!" I smiled as I read the article. Doc sure knew how to break the tension. "Dr. Delicious! Dr. Delicious!" he squawked excitedly.

I glanced up and looked at Doc. "He's here?" I asked, and in answer the front door to our suite opened and we heard a "Good morning!" from the lobby.

Gil stopped his pacing and visibly tried to

look more relaxed. "We're in here," he called.

I quickly put the magazine I'd been reading in a drawer and pulled my laptop closer, resting my fingers on the keyboard. After a moment, in walked six feet or so of tall, dark, and really delicious, or Dr. Steven Sable, the third partner in our ghostbusting business. "Hello, team," he said in a deep, gravelly baritone laced with an accent that is an odd blend of German and Spanish.

"Morning," Gil and I said in unison. "I didn't expect you this morning," I added. "I thought you had a lecture." Steven had just begun working at the University of Massachusetts as the summer semester's guest lecturer on cardiovascular thoracic surgery.

"It was canceled. A pipe burst in the lecture hall. There was water everywhere, and the administration called off classes until further notice."

"It's June," Gil pointed out. "How does a pipe burst in June?"

"I am not knowing this," said Steven, taking a seat across from me. Our eyes met, and I felt a little zing of electricity pass between us.

"You got your bandage off," I said, noticing his swollen and scarred hand, now free of the thick bandage he'd been walking

15

around with since he'd been shot in the hand on a ghostbust that had gone bad several weeks earlier.

"Good and new," Steven said, turning his hand this way and that.

"Good for you," I said to him. "And it's nice to see you, but there's not much going on today. No ghostbusting to be done, I'm afraid."

"No new cases?"

"Not a one," said Gil. "It looks like we've hit a dry spell."

"What about the Hendersons?" Steven asked, referring to the last case we'd worked. "Have they had any more trouble?"

"Nope," I said. "In fact, Mrs. Henderson sent over a fruit basket with her thanks. The house has been totally quiet for over two weeks now."

"This is a major bumming," said Steven. I should mention that English is his fifth language, and not one that he's even remotely mastered yet.

I glanced at Gil and noticed that he'd started sweating. By the clock on the wall his Diet Coke was now officially ten minutes late. "Gil," I said gently. "Why don't you just drive to the deli and get your breakfast?"

Gilley gave me a curt nod and bolted out

of the office suite. "What is his problem?" asked Steven.

"He's gotta have his caffeine fix by ten a.m. or we all suffer for it," I said.

"At least now we have some time alone," Steven said, with a bounce of his eyebrows.

I squirmed in my chair. "Now, now," I said, wagging a finger at him as he got up from his chair and came around the desk. "Steven," I protested as he twirled my chair around to face him and leaned down to hover his lips over mine.

"What is the harm, M.J.?" he asked. "We are alone. Gilley is off getting fixed, and there are no clients coming in. . . ." And that was when we heard the front door open.

Steven sighed as his lips brushed mine, and then he straightened up and took a glance out into the lobby.

"Hello?" I called.

"It is your friend," Steven whispered. "The one who knocks out the men."

I gave him a quizzical look, but understood what he meant when my good friend Karen O'Neal came into the office. When Gilley first met Karen he noted what a knockout she was — blond, blue-eyed, and boobs out to there. He nicknamed her TKO for *total knockout,* and that evolved into Teeko.

"Hey, M.J.," she said when she saw me.

17

"And hello, Dr. Sable," she added.

I noticed right away that Karen seemed upset about something, which was alarming, because in all the time I'd known her I'd never seen her look anything other than cool as a cucumber. "Hey, Teek," I said as I stood up. "What's happened?"

Karen smiled tightly. "It's that obvious, huh?" Steven moved to pull out a chair for her, and then he took a seat as well. "I need your help," she said, getting straight to the point.

"Of course," I said. "Anything. You name it and I'll help."

"It's about my niece," she said, wringing her hands and referring to her niece, fourteen-year-old Evie O'Neal. "She's been attacked."

"Oh, my God!" I gasped. "Teeko, that's horrible! I'm so sorry!"

Karen nodded, and I could tell she was struggling with her emotions. "It happened at her school," she said raggedly, looking down at her lap. "She can barely talk about it."

"Is she all right?"

Karen looked up at me, her eyes haunted by the trauma that her niece had been through. "God, I hope so, M.J.," she said.

"Did they catch the guy who attacked her?"

Karen shook her head no. "That's why I need your help. All Evie could tell us was that shortly after first period began this morning, around seven thirty, a man wielding an ax chased her through the hallway at school. He cornered her in one of the old classrooms, and as he came at her she closed her eyes and screamed. And then she felt something strike the chalkboard right next to her, but when she opened her eyes, no one was there."

I cocked my head to the side. "How long was the time between the strike she heard and when she opened her eyes?" I asked.

"Instantaneous," Karen said. "She said the sound made her snap her eyes open."

"Was there a mark on the chalkboard?"

"I don't know. My brother was called to the school to collect her. She's hysterical. She insists she saw what she saw, but . . ." Karen's voice drifted off.

"But what, sweetie?" I asked softly.

Karen sighed. "At the beginning of the school year the school had security cameras installed in every hallway and in the classrooms, just in case an intruder ever entered the school. They played the tapes back to see who this guy was. My brother says that you can clearly see Evie running down the hall as if she's being chased, and into a classroom, where she appears to see someone who terrifies her. But there's no man with an ax on the tape. There is no man at all. She's completely alone."

"Have you seen this tape?" I asked, my curiosity piqued.

"No. Not yet. I just got off the phone with Evie. She called me from the car as Kevin was bringing her home, and she was crying so hard I could barely make sense of what she was saying. When I couldn't calm her down I asked to speak to Kevin. He's lost all patience with her," Karen said with a sigh. "Of course, he never really had that in abundance anyway."

I kept my opinion about Karen's brother to myself, even though I was itching to add a similar sentiment. "What is he going to do about Evie?" I asked, feeling a sense of dread in my stomach.

"Bah," she said with an impatient flip of her hand. "My brother is an idiot! He's convinced that Evie has some sort of psychosis that is causing her to hallucinate, and he's considering taking her to a psychiatrist."

I frowned. I knew how close Karen was to her niece, and I also knew how skeptical her brother was of anything that science couldn't precisely quantify. He didn't believe in ghosts, mediums, psychics, or anything spiritual. I'd met him only once, and I'd instantly disliked him. "I'll help you any way I can," I said to her. "Just tell me what you want me to do."

"I want to hire you," she said, reaching inside her purse for her checkbook. "And I want you to hunt down whatever evil demon attacked my niece, and then I want you to send him to hell, if that's possible."

Steven and I glanced at each other. He gave me a slight shrug, as if to say, *Why not?* "You don't have to hire me," I said. "I'll do it for free."

Steven coughed loudly and widened his eyes at me. Karen smiled. "Don't be ridiculous," she said. "You need the income, and I need your professional ghostbusting services. I pay you, or it's no deal."

"Okay," I said, throwing up my hands. "If you say so."

Karen removed the cap from her pen, hovering it over her checkbook, and said, "Good, I'm glad you're being reasonable. How much to retain your services?"

"It's a hundred dollars a day, Teek," I said. Again Steven sputtered a cough. I gave him a warning glare. There was no way I was

21

charging my dear friend full price.

"Really?" Karen said skeptically. "Because your Web site says it's two-fifty a day."

"Must be a typo," I replied easily.

"You must think I'm gullible," Karen said as her hand scribbled out a number on the check. She tore it off with a flourish and handed it to me as she got up. "That should hold you for a week or so," she said. "And don't even think about not cashing it."

I looked at the check on my desk. There were far too many zeros there for my comfort level. I opened my mouth to protest, but Karen held up her hand in a stop motion. "I don't want to hear about it, M.J. This is business."

"But Teek —"

"No," she said firmly. "It's settled. I'll call you in an hour to confirm the time of our departure. The school is in upstate New York, just outside Lake Placid. If we leave tonight we can make it halfway there and stop for the night at this really nice hotel I know along the way. Would you mind sharing a room with me?"

"Not at all," I said, then glanced at Steven. "As long as you don't mind sharing a room with Gilley?"

"This is not a problem," he said agreeably.

Karen gave him a smile. "Perfect. I'll book two rooms with double beds. If we leave around five we can be there by eleven. I hope traveling that far isn't going to be a problem?"

"It's no problem," said Steven. "We can break into the new van."

"Break *in* the new van," I corrected gently.

"What is this difference?" he asked.

"If we did it your way, we'd get arrested." Turning to Karen I said, "We'll need clearance from the school, Teek."

"Leave it to me," she said confidently.

"I'll also need to talk to Evie," I added.

"Consider it done. My brother and his wife live about an hour away from the school. And my family has a ski lodge only twenty minutes from there. It's large enough to accommodate all of us, and we can use it as a home base."

"Are you sure Kevin will let me near Evie?" I asked.

"He will if I have anything to say about it," said Karen.

Just then Gilley came back in from his trek to the deli. He was with the delivery guy and laughing and giggling like the girlie man he was. "Oh, it's really okay, Jay," he said to the deliveryman. "Sleeping through your alarm happens to everyone." When he saw

23

Karen standing near my door he said, "Teeko! Great to see you, dahling. And the ladies look extra sumptuous today. I love the sweater," he added with a hand flourish. "Shows off the mounds something *fierce.*"

I cleared my throat loudly, knowing Karen was not in the mood for Gilley's usual banter. Karen smiled at Gilley anyway. "Hey, Gil. M.J. will catch you up. Talk to you all in an hour," she said, and she hurried out the door.

Gil gave me a curious look as the delivery guy stood there, patiently waiting for Gilley to pay him for his bagel and Diet Coke. "Gas up the van, Gil," I said, standing up. "We've got a job!"

Gilley took his time polishing off his bagel and downing his Diet Coke before heading out to the van to gas it up and load some of our equipment. The great thing about adding Steven to our little business was that he'd helped finance some of the very best ghostbusting equipment available.

We had two night-vision cameras, two handheld computer thermal-imaging devices, three electrostatic energy detectors, some brand-new state-of-the-art walkie-talkies, video monitors, digital cameras, and laptops, not to mention a shiny new van to put it all in. Hooking up with Dr. Sable and all his money was like being at the top of Gadget Santa's good list.

"Are you bringing the bird?" Steven asked me as I hurried around the office with a list, checking off items to take with us.

I nodded. "Can't very well leave him in the condo alone," I muttered. Out of the corner of my eye I caught Steven's frown. "What?" I asked, looking up from my list.

"It is nothing," he said in a way that told me it was definitely something.

I sighed. Obviously I was going to have to draw it out of him. "Really? Because the look on your face is suggesting otherwise."

"It is only that Doc can be a bit of a mood murderer."

I hid a smirk. "Mood murderer," I repeated. "That sounds serious."

Steven got up from the chair he'd been sitting in and came over to hover next to me, where he traced my jawline with his finger. "Remember the last time I came over?"

I smiled at the memory of him in my condo and Doc dive-bombing his head the moment Steven tried to show me some affection. "So he got a little jealous," I said. "He just needs to get used to you."

Steven sighed. "All right," he said, kissing

25

me lightly before stepping away. "I will go home and pack for the trip. I'll be back by five."

I nodded and got back to my list. While I was finishing up Gilley came in. "It is wet out there!" he exclaimed, shaking off the rain from his coat.

"Have you heard the weather report?" I asked.

Gil frowned. "Yes." He groaned. "Supposed to rain through next Tuesday."

"Makes for good ghost hunting," I said. Ghosties love the rain. The more moist the atmosphere, the easier it is for them to appear.

"Yeah, well, it also makes for some long, cold nights. It's June, for cripes' sake!"

"It's the third week of June, Gil," I said with an eye roll. "And this is New England; you know that the only way to predict the weather is to expect the unexpected."

"Maybe it won't be as bad in New York," Gil said, brightening up.

I gave him a sad smile. "Sorry, pal. I checked. This storm is supposed to track straight through the way we're heading. Looks like it's going to hang out with us for the duration."

"We need a vacation," Gil mused. "M.J., when we're done with this gig let's book a trip to Cabo San Lucas or something."

"I thought we were in a money crunch?"

Gilley gave me a sideways glance. "I've done some creative accounting."

That stopped me. "You've what?"

"It's no big deal," Gil said, playing with the zipper on his coat.

"Gil," I said evenly. "What's going on?"

"Well, our friend the good doctor happened to shove a teensy bit of extra money into our petty-cash fund, just in case of emergencies."

"How much is this 'teensy bit'?"

Gil mumbled something that I didn't catch.

"How much?" I asked again, laying my hand on his shoulder.

"Ten thousand."

"*What?*" I gasped. "Gilley Gillespie, you give that money back!"

"No," Gil said stubbornly, walking around to his desk.

I followed after him and cornered him in his chair. "I am not kidding, Gil! You give every penny of that money back!"

"What if we invite him along to Cabo?"

"Oh, you'd like that," I snapped. "Steven would no doubt feed your petty-cash fund there, too!"

"What's the harm, M.J.? The man is rolling in money! He certainly didn't invest in our little venture for the great earning potential."

"You're taking advantage of his generosity, and I won't have it."

"I am not taking advantage," Gil insisted. "He thinks of us as a form of entertainment. I'm merely providing him with his source of amusement, and if he wants to pay us generously for that, then that's his choice."

"Great," I snapped. "Tomorrow you'd better show up in a pair of stilettos and some skimpy leopard-print number, because you've just pimped us out, my friend."

"Oh, come on, M.J.!" Gil complained. "Don't think of it like that. Think of it like we now have a patron for our art."

"Our *art?*" I said, giving Gil a look that suggested he'd gone off his rocker.

"Yes!" Gil insisted, no doubt believing he was onto something. "What we do is rare and exceptional, and it takes a certain level of talent to be able to offer our services. I would call that art."

I gave Gil the full eye roll and shook my head. "And I suppose that little dance you do every morning before your deli guy gets here is your idea of performance art, hmm?"

"If it gets ten grand thrown into the petty-cash fund, we can call it whatever the good doctor wants."

"Gil," I said, giving him a level look.

"Yeah?"

"Give the money back."

Gilley sighed like he'd just been told he had a terminal disease. *"Fiiiine,"* he said, and stomped off to continue packing the van.

Later that afternoon we were on our way. Gil was at the wheel, following closely behind Teeko's Mercedes. Steven was in the passenger seat next to Gil, and I was in the back, testing our equipment one gadget at a time. "How's that new thermal imager working out?" Steven asked me.

"It is the coolest thing ever," I said, looking at the display while I held up the gadget. The thermal imager showed variances in temperature through color imagery. It could show the shape of people and various objects by how much heat or cold they were giving off. As I held the imager up I could see the outline of Steven and Gilley in various shades of yellow and red, and their clothing in a slightly cooler tone. "I love this thing," I said, and pointed it out the window. The landscape opened up in shades of cool blue or green, and a hint of warmer yellow, but up ahead I noticed the distinct image of a person just off the road, walking erratically.

I lowered the device and looked up as we passed by, but there was no one there. Quickly I turned and held up the imager again. Fiddling with the focus I could see the stranger's outline clearly on the imager, but no person was physically there. "Gilley!" I shouted. "Pull over!"

Gil pressed hard on the brakes, and we skidded slightly before stopping on the shoulder. One of the walkie-talkies we'd brought with us beeped, and Teeko's voice asked, "What's going on?"

"M.J. just yelled at me to pull over," Gil said into the walkie-talkie.

"There's someone back there," I said, still holding up the imager to watch the figure teeter around on the opposite shoulder.

"Who?" Steven asked, squinting at the barren landscape.

"Look," I said, holding up the imager so that they could both see.

"Whoa," Gil said.

"Cool," Steven added.

Unhooking my seat belt I said, "I'm going back there."

"Hold on, M.J.," Gilley said. "There's not a lot of traffic. Let me see if I can back up." And he began to carefully reverse along the shoulder. Unfortunately, that was exactly when a cop came around the bend and spotted us.

"Crap," we all said at the same time.

The walkie-talkie beeped again. "You guys are officially in trouble," Teeko said, and on cue the patrol car's lights flicked on and the cop pulled up right behind us.

"Great, now my insurance is going to go up!" Gil complained as he fished around in his wallet for his driver's license and insurance card.

I looked out the window at the shoulder across the highway and opened up my sixth sense. There was a little tugging sensation in my solar plexus, and I knew I'd zeroed in on the ghost wandering anxiously around in circles. "I've got to go help him," I said, feeling that familiar sense of panic that I sometimes get with grounded spirits.

"M.J.," Gilley snapped. "You'll stay right here until we deal with this cop."

I handed Gilley the thermal imager. "He's frantic, Gil," I said. "Look at how he's pacing around and around!"

Gil held up the imager, and that was when I realized I'd done the dumbest thing ever. "Drop your weapon!" the cop shouted from just outside our van as he raised his big silver gun.

Gilley screamed and dropped the imager.

"Don't shoot! Don't shoot!" he wailed.

All three of us threw our hands up in the air. "Step out of the car one at a time, and keep your hands where I can see them!" the cop demanded.

Gilley shrieked again. "He's going to kill us!" he cried.

"Just do as he says, Gil," I said quietly. "We can sort this all out once he realizes we don't have a weapon."

Shaking like a leaf, Gilley slowly opened the van door and stepped out. "I'm next," said Steven when Gilley was shoved violently up against the side of the van by the cop. "Maybe the officer will find the cash in my back pocket and let us go?"

"Steven!" I hissed. "Don't even *think* about bribing him!"

"Why not?"

"It's not how it's done here!" I hissed again, but went very quiet when the cop stuck his head into our van and pointed the gun right at Steven.

"You," he said. "Out."

Steven got out and came around the front of the van with his arms in the air. The walkie-talkie pipped again, and I heard Karen say, "I'm calling my lawyer; you three just go along nice and cooperative-like."

As if I needed the encouragement. The

cop threw Steven up against the van and gave him a one-handed pat-down; then he motioned to me, and I also stepped out. "We don't have a weapon," I said as I was whipped around and thrust forward against the van.

"I saw what I saw," growled the cop as he felt along my body, lingering slightly across my front.

I sneered distastefully but managed to keep my voice level when I said, "The device you thought was a weapon was a thermal imager. It's used in our line of work."

"Oh, yeah?" said the cop in a sarcastic tone. "Well, then, please accept my apologies. You all can go on and have a nice day."

"Really?" Gilley asked hopefully.

"No," said the cop. "Not really."

"Excuse me, Officer," said Steven. "But I believe you may have left something in my back pocket when you were frosting me."

"Frosting?" said the cop.

"He means frisking," I said, giving Steven a warning look. "And no, you didn't leave anything in his back pocket. He's from Argentina. They take care of situations like this a little differently."

But the cop had already reached into Steven's back pocket and was holding a big wad of cash in his hand. There was a moment in which no one spoke, and then the cop reached for his handcuffs and slapped them on Steven. "You're under arrest, big guy," he said.

"Yoo-hoo," came a feathery female voice. I turned my head and saw Teeko standing near our van, her mohair sweater gently off one shoulder and her hair fluffed up and teased to within an inch of its life.

The cop cinched the handcuffs tightly around Steven's hands and stepped back. "This doesn't concern you, ma'am," he said. But I noticed his voice wasn't as barky as when he'd been ordering us around.

Karen giggled and flipped her hair. "Oh, I know what you must be thinking. But I can assure you, these three aren't criminals. They're ghostbusters, and I've hired them for the week."

The cop seemed to take that in for a minute. "You know them?" he asked, and I could see by the set of his chin that he appeared to be addressing Karen's boobs.

Karen giggled again and did something with her shoulders that pushed the ladies out even farther. "Yes, I'm afraid so. I can't take them anywhere these days without attracting all sorts of attention."

Just then I felt a real tug on my solar

plexus, and right next to me I felt a presence. "Does anyone here know a Randy Donald, or Donaldson?" I said. The name had bulleted into my head, and I'd spoken before I'd had a chance to think about what I was saying.

The cop whipped his head around to me. "What did you say?"

I closed my eyes. Randy was standing right next to me, shouting in my mind to speak his name. "Randy Donaldson," I said slowly. "He says there's been an accident, and he's called for backup. He says you're late."

I opened my eyes and the cop had gone pale. He blinked several times stupidly; then he seemed to look around, noticing for the first time where we were standing. He glanced across the street exactly at the spot where I'd first picked Randy up on the thermal imager.

Randy was still yelling at me so loudly that it was becoming uncomfortable. "He says that he needs to get home to Sarah and the baby. The baby's had a bad cough or something and he's worried about her."

The cop, whose name tag read, MICHELSON, pivoted his head back to me, his mouth slightly agape. "How do you *know* that?"

Karen took a cautious step forward. "This

is M. J. Holliday. She's a psychic medium, and I believe she's talking to the deceased Randy Donaldson."

"Randy was a cop," I said, seeing the familiar badge flash in my mind's eye. "He says a woman's been hurt in some kind of accident. He's called for backup and an ambulance, but he can't seem to find the woman, and he doesn't see the ambulance."

"Okay," said the cop, and he stepped angrily away. Drawing his weapon again, he raised it at us. "That's enough out of all of you! I'm calling for backup, and until they get here I need everyone to just face the van and shut up!"

Karen obediently turned toward the van and placed her hands on it. "The imager's still in the van, right?" she whispered to Gilley.

"It's on the front seat," he said.

"Officer," Karen said evenly. "The thermal imager is right there on the front seat. You can pick it up and see what M.J.'s talking about."

Out of the corner of my eye I could see the cop hesitate as he raised his microphone to his lips. Randy, meanwhile, was still over my right shoulder, dazed, confused, and really furious that it had taken so long for his backup to show. "Randy is telling me that he's had enough of this mandatory overtime," I said. "He says it really sucks to be forced to work on Christmas Eve."

The cop behind me gasped, and then he did come forward and peek into the van's window. Seeing the imager on the front seat, he lifted it out and looked at it. "Randy is over my right shoulder," I said. "If you raise the imager up you'll see the outline of all of us. Test it first on those three, then point it at me."

The cop stepped back and raised the imager, seeing the outline of everyone leaning against the van. I then saw him swivel it toward me, and he gasped again. Randy was becoming more and more agitated. He wasn't getting anyone but me to listen to him, and this was pissing him off royally. I heard him shout at the cop behind me, then stomp off in his direction. The cop obviously saw through the imager the shape of a tall man charging at him, and he dropped the imager, raising his gun again. "How is that happening?" he asked when he saw that no one was there.

"Randy died on Christmas Eve," I said calmly. "He was responding to an accident with a woman in a car. I think it was icy that night, right?"

The cop nodded dumbly at me. "We had

accidents all up and down the highway."

"Something happened," I said, feeling out the event that Randy was describing. "He said he checked on the woman in the car, and she was okay but had a bad cut on her forehead. He called for backup and was setting up road flares when . . ." My voice trailed off. The imagery got intense as I saw a pair of headlights coming right at me.

"Another car hit him," said the cop.

"He's stuck here," I said. "He thinks he's still alive, Officer."

Michelson lowered his weapon and holstered it. He then walked over to Steven and clicked open the handcuffs, handing him back the wad of money he'd found in his jeans. "Sorry," said Steven sheepishly.

"You have to help him," said Michelson to me with a rather pained look. "He was my best friend, ma'am."

"I'll need to go over there," I said, pointing to the spot where the accident had occurred. "Can I take my hands down and do that?"

The cop nodded. "Yes, go ahead."

Teeko gave me a warm smile, while Gilley was still shaking. "It's okay, Gilley," said Steven. "We are not going to be shot."

I waited for a car to pass, then jogged across the road. To my left there was a small piece of taillight, and up ahead what looked like a shard of rusty metal. Randy had followed me, and as I glanced over my shoulder I could see Gilley holding up the imager, and everyone — including the cop — staring over his shoulder to watch what happened next.

I closed my eyes and said mentally, *Randy, I know you can hear me. I want you to know that I can hear you too.*

You need to get back in your car, ma'am. The shoulder's not safe tonight, Randy replied.

No, Randy, you're right. The shoulder wasn't safe, I agreed.

I need to put down some flares. I wish those salt trucks would get here already.

"Randy," I said aloud. "Hear what I'm telling you. It's no longer Christmas Eve."

I'm glad Bruce is here. He can keep the gawkers moving while I put down the flares. . . .

"Randy!" I yelled, and felt his energy snap to attention. "Last Christmas Eve, when you were setting down road flares, something happened, didn't it?"

Randy's energy seemed to hesitate. *A woman had an accident. She's hurt pretty bad.*

"No, Randy," I said patiently. "I'm not talking about that. I'm talking about what

39

happened when you were setting down flares. Do you remember?"

There was a car . . . , Randy said, and I could feel him do something like a wince as the memory floated back. *It slid on the same patch of ice and it hit me.*

I smiled. "Great job," I said. "You remember. But what you don't remember is what happened next."

The lady in the car is missing, Randy said, and I could feel his energy growing agitated again. *Where did she go? I called for an ambulance. She must have driven away while I was setting off the flares!*

"No, Randy, that's not how it played out. What happened was that you were hit by that car so hard that your body died."

Good one, he said. *I'm here talking to you, aren't I?*

"Yes," I said. "Yes, you are. But here's the deal: Your soul survived the crash. Your body didn't. Sarah and the baby buried your body almost six months ago, Randy."

Randy's energy vibrated, almost like a shock wave. *That's not possible,* he said, but I could tell he was starting to realize the truth of things.

"Randy," I said gently. "Your body is gone. There's nothing left for you here. If you'll listen to me and do as I say, I can get you where you need to be. Will you agree to that?" I felt something like a nod in my head, and I continued. "Above you there should be a bright white light. Can you look up and see that?"

In my head I heard a gasp, then, *I see it!*

"Excellent! Now, Randy, this is so important: When I tell you to, you've got to mentally pull that energy down around you. When you do that you'll feel like you're in a tunnel, or there may even be a path. Once you see that it will lead you home. Just let the white light carry you along, and you'll be home in no time."

But Sarah . . . , Randy said, protesting.

"Will be just fine," I reassured him. "I think Bruce will make sure to look after her and your daughter. And where you're going you'll be able to check in on both of them anytime you want. Don't you want to see them again, Randy?"

I do, he said.

"It's been six months since you've seen them, my friend. But where you're going you can see how your daughter is growing up and help keep her out of trouble."

Okay, he said. *I'm ready.*

I stepped back and closed my eyes, seeing in my mind's eye a huge ball of white light cover up his spirit and whisk him away. A

41

moment later his energy was just gone.

Across the street came a round of applause, and I opened my eyes. Gilley, Steven, and Teeko were whooping it up for me, and Officer Bruce Michelson was gripping the thermal imager tightly and looking every bit like he'd just seen a ghost. Which, of course, he had.

CHAPTER 2

We got back on the road a short time later, leaving Officer Michelson in a bit of a stupor and heading, no doubt, straight to the bar after his shift. Gilley had managed to avoid a ticket, and even better, Steven had avoided arrest — this time. "From now on, Steven, try to keep your wad of cash in your back pocket, where it belongs," I said, irritated that he'd nearly caused us so much trouble.

"Can I keep the roll of quarters in my front pocket?" he asked smartly. Gilley burst out laughing, but I wasn't so easily amused.

"You're just lucky that cop let us off," I groused.

"That was pretty brilliant work back there, M.J.," Gil said. "I mean, you should have seen that thermal imager the moment that cop crossed over. It was awesome!"

"What'd it show?" I asked curiously.

"Well, we could see you on the imager,

43

and the outline of Randy — he was a greenish blue with a little hint of yellow around his outside. But then all of a sudden there was this flash of yellow all around him, then *zap!* He was gone!"

"Yep," I said, nodding at him in the rearview mirror. "Pretty close to what I saw in my mind's eye too."

"These thermal imagers are very good, no?" Steven asked as he held one up.

"They are the bomb," said Gil. "I about had a heart attack, though, when that cop dropped it on the ground. I thought for sure he'd broken it."

Steven turned the gadget over a few times, inspecting it for damage. "Looks good," he announced.

"That's a relief," I said. "That thing works great, and I'd really like it along for this job." Thinking of something, I opened up my laptop and began typing.

"Whatcha doin'?" Gil said, studying me in the rearview mirror.

"Seeing if I can find something on this boarding school Evie attends. Maybe there'll be something out there that will point a finger at who this guy with the ax is."

I plugged the name of the school into a search engine and opened the link. Northelm Boarding School was located in a valley

44

by a large pond at the foot of the Adirondack Mountains. The school was founded in the early nineteen hundreds and on its home page listed several notable people in a stream of alumni, including two New York governors, several U.S. Congressmen, senators, and a half dozen journalists and authors.

The school itself was reflective of its surroundings, built to resemble something like a long ski lodge, with a main building holding classrooms for grades nine through twelve, and two flanking buildings, one housing grades six through eight, and the other, the old elementary wing, was to be turned into a large dormitory for the boarding students by the end of the year.

According to the school's Web site, it currently housed ninety-eight boys and forty-two girls, and there were a little over a hundred kids in total boarding there full-time. Tuition was in the forty-thousand-dollar range, and of course that didn't include miscellaneous expenses that comprised an average of an additional four thousand dollars a year.

Sports seemed to be a big attraction at the school, with miles of ski trails, a hockey rink, tennis courts, a track-and-field arena, and Lake Placid just twenty minutes away.

The place was a young jock's paradise.

"What's it say?" Gilley asked me, and that's when I noticed I'd been quietly reading for a while.

"It's pretty much a country club for rich jocks," I said. "A hundred and forty kids attend, and most of those board full-time."

"Does it talk about the school's history?" Gilley asked.

"Not much," I said, skimming over the site. "Just that it was founded in the early nineteen hundreds by the Habbernathy family, who've had control of it ever since."

"Nothing on our mysterious ax man, huh?" Gil said.

"Not on the school's Web site, but then, that might be a bit of a turnoff to parents looking to board their kiddies."

"Good point. Try plugging the school's name and the word *ghost* into the search engine and see what it says."

I did and came back with nothing but a few more links back to the school's Web site and a couple of articles on ghosts. "I got bupkes, Gil," I said. "There's no mention of a ghost sighting on the school grounds, and since we already know this is a fairly active ghost, I'd be willing to guess that the school administration is working hard to keep it off-line."

Gil sighed. "This stuff is never easy for us," he said.

"Why is this such a bad thing?" Steven wanted to know.

"If there had been some information on this mysterious ax man, we could have had a starting point; even a name would have been handy. Sometimes the only way you can get a ghost's attention is to call it by name," I said.

"The fact that this guy is wielding an ax is really bizarre," said Gil. "I mean, who goes around with axes these days?"

"Could be someone from the sixteen or seventeen hundreds," I said. "Maybe one of the first settlers had a house where the school is, and he's trying to get people off what he perceives to be his land."

"Why the sudden activity, though?" Steven asked, swiveling in his seat to look back at me.

"Could be the renovations," I said, and clicked back to the school's Web site. "It says here that the school is about to undergo a massive reconstruction of its old elementary wing. They're turning it into better housing for the students, and a new dining hall."

Steven looked at Gilley, rather perplexed. "I am not understanding her," he said.

"Ghosties hate construction," Gil said. "It's bad enough when you start rearranging furniture, but when you begin to tear down walls and whatnot it drives them crazy and they get wicked mad. That's when you hear a lot of doors slamming and things being tossed around. The grounded spirit can actually throw a temper tantrum."

Steven nodded his head; he understood. "Still, it is strange that such a violent ghost would wait so long to make an entrance, no?"

"Maybe not," I said as my eyes flew back and forth across the screen of my laptop. "Guys, listen to this headline just posted on the school newspaper: 'Hatchet Jack Returns.' "

"Read it!" said Gil.

I cleared my throat and read, " 'The ghost of Hatchet Jack has returned to Northelm Boarding School. This reporter has learned that ninth grader Evie O'Neal was picked up by her father this morning after being attacked in the elementary wing by everyone's least-favorite bogeyman, Hatchet Jack.

" 'Jack makes a return to the school after almost ten years of relative silence. The last notable encounter between Northelm's resident ghost and a student ended when Ricky Tamborne was sent to a mental hospital after suffering a breakdown when he was cornered by the evil demon. This reporter is further convinced that the old wing is more in need of an exorcist than a face-lift.' "

"Well," said Gil, "at least we have a name."

"Somehow I can't see myself reaching out politely to Mr. Hatchet," I said with a scowl, and closed the lid to the computer. "Something tells me this is going to be a tricky bust."

"Aren't they all?" Gil said.

We drove in silence until eleven o'clock, when Teeko pulled off an exit and led us to a lovely hotel. Wearily we checked in and each headed off to our rooms. Teeko and I shared one room, and the boys were left with the other.

Even though I was tired, I still caught the look of glee on Gil's face as he was handed his key to the room he'd share with Dr. Delicious. Gil had a major crush on the man.

The next morning we were up early and headed to our cars. Teeko waved me over to her Mercedes and asked if I would ride with her to keep her company. I agreed and we got in. As I waved to Steven and Gilley, I noticed Steven pouting a little that I wasn't riding with him. "What's going on with you two, anyway?" Karen asked me.

"Hmm?" I said coyly. "Nothing."

Karen gave me a look that said she wasn't buying it.

"Really. We're colleagues."

This got me more of the same look from Karen.

"There's honestly nothing going on," I said, giving her my most innocent face.

"Can you check my driver's license?" she asked. "I think I might have been born yesterday."

"Fine," I said with a laugh. "So I like him."

"Ah," she said.

"And I think he might like me."

"I see."

"And we have really good chemistry."

"Hadn't noticed," she said with a smirk.

"But we haven't done . . . er . . . anything about all that yet," I said, feeling myself break out into a sweat.

"Why not?" she asked, giving me a quick quizzical glance.

"Because we work together, for one," I said. "And as Steven is an investor in my company, romance might make things a bit sticky."

Karen laughed. "I've had a few sticky nights of romance, honey, and trust me, they were memorable in a good way."

I rolled my eyes and tried to turn the tables on her. "So, have you heard anything from John?" John Dodge was Karen's ex-boyfriend. Dodge was a *major* financial player, voted one of the top bachelors in Boston two years running. He and Karen had dated seriously for about three years when she'd given him an ultimatum. Against expectations he'd proposed, but to everyone's surprise she'd actually turned him down flat.

Later Karen claimed that she realized the moment he got down on bended knee that he was doing it only to please her. She didn't want to get married because she'd forced his hand, so she'd broken it off then and there.

Since then, rumor had it the guy had dated every blond, blue-eyed Karen look-alike he could find. And when that didn't ease his apparent broken heart, he started sending her flowers by the truckload. When *that* didn't work the jewelry arrived. We're talking bling that could be seen from space, it was so sparkly. She'd sent it all back.

"Oh, I hear from John every day," she said, shaking her head. "He doesn't give up easily."

"Are you sure you want him to?" I asked.

Karen didn't answer me. Instead she adjusted the volume on the radio and said, "Oh! I love this song!"

I let it go, and we drove for a while just listening to the radio. Finally she asked, "What's going to be your first step, M.J.?"

"Hmm?" I said, coming out of the haze I'd been in while staring at the road ahead.

"For busting the school. What will you do first?"

"Oh," I said with a giggle. "Yeah, I almost forgot why we were driving. Okay, so my first step will be to talk to Evie, try to get a feel for things from her perspective. Typically there's a point right before a ghost shows himself when the victim senses something is off. Sometimes it can feel like they're being watched, or that there's an overwhelming sense of emotion emanating from a room, like a heaviness or sadness or even anger."

"My poor niece," Karen said. "Her father is such an idiot. I know he's telling her that it's all in her head."

"If he's so resistant to this stuff, how do you think you're going to convince him to let me talk to Evie?"

"I don't have to convince him," Karen said. "Leanne will let us talk to Evie," she said, referring to her sister-in-law. "The one good thing my brother did was to marry such a fantastic woman," she added. "It's a wonder she's still with him."

I smiled. I had my own family struggles, so I definitely got where she was coming from. "After I talk to Evie, I'll need to talk to some of the teachers at the school, see if they've seen anything they can't explain. I'll also want to hunt down that reporter who posted the story on the school's Web site."

"The one you told me about last night?" she said. "I can't believe it's already been taken down."

I'd logged back onto the Web over our continental breakfast at the hotel and was shocked to learn that the story I'd read the night before about Hatchet Jack had been removed from the school's Web site. "I wish I could remember the kid reporter's name," I said. "That way we could track him down at the school and get an interview with him. Still, Gil said he could work his computer magic and dig up the old article once we get off the road."

"What do you make of that?" Karen asked.

"What do I make of what?"

"The fact that the story was removed so quickly. It's like Northelm is really nervous about their reputation."

"At forty grand–plus a year per student, I

can see why," I said. "They're making a killing off their students."

"No pun intended," Karen said with a laugh.

"Right," I said, laughing too.

"So then what?" Karen asked.

"Well," I said, "after I interview everyone I'll want to set up a baseline test —"

"A what-line test?"

"Baseline. It's a test where Gil and I map out the area and measure temperature changes and electrostatic output. It helps us identify where there might be hidden pockets of electrical energy, like wiring in the walls or outlets that aren't easily seen. These can make our meters go off, and if we know where they are ahead of time we can differentiate between what is normal and what is not normal. The same is true for temperature."

"Sounds very scientific."

"It can be," I admitted. "After we get our baseline measurements, we'll set up some trigger objects."

"The objects you hope a ghost might want to play with, right?"

I nodded. "Exactly. Gil's favorite is a house of cards; ghosts love to take them down, and we've even had one instance when the ghost put the cards back into a deck, arranged by suit and number."

"That is so cool," said Karen.

I nodded again. "After that comes the hard part."

"Which is . . . ?"

"We'll need to camp out and wait for something to happen. I'll do my best to make contact, but if I don't get an initial reaction we might have to wait for the ghost to make the first move so I can follow his energy back to his portal and shut his ass down."

"His portal?"

"Yep," I said. "A portal is a window that nasty energies like him go through. It connects him with a lower realm or another plane of existence. I've found that most ugly energies like to hang out in the lower realms, where they can learn from other beastly energies, and often they become more powerful over time."

Karen shivered. "That sounds so creepy," she said. "How will finding his portal help you to bust him?"

"I can block his return from the portal with a couple of magnetic spikes. Magnets create a barrier of electrostatic energy, and as long as Jack's portal is located in something I can drive some spikes into, it should be a fairly easy thing to do. This bust might be easier than most, in fact, especially if Jack's as aggressive as he sounds. They hate to be provoked, and when you start insulting them they can't handle it."

"What can he do?"

"A variety of things," I said. "He could appear in shadow or in full form, which would be great, or he could stay invisible and throw something at me, or resort to shoving and pushing."

"They can *do* that?" Karen asked.

"They can do worse," I admitted. "I've seen them drop a hundred-eighty-pound man and pummel him black and blue."

"No way!"

I grimaced. "Way. Some of the worst ghosts are incredibly violent. That's why this stuff isn't a game. We're always careful . . . well, except that time we were at Steven's grandfather's."

"When Gil got hurt, right?"

"Yeah, and that was my fault. I'd forced Gilley along and left him alone on the stairs. We got lucky that he wasn't hurt worse."

"So if this ghost is wielding an ax, does that mean he can kill you?"

I smiled. "No, Evie said that when she opened her eyes she saw nothing. If Jack were toting a real ax it would have been left in the chalkboard. Still, the ax or hatchet or whatever it was is very real to Jack, and that means that while it probably couldn't kill me, he might be able to give me something like a slap with it. I'll be sure to keep on my toes for this one."

"You can back out," Karen said to me seriously. "I can talk to Leanne and convince her to find another school for Evie and call this whole thing off."

"That's just it, Teeko," I said. "Who's going to protect those other kids? If a demon like Hatchet Jack is loose in that abandoned wing, and they're about to put up a dorm there, it means none of those kids are safe."

"Good point," Karen said with a heavy sigh. "Be careful, honey, okay?"

I winked at her. "Aren't I always?"

"No," she said flatly.

I smiled. "True enough, and point taken. This time I promise to be careful."

Karen still looked worried, but she let the topic drop. "We should be at my brother's in an hour."

"How far is the school from his place, again?"

"About an hour. He lives in this really snotty neighborhood, and a few of the residents send their kids to Northelm."

"It's so weird that they make the kids board at the school when home is so close at hand."

"Not for these folks," said Karen. "I tell you, it's like out of sight, out of mind with some of those parents. They pay more attention to their pets than their kids."

"I'm assuming having Evie board at the school was your brother's idea?"

Karen gave me a wry smirk. "Actually, it was Evie's idea. That girl is a feisty one, and at the end of last year she told her parents she wanted to live at the school full-time. My brother was only too happy to ship her off, but Leanne's had a tough time of it."

"What does your brother do, again?" I asked.

"He's a day trader," Karen said. "The man doesn't give a single ounce of credence to intuitive ability, and yet he's never been wrong on a stock."

I laughed. "I know! I hate it when people start telling me how unscientific intuition is, and yet they're the ones going around advertising that everyone should trust their gut, or rely on their instincts, or my favorite, 'listen to that voice inside.' "

"Like there's a *major* difference between those things and intuition," Karen said with a roll of her eyes. "People are so dumb."

"Agreed," I said.

"Anyway, let me handle my brother. You

guys hang out in the van and I'll give you the signal when it's okay to come in."

"Sounds like a plan," I said.

We drove for another hour in companionable silence, sometimes pointing out the increasingly beautiful scenery even though it was a drizzly, rainy day out.

The Adirondacks came into view about a half hour from Karen's brother's house. "Whoa," I said as I spotted them. "Those are spectacular."

Karen nodded. "My family's ski lodge is up here right on Echo Lake, which is on the east side of Lake Placid. We used to come up here to ski when I was a kid. I think that's why Kevin wanted to move up here. He was addicted to winter sports, and if you like to ski and play hockey and hang out where it's cold, the Adirondacks are the place to be."

"Does he live in Lake Placid?" I asked.

"No. He lives in Meridian; it's about forty-five miles southeast. Many of Lake Placid's superwealthy live there. It's very chi-chi."

"I would have thought the rich folks would be living closer to town," I said.

"Oh, there's still plenty of money close to Lake Placid proper, but it's a bit more pretentious, if you can believe it. Meridian also has a lake, but it's much smaller, and yes, Kevin and Leanne live on it."

At that point Karen flipped on her turn signal and took the next exit. In my side mirror I could see Gilley and Steven following close behind. "We'll need to shop for groceries before we settle in at the ski lodge, but it's probably going to be more comfortable than staying at a hotel in town, and the commute to the school isn't bad."

"Is your family's place big enough for all of us?" I asked.

Karen smiled. "I think so," she said with a wink. "I'll take you there after we meet with Evie. The school is only a fifteen- to twenty-minute car ride from there."

We took another few turns and headed southeast for a while. The scenery outside continued to dazzle me. It had started to rain hard, but that didn't diminish how spectacular the mountains were, or the beautiful views of greenery. Finally Karen turned onto a road that had a private gate and guardhouse attached. She drove up to the guardhouse and lowered her window.

"How can I help you, ma'am?" a pleasant old man in a gray uniform asked.

"I'm Karen O'Neal, here to see my brother, Kevin O'Neal," Karen said. "And the van behind me is also with me."

"Mr. O'Neal is expecting you?" the guard asked, looking a bit nervously at our big black van.

"Of course," Teeko said confidently, flashing a winning smile at him.

The guard told us to hold on while he called Karen's brother; then he waved us through. "Lots of crime around here?" I asked.

Karen laughed. "Not with Deputy Dog back there on high alert," she said.

I glanced out my window as we drove and was surprised by the enormity of the subdivision. And by *enormity,* I'm not referring to the actual size of the subdivision as much as I'm referring to the size of the mansions making it up.

The neighborhood was full of them. Not one house looked to be under five thousand square feet; in fact, those under ten were clearly in the minority. I tried not to ogle, but it was hard, especially when we pulled into Kevin and Leanne O'Neal's driveway. "Good Lord," I said when we came to a stop. "This place looks like a hotel!"

Karen smirked. "I know, right? It's like he's trying to compensate for something."

The "house" was enormous, at least twelve thousand square feet. A large white structure with triangular windows and a huge front door, it had some sort of ivy with large purple flowers growing up the front on white latticework. Lining the house were rows of well-tended flower beds and gardens. To the side I could see a small lake and a boat dock with two boats and three Jet Skis in attendance. The garage was detached, with three large bay doors and what looked to be a studio on the second floor. A light was on in the studio, and as I glanced up I saw a beautiful blond woman with curly hair staring down at us. When she saw me glance up, she waved.

I waved back and asked, "Is that Leanne?"

Karen leaned over and looked up. "Yep," she said, and waved as well. "She's probably painting today, since its raining. Kevin works from home, which means she's usually in her garden or up in that studio."

"They get along okay?" I asked, noting a hint of sarcasm in her voice.

"No one gets along with Kevin okay," said Teeko. "But Leanne probably does it better than anyone." Picking up the walkie-talkie, Karen clicked the button and said, "Gil, I'm going to talk to my brother first and clear our visit with Evie before I bring you guys in. Sit tight until I get back, okay?"

At that moment the front door opened, and an incredibly tall and imposing figure stood in the doorway, his arms folded crossly and a scowl on his face.

"Oh, look," Karen said when she caught sight of him. "He's in a good mood today."

Karen got out of the car and hurried through the drizzle to stand next to the big guy on the front stoop. To the right of me a door on the side of the garage opened, and Leanne hurried over to join her sister-in-law and her husband. Hugs were exchanged with the two women, but no warmth passed between Karen and her brother.

Some sort of debate ensued, with lots of hand waving on Karen's part, Leanne nodding vigorously, and Kevin's frown deepening. At one point Teeko turned to her car and pointed at me. I waved and smiled broadly. Leanne waved back, and Kevin's scowl deepened. "Fabulous," I said at his reaction. "I love it when people are so open-minded."

Finally Leanne said something to Karen, and she turned to her husband and placed an arm on his shoulder and spoke to him. He seemed to want to argue with her, but she only gave him a gentle pat on his arm and motioned for us to come in.

As I opened up my car door, I saw Kevin throw his arms up and stomp away into the house. Teeko flipped the bird at his retreating back, and Leanne giggled, putting her hand over Karen's sign language.

Gilley and Steven also got out and approached the house. "Hello!" Leanne said as I came up the stairs. "I'm Leanne."

"Good afternoon," I said, shaking her hand. "I'm M. J. Holliday."

"I've heard so much about you, M.J.," Leanne said. Turning to Teeko she added, "You were right, Karen; she does look just like Sandra Bullock."

"Oh!" Gil said, jumping in on the action. "Who do I look like?"

Leanne laughed. "You must be Gilley," she said, and was rewarded with some enthusiastic head nodding. "Well," she said, taking an appraising look at my partner. "I'd say that you must be related to Josh Hartnett."

Gilley beamed, and I hid a smile. For the record, Gil looks *nothing* like Josh Hartnett. He doesn't even look like Josh Hartnett's fifth cousin. On a good day Gil is five foot seven (on a bad he's a little closer to five-six), with thick, unruly brown hair, a strong Roman nose, and eyebrows that dominate his face. His strong suits are his broad shoulders and something of a bubble butt, which he makes sure to swish every time he's within eyesight of a good-looking man.

Still, the ego boost seemed to be good for him, given the way he was puffing out his chest and batting his eyes at Leanne. "And this must be the good doctor?" Leanne added, turning to Steven.

"I am like Antonio Banderas, no?" he said, sweeping up her hand and giving it a kiss.

Leanne blushed and waved her free hand in front of her face. "Oh, my," she said. "Handsome and an MD. May I ask, what is a doctor doing on a ghost expedition?"

"I am a Jack of trading," said Steven.

I smirked. Steven never met a woman he didn't flirt with. "Dr. Sable has taken an interest in what Gilley and I do and has become our newest partner."

"But you're the medium, right?" Leanne said, pointing to me.

"I am," I admitted.

"I'm so grateful that you've agreed to help Evie out," Leanne said.

"Happy to do it. Is she here?"

"She's up in the studio. I thought it might be a good idea for her to sit with me and paint this afternoon, anything to take her mind off what happened yesterday."

"Is she up to talking with us?" I asked.

Leanne nodded. "I hope so. Come on; I'll take you up."

We headed back down the few steps leading to the front door and hurried through the rain to the side door I'd seen Leanne come out of. "It's up these stairs," Leanne said as she held the door open for us.

We trooped up the narrow staircase and came to a huge room with high ceilings, white walls, light hardwood floors, and fantastic lighting. Enormous windows on the left side of the studio gave an incredible view of the lake and garden behind the garage. Up against many of the windows were a half dozen easels, most with paintings of the lake, gardens, and mountains. Cluttering the space were canvases, empty easels, and drop cloths. "It's a bit of a mess in here," Leanne said as she hurried into the room and began straightening up.

On the other side of the studio, in front of the very last easel, sat a thin girl with long, wildly curly hair and overalls. She was looking at us with big brown eyes and a face that was as beautiful as her mother's. "Hey, there," I said, heading across the room toward her. "My name is M.J."

"Hi," she said in a voice that wasn't much above a whisper. "I'm Evie."

"That is one beautiful name," I said.

"Thanks."

I pulled a stool over to sit close so we could talk. "You like to paint?" I asked, noting her easel, which was turned away from me.

Evie nodded.

"I have no artistic talent at all," I said. "It must be great to be able to draw something your mind imagines."

Evie shrugged.

"You're probably wondering why I'm here," I said.

I got another shrug.

"I'm a friend of your aunt's," I said, pointing behind me to Karen, standing with Leanne and my two partners. Evie gave her aunt a shy smile, and Karen waved and gave her a big, encouraging grin. "She came to me and said that something bad happened to you yesterday."

Evie's posture stiffened. Still, she managed to give me another shrug.

"As I was saying," I continued, trying to soften my voice as much as possible, "your aunt came to me and asked if I might be able to help with what happened to you. You see, I have this really cool ability to talk to people who are no longer here."

Evie's head cocked to the side like a trusting puppy's. "What do you mean?"

"Well," I said, thinking how I might explain what I did in a way that wouldn't sound creepy. At that moment I felt a thump on my energy, but it was very low. I looked down at the ground, momentarily distracted, and said the name that had entered my brain: "Paddington."

Evie's tone became sharp. "What?" she demanded.

I glanced up at her and noticed that those big wide eyes were staring at me with so much emotion. "Paddington Bear," I said again. "You had a dog named Paddington Bear, right?"

Instantly Evie's eyes watered and her lower lip began to tremble.

I smiled. I was in. "He keeps doing figure eights around you," I said. This got me another gasp. "And he says you dream about him all the time."

"I do!" Evie said as she looked down at the ground, trying to see the energy circling her even now.

"Paddington says he's hanging out with . . ." I hesitated, trying to sound out the name. "Me-ma?"

That brought me another gasp. "My grandmother!" she squealed.

I grinned broadly and gave her a nod. "She and Paddington are having a great time. And your Me-ma is saying she knew you'd learn to knit eventually."

"I just learned that at school!" Evie said.

"One of the other girls taught me, and we made these really cool scarves! Except we can't wear them until it gets cold again."

I laughed. "So now you know what I do," I said. "I talk to people who are no longer here."

"You talk to dead people," Evie said succinctly. "It's cool. I've seen *The Sixth Sense.*"

I laughed again. "Thank God for that film or I might be considered particularly freakish."

"How did you learn to talk to dead people?" she asked me with those big, inquisitive eyes.

"I didn't so much learn as I discovered," I said. "I was about your age when my mother died. Just before her death, her parents, who were both dead, came to my bedside and said that my mother was coming to see them, and that she wouldn't be back. And they kept coming to my bedside for many nights, long after she'd passed away, to let me know that she was doing well and that they were happy to have her with them again. From there I got visits from other people's grandparents and uncles and aunts and parents and friends. For a while there in high school my bedroom was a major gathering place for the dead."

"That is so cool," Evie said.

"It can be," I said smugly. "My partner — that's him over there," I said, pointing to Gilley, who waved back at us. "He's the one who encouraged me to start reading for people professionally."

"Like that guy on the cable channel, what's his name?" she said, and tapped her chin thoughtfully with her forefinger. "John Edwards?"

"John Edward," I corrected, referring to one of the more famous names in professional mediumship. "Yep, I'm a little like him. So, Evie," I said, trying to get back to the topic at hand, "about what happened to you . . ."

"It was Hatchet Jack," she said, with those big, wide eyes. "He came after me."

"Is it all right if we talk about it?"

Evie went back to shrugging. "I guess," she said.

"Tell me what happened, and try not to leave anything out."

Evie picked up her paintbrush and began painting while she talked. "It was during first period science class," she said. "I have Mr. Vesnick — he's way cool, and a bunch of us think he's really cute." Evie blushed slightly when she realized she'd said this out loud.

"I had a good-looking science teacher once too," I said, trying to make her feel at ease.

Evie smiled shyly and continued. "So, Mr. Vesnick was giving us our final. Part of the test was about finding these certain types of plants on the school grounds and bringing them back to hand in at the end of class. I'd found a really cool sample of clematis out behind the old wing, and I didn't have a lot of time left before Mr. Vesnick was gonna call time, so I cut through the elementary building instead of going around it."

"I'm following," I encouraged.

Evie's voice became shaky as she got to the next part. "So, I'm, like, walking through the hallway, and I hear someone coming down the hallway behind me. I thought it was Alice Crenshaw — she's my lab partner — but when I looked behind me, nobody was there."

"But you still heard the footsteps approaching, am I right?"

Evie glanced at me. "Yeah, I did. Anyway, I'm, like, really scared, so I start running, but the footsteps start running too, and I look back again and that's when I see him."

"Who?" I asked gently.

Evie swiveled her easel around to show

me what she'd been painting. Her artistic skills were quite extraordinary for a fourteen-year-old. The painting was straight out of a horror flick. It portrayed a man with a crazed look in his eyes, sharp, angular features, a receding hairline, and a hatchet raised high and threateningly above him as he ran down a long hallway. "Yikes," I said as I looked at the picture.

"I can't get him out of my head," Evie admitted, her eyes watering.

I stood up off my stool and wrapped my arms around her. "I know the feeling, babe," I said. "But here's the good news. One of the other things I do is send ghostly types like Hatchet Jack to a place where they can never scare anyone again."

Evie squeezed me hard, and I held her for another moment. Finally she pulled back and said, "The other kids are really scared to move into the new dorms. We all know Hatchet Jack haunts that old building."

"Do you know when they plan to complete the renovations?"

"They were waiting for the kids to be let out for the summer to do the heavy stuff."

"When is that?"

"The last day of class is tomorrow. Everyone's going home either tomorrow or Saturday."

"That's actually a good thing," I said. "The last thing I want is to try to chase this guy all over campus with kids around."

"The teachers don't believe us," Evie said. "The dean was really mean to me. He said that I was making the whole thing up to get out of my finals, but I wasn't, M.J.!"

"I believe you, Evie," I said, meeting her gaze. "I know that what you experienced was real. And like I said before, I won't leave Northelm without sending that monster back where he belongs."

"Are you going to send him to hell?"

I grinned. "Not exactly, but it might feel that way to him. Listen, can I take that painting with me?" I asked, pointing to her portrait.

She nodded and gave it to me. "Sure. And don't worry about giving it back. I don't think I want to see it again."

"You got it, kiddo." It was then that I noticed the dark circles under her eyes and how tired she looked. "Didn't get much sleep last night, I'll bet, huh?"

"Nope," she confirmed.

"Well, that makes sense, then."

"What?"

"Why Paddington is all over you. He's around to protect you from now on. You won't have to worry about the likes of

Hatchet Jack showing up around here, Evie. Paddington's going to keep anything bad away, so you can get some sleep and not worry about it, okay?"

Evie seemed to brighten. "Really?" she asked me. "He's really around me?"

I focused hard on the little energy that had been running in figure eights around her earlier. "He was a cocker spaniel, right? Kind of caramel colored?"

Evie broke into a huge grin. "Yes!" she said, and clapped her hands. "I really miss him. He died last summer."

"Well, his body might not be around anymore, Evie, but his spirit is sticking close to you. I promise, it's safe to fall asleep, okay?"

"Thanks," she said.

I got up off my chair and gave her another squeeze. "I gotta get going, but it was really nice meeting you. And if there's anything else you can think of that might help me you can call me anytime." And with that I handed her my card.

Evie took my card and looked up at. "M.J.?" she asked.

"Yes?"

"I can't go back there if he's still there. You have to get rid of him, okay?"

And that was when I did something I

never do. I promised with a cross over my heart that I would make sure I rid the school of his evil presence. It was a big promise on my part, because sometimes an energy is so vile, so evil, so intent on staying put that there's little we humans can do about it. I only hoped that this thing wasn't one of those, because if it was, I was in deep doo-doo.

CHAPTER 3

Shortly after I talked with Evie we all took our leave. As we piled back into our vehicles Karen asked me, "What'd she paint?"

I had propped the canvas up in the van, because the paint was still wet and I didn't want it to get on Karen's leather upholstery. "It was a pretty horrifying rendition of this Hatchet Jack character who's haunting the old elementary wing of the school."

"Lovely name," Karen said. "Wonder who thought it up."

"The name Jack is pretty curious," I said. "It might indicate that someone somewhere knew who this guy was."

"Evie never talked about any ghost at her school before yesterday."

"Probably because he wasn't active until the construction started. Plus, it sounds as if there haven't been many people hanging out in the elementary wing for a long time."

Karen nodded. "According to Leanne,

when the school was first built that was the only building. The others have been added on with time, so you can imagine the electrical and plumbing problems a hundred-year-old building would have. A small electrical fire broke out there the first year Evie attended, and since then they've pretty much kept the kids and faculty out of there."

"I'll want to talk to some of the older students; maybe some of them can fill me in on anything that went on in the years before the fire. Some of the faculty might be willing to talk as well."

"I'll take you guys to the ski lodge and get you settled first; then we'll head over to the school. The kids get out after finals tomorrow, so hopefully we can talk to a few of them before they head home for the summer."

We arrived at the O'Neal family ski lodge a short time later, after we'd picked up some groceries. The place was gorgeous. It was classic A-frame construction made of cedar wood, with huge windows that allowed you to see from the front of the house straight through to the lake behind. "That's Echo Lake?" I asked as we got out of the car and Gilley and Steven pulled in behind us.

"It is," she said.

"Whoa," I heard Gil exclaim. "Is this

77

where we're staying?"

I nodded. "Yep."

Gilley sidled up next to me, and out of the corner of his mouth he said, "Don't rush this job, okay? I'd really like to stay here awhile."

I laughed and gave him a pat on the back. "Champagne taste on a beer budget again, Gil?"

"It sure beats our condos," he said, and I had to agree. Gil and I lived one floor away from each other in two tiny condos in Arlington, Massachusetts, about fifteen minutes from downtown Boston.

We headed inside, and the smells of the wood and the mountain air were so refreshing that I paused in the spacious den that overlooked a boat dock and sighed happily. "You like?" Steven said from behind me.

"I could definitely get used to it," I said. "It's beautiful up here, don't you think?"

Steven nodded. "I had a friend in Germany who had a ski house in the Swiss Alps. Someday I will take you there and you can tell me which you like better."

I swiveled and gave him a smile. "You're going to take me to Switzerland?"

He nodded. "Someday," he said.

"Whoo-hoo!" we heard from one of the bedrooms. A moment later Gilley came bounding out into the hallway. "M.J.! There's a hot tub!"

"There's also a sauna," said Karen from the kitchen. "And downstairs there's a full game room, complete with a pool table and Xbox 360."

"Teeko," Gilley said seriously, "I've never had feelings for a girl before, but you may be the one to convert me."

We all laughed; then I glanced at the clock on the wall. It was getting close to one o'clock. "We'll need to get rolling if we're going to get to the school and do some interviews."

Everyone hustled to unload the van. I got Doc settled into one of the bedrooms and went back out to get my luggage. When I returned to the bedroom I noticed Steven's Gucci valise next to the bed. Crap, he wanted this room. Picking Doc up I carried his cage into one of the other bedrooms, and, after putting his cage on a table near the window, I set my luggage on the bed. I then took my toiletries into the adjoining bathroom and returned to the bedroom for one more check on Doc before going back outside to the car.

It was then that I noticed Steven's leather valise parked next to my luggage on the bed. I rolled my eyes and decided to deal with him later.

We were on our way five minutes later, me riding shotgun, with Karen and the boys following in the van behind us. My stomach gave a terrific growl, and with a knowing smile Teeko made a quick stop at the local Burger King drive-through.

Not long after we got back on the road and were scarfing down our junk food, we saw the first sign for Northelm. "This place is out in the boonies," I said as I looked around at nothing but forest on either side of the highway.

"Typical boarding school mentality," said Karen. "Isolate the kids to keep them out of trouble."

"Wonder if it works," I mused.

"Never did for me," she said.

"You went to boarding school?"

Teeko nodded. "Marymount International, in London. Hated every single second of it."

"Wow, I had no idea you were so cosmopolitan."

Karen bounced her eyebrows at me. "Oh, I'm a *Cosmo* girl, all right. But I only read it for the articles."

I smiled, then saw another sign for Northelm. "We're close," I said, pointing to the sign. "It should be the next turnoff."

Five minutes later we were driving down a long and winding slope on our way to a row of large buildings at the base of a valley. To our left was a huge pond with a scrubby island in the center. Straight ahead were several side-by-side fields of green marked off for what looked like soccer, lacrosse, and football. To the far right were rows of tennis courts, and next to those a track and field.

The backdrop to all this was, of course, the Adirondacks, which loomed large and panoramic in the background. "Wow," I said as I took in the breathtaking view. "What a gorgeous place to put a school."

"I was here last year for Evie's graduation from eighth grade," Karen said. "The kids rave about living here."

"I can see why."

We parked in a large lot to the side of the main buildings and hoofed it through the drizzle to the main entrance. Steven got the door for us, and we walked into the school.

A sign overhead with an arrow pointed us to the admin office, and we followed after Karen as her heels clicked on the parquet flooring, passing row upon row of trophy cases lined with all sorts of medals, ribbons, plaques, and trophies.

We stopped at a set of double doors, and again Steven held these open for us as we trooped through. A receptionist behind the desk glanced up over her half-moon reading glasses and said, "Miss O'Neal?"

"Yes," said Karen.

"Dean Habbernathy is expecting you. Please follow me."

I was a little surprised that the dean was expecting us, but when we went into his office and saw Leanne sitting there, I understood.

Behind a large cherrywood desk a tall, thin man with white-blond hair and sparkling blue eyes, who appeared to be in his mid-forties, stood to greet us. "Good afternoon," he said, extending his hand.

One by one we shook it, gave him a brief introduction, and took a seat in one of the chairs in the room. Luckily there were just enough to accommodate all of us. "Mrs. O'Neal has told me of your request to perform some sort of ritual here at the school, Miss O'Neal," the dean began. "But I'm afraid I cannot allow it."

Karen looked completely unfazed. "I appreciate your hesitancy, Dean Habbernathy," she said in a calm, even voice. "However, I'm hoping you'll at least hear us out before making your final decision."

The dean smiled uncomfortably. "Yes, but you see, I've already made my final decision," he said. Turning to Leanne he added, "I appreciate that your daughter was upset by something she thought she may have seen in the old building, Mrs. O'Neal, but the school's integrity is at stake here. If word got out that I had allowed some sort of exorcism on school grounds, we'd have parents questioning my decision making and pulling their children out of school right and left."

"Dean Habbernathy," Leanne said, growing visibly furious. "My daughter saw something on school grounds that terrified her. She saw it in a wing that is rumored to be haunted, and which none of the students want to go near. That same wing is the area you intend to board them in next year. What could be worse for morale than forcing students to live in a haunted environment where they are constantly in fear of invoking some demonic force?"

I saw the dean inhale and exhale. He wasn't a believer; I could tell. In a quiet but firm voice he said, "I'm so terribly sorry, Mrs. O'Neal, but it is not something I am willing to entertain considering at this time."

Karen looked thoughtfully at the dean. "I have a question," she said. "When will construction begin on the new dorm?"

The dean seemed to blanch. He dropped

his eyes and shuffled papers around on his desk. Clearing his throat, he said, "We're waiting on the children to leave for the summer recess to begin construction. That way the noise won't disturb classes," said the dean.

Something in the dean's mannerisms about when the construction would begin alerted me, and Karen must have picked up on it too, because she boldly asked, "Have you secured the financing for this construction yet, Dean Habbernathy?"

The dean scowled. She'd struck a nerve. "We expect to hear from our bank any day now," he said. "As soon as the children have left for the summer and the bank approves our loan, construction will begin."

"Aren't you concerned about getting a construction crew out here on such short notice?" Karen asked. She'd dated John Dodge of Dodge Construction for three years — Karen knew about construction crews.

"I'm sure that won't be a problem once we've secured the financing," the dean said firmly, and we could all tell that his patience was wearing thin on that topic.

Karen changed tack. "How many children will the new dorm accommodate once it's complete?" she asked.

"It will allow us to double our numbers," said the dean smugly. "And as we are at max capacity and are having to turn away potential applicants every year, adding accommodations makes good business sense."

Karen was quiet for a long moment as she tapped her chin and looked at the dean. Finally she stood up and said, "Thank you for your time, Dean Habbernathy. We'll be taking our leave for the time being."

I was startled that Karen had called such an abrupt close to our meeting, especially since I had my own argument for the dean lined up. "You're giving up that easily?" I asked once we were out in the hallway.

"Hell, no," she said, a look of determination firmly planted on her face. Once we were at the front door Karen handed me her keys and said, "You go wait out in the car. I've got a call to make. I'll join you in a minute."

I looked quizzically at her but followed her directive. Leanne trotted next to me, lending me her umbrella while the boys ran through the rain back to the van. "What do you think she's up to?" Leanne asked me.

"Not sure. But knowing Karen, it's bound to be spectacular."

Little did I know the half of it. Karen joined me in the car a short time later and

85

immediately began fluffing her hair and checking her reflection. "Want to let me in on what's going on?" I asked.

She gave me a broad smile in return. "I've set up another meeting with the dean," she said. "But this one's going to be a little more private."

My jaw dropped. "You're going to seduce him?" I gasped.

Karen tilted her head back and laughed heartily. "Hardly," she said. "No, the seducing is for someone else." With that cryptic remark she started her car and drove us back to the lodge, where Karen ducked into her bedroom while Gilley got to making us some sort of lavish feast for dinner and Steven and I headed downstairs to check out the game room.

"Look!" said Steven, pointing to an air hockey table. "Hockey!"

I giggled at his enthusiasm. "Do you play? 'Cuz I'm good."

"Yes, I play," he said confidently. "I will be mopping the flooring with you."

I smiled wryly. "*Really?* Well, then, how about a little wager?"

"You want to bet some money?" he asked.

"I surely do," I said, picking up one of the handles and flipping the switch for the air.

"How much?"

"How much do you have in your pocket?"

"Couple grand," he said nonchalantly.

I frowned. "Okay, so an amount significantly less than that," I said. "How about a hundred bucks." That was my allowance for the week. If I lost it, I'd have to mooch off Gilley.

"You are on," he said, picking up his own handle.

We played furiously for the next hour, and I had to admit Steven was good, but not as good as *moi.* I was one point away from collecting my moola when a loud *thump, thump, thump* came from outside. Steven looked up at the noise, and I smashed the puck with all my might. It slid into his goal and I threw up my arms. "Whoop!" I yelled.

"That is no fair!" Steven cried, and it was then that I realized he was shouting. The *thump, thump, thump* from outside was getting louder. "What *is* that?" he asked.

"Not sure," I yelled. "Come on!" And we headed upstairs. Gilley was staring out the front window, a bowl cradled in one arm, a spoon in his other hand.

"What's going on?" I shouted, and it was then that I noticed the trees across the large lawn were blowing and bending away from the house.

Gilley didn't have to answer me, because

the next moment a helicopter dropped down onto the front lawn. On the side of the helicopter it read, J. DODGE INC.

"Uh, Karen?" I yelled. "You need to come here, quick!"

Karen appeared a moment later looking so gorgeous it hurt to look at her. "Oh, good," she said, glancing outside. "My ride is here."

We were all just staring at her with open mouths and wide eyes when the doorbell rang and we jumped.

Karen opened the door, and a man in a pilot's uniform stood there on the front step. He tipped his head to her and said, "Miss O'Neal."

"Charlie," Karen said warmly. "It's so nice to see you again."

"We've missed you, ma'am," Charlie said with a slight blush.

"That's sweet of you, Charlie. Is Mr. Dodge waiting out there for me?"

"Yes, ma'am. He's in the chopper. Oh, and these are for you," he said, handing over a gigantic bouquet of flowers.

"They're lovely, Charlie. I'll have to thank John's assistant for picking them out for me."

"Oh, no, ma'am," Charlie was quick to say. "Mr. Dodge selected that arrangement himself."

Karen cocked an eyebrow at him. "Really?" she said, but I could tell she was secretly pleased at the revelation. Handing the bouquet to me, she said, "M.J., would you do me a favor and put these on the counter in the kitchen? I don't want to be late for our meeting with the dean."

I grinned, finally understanding why Karen had asked Dean Habbernathy if he'd already raised the funding for the new wing. "You got it, gal pal. Now go on and have fun, and we won't wait up for you."

Karen cut me a look that said that might be a good idea, then ducked under the umbrella Charlie had opened for her and crossed the lawn to the helicopter. The door opened and out jumped a tall, absolutely beautiful man with impossibly broad shoulders, a thin waist, ebony hair, and a strong jaw. He planted a quick kiss on Karen's cheek and helped her into the chopper. A moment later they were gone.

When the trees had settled down again Gilley turned to me and demanded, "Dish!"

I shrugged my shoulders. "She hasn't told me any more than she's told you," I said. "But my guess is that on the way over to that school Karen is going to convince John of the importance of receiving a decent education. And what better place to get a good education than at a boarding school. And every child who boards away from the safety and comfort of their own home needs to feel safe in that environment.

"She'll point out that it's too bad the children at this particular boarding school are in fear of their lives and are terrified to return to a school next year where they could at any moment be attacked by some wild demon!" I added with a dramatic flourish.

"She's going to convince him to donate the funding and the construction crew to the school," Gilley summed up succinctly.

"That'd be my guess. Dodge made *Forbes*'s Wealthiest Men in America list last year, so my guess is that man has money to burn. He'll fork over a few hundred thousand like it's nothing, and that will give Karen the leverage she needs to convince the dean to let us go in and do our thing."

"She is very clever," said Steven.

"She is," I agreed. "Now hand over my hundred."

Steven slanted his eyes at me. "You cheated."

"I did not cheat," I insisted. "I merely took advantage of a lapse in concentration from my opponent to score the winning point."

Steven reached into his pocket and pulled out his money clip. Peeling off one of the bills, he handed it to me. "I will want to rematch," he said.

I snapped the money out of his hand. "Anytime, anywhere, Doc."

"Snap, crackle, and pop!" said Gilley, swiveling his eyes back and forth between us. "You two have enough chemistry going on between you to be hazardous. I'm heading back to the kitchen. Dinner will be ready in twenty minutes."

We ate a delicious meal of veal piccata and retired to the living room to watch television and wait for Karen to get back. By eleven thirty I gave up and stood, ready to call it a night and head to bed. "Looks like Teeko and John are hitting it off," I said, stretching. "I'm going to bed."

Gilley was on the other couch, and he gave a loud snore. I glanced over, surprised that he'd dropped off so early. Gil was usually the last one to bed. "He fell asleep an hour ago," Steven said.

"Must be the mountain air," I said. "Well, I'm off to sleep too. Good night, Steven."

"I will join you," he said, getting up from the couch. With a smile I noticed that he paused next to Gil's couch and pulled an afghan from a nearby basket. After draping it over my friend, he followed after me. When we got to my bedroom I turned and said, "Good night," again.

Steven looked over my shoulder. "Are you sleeping in here too?" he asked me with mock surprise.

"You know I am." I giggled.

"Oh, well, my things are already in here, so we might as well share."

"Doc's a pretty bird!" Doc said from his perch. "Doc's cuckoo for Cocoa Puffs!"

"He's got a million of 'em," I said, glancing at my bird. "He'll keep it up all night if he wants to."

"He is not liking me?" Steven said.

"He is not liking you *with* me," I replied. "Doc's pretty possessive. You should have seen what he did to a few of my ex-boyfriends. It takes him a while to warm up to the idea of someone else in the room."

"We could leave him here and go into one of the other bedrooms."

"Doc's lonely!" my bird squawked as he fluttered his wings and started pacing along his perch. I could tell his agitation was increasing the longer Steven hovered near me. "Doc wants Mama!"

I sighed. "Better take a rain check on that one, my friend," I said. Inching up on my toes I gave Steven a light kiss, and that was the wrong thing to do because Doc went ballistic. *"Pow!"* he yelled, and the sound was eerily similar to a gunshot. "Gilley! Gilley, come quick!" he shouted, fluttering about and flapping his wings. "Doc's been shot! Doc's in pain! Doc's going to the light!"

We heard footsteps running down the hallway toward us, and a bleary-eyed Gilley appeared. "What's wrong with Doc?" he asked as my bird fluttered and squawked around in his cage.

"Nothing," I said, giving Steven an apologetic look. "He's just doing his possessive bird bit."

Gilley blinked and seemed to take in how close Steven and I were standing. "Oh," he said. "Well, he's making a hell of a racket, M.J."

"I know," I said, moving across the room to open up Doc's cage. "He's just a little — Ack! Doc, no!" But it was too late. Doc flew out of his cage and headed directly toward Steven. Squawking and fluttering about Steven's head, Doc bit him on the ear.

"Ow!" Steven said; then he started speaking angrily in Spanish.

"Gilley!" I said as I ran to Steven's side. "Help me get Doc!"

But Doc was having none of it. He circled the room and aimed straight for Steven's head again; this time, though, Steven got his arms up in the nick of time and Doc only scratched his arm.

"Your bird is *loco!*" Steven shouted and fled from the room. I quickly closed the door behind him, and Doc settled on the bedpost. Gil leaned against the door and said, "Maybe you're going to want to keep Doc in his cage for this job?"

I nodded. "And I wonder why I've been single all these years. Come here, Doc," I said. *"Now."*

Doc whistled long and low and twirled around on the bedpost twice before flying to my hand. I stroked his feathers and gave him a kiss. "Silly bird," I said, and put him gently back into his cage.

"Did Teeko call?" Gil asked me, and at that moment my cell phone rang. I hurried over to it and answered.

"You're in," Karen said. "John and I have cleared everything with the dean. The only stipulation is that you three will have to wait two days to go in and do your ghostbusting. The dean doesn't want any of the students exposed. Most of them should be gone by the end of the weekend, but if you see any kids left on the campus, you can't tell them what you're doing."

"Got it," I said. "Can I still talk to the faculty?"

"Yes, if you can find any. The dean said there really wouldn't be anyone left on campus beyond Sunday. Most of the teaching staff will have cleared out as well."

"Well, that makes things a little tougher, but we'll deal with it," I said.

"And there's one more thing," Karen said, and I could tell by the tone in her voice that she was pissed about the next bit of news. "You'll have to get in there, M.J., and get rid of Jack in five days. We can't go beyond a week from today."

"Why not?" I asked, feeling like the pressure was really on now.

"John's crew is available for only a few weeks between the week after next and the second week in July. He thinks he can complete the renovations by then, but he can't delay construction by a minute past midnight next Friday."

"Okay," I said reluctantly. "Then we'll have to make sure we work this one quick." In the background of our call I heard birds chirping and singing. Glancing outside at the dark I asked, "Where are you that birds are awake and singing?"

"Paris," Karen said. "John chartered a jet

and we made it here about twenty minutes ago."

"Ah," I replied. "Then I guess we won't wait up for you."

"Probably a good idea," she said. "Do you remember your way to the school?"

"Gilley's got his mapping gizmo in the van. We'll find it just fine."

"Good. I'll be back as soon as possible," she said, and we said our good-byes.

"We've got the okay?" Gil asked from behind me.

"Yep. We'll have to wait it out here until Monday, and we're not allowed to talk to the kids if we see any, but we can do our baseline this weekend."

"Perfect!" he said happily. "I can spend the weekend in the hot tub."

The next two days passed slowly. It continued to rain, which left us all a little on edge. Gilley hung out in the hot tub, and Steven and I spent a lot of time in the game room. By five o'clock on Sunday we were all climbing the walls. "Let's go into town for dinner," said Steven. "My treat."

We made our way to town and pulled into the Mirror Lake Inn, then headed toward the View Restaurant inside. We were seated at an elegantly dressed table overlooking the spectacular Mirror Lake.

This early in the evening the restaurant was only half-full, and most of the diners were of a somewhat older demographic. "Early-bird special," Gilley teased, snapping open his menu.

"Good evening," said a soft male voice next to me. I looked up to see a handsome waiter in a crisp white coat and black pants, with a name tag that read, ANDREW.

"Hi, Andrew," Gilley said quickly, setting his menu down and sitting up straight in his chair. Gil never met a handsome man he didn't flirt with.

Andrew greeted him warmly, then asked us for our drink orders, promising to be back shortly to tell us about the specials. "He's nice," Steven said when Andrew had gone.

"Years from now I'll tell people about the first time I laid eyes on my husband," Gil said dreamily.

I smirked and reopened my menu, and that was when I got a hard thump on my shoulder. I scowled and ignored the thump. But whoever was bumping up against my energy wasn't having it and kept thumping. I sighed heavily and closed my menu. I couldn't concentrate with the constant bumping.

"What is the matter?" Steven asked, noticing my irritation.

"Someone's trying to get my attention," I said.

Steven and Gilley both looked around the restaurant. "Who?" Gil asked.

"Not sure," I answered. "But it began right after Andrew showed up, so my thinking is, it's connected to him."

My feelings were confirmed the moment Andrew came back to our table and set down our wineglasses. The thumping was so intense that I finally opened up my energy and thought, *Fine! You win. Who are you and what can I do for you?*

The name Richard impressed itself firmly on my mind. Glancing up at Andrew, who was reaching into his inside pocket to pull out a small notepad, I said, "Andrew, do you happen to know a Richard?"

Andrew smiled. "Yes, he's working the back section. Would you prefer to sit at one of his tables this evening?"

In my mind I got the sensation of a vigorous head shake no. I reached out to the energy again and asked him for clarification. Again I got the name Richard, and I felt like the name in question belonged to this spirit who had crossed over. I smiled tightly at Andrew and tried again. "I'm sorry, Andrew, but I think I've asked this question incorrectly. Do you know someone who's *deceased* named Richard?"

Andrew blinked dumbly at me for a moment, and then the look was replaced by one of confusion. "No," he said carefully.

Inside my head I got an *intense* feeling he did. I glanced at Gilley, not knowing how else to proceed. "Andrew," Gil said calmly. "I don't want to upset or alarm you, but my friend here is a professional medium. Sometimes when she encounters a total stranger, someone from the other side will attempt to make contact through her. It appears that's happening right now, and my friend here needs you to think hard, because if we don't identify this person trying to make contact with you, none of us will be able to enjoy our meal."

Andrew stood mutely for a full minute, looking from me to Gilley and back again. Finally he said very quietly, "I had an older brother," he said. "He ran away when I was seven, and we never heard from him again. His name was Richard."

Inside my head there was an explosion of emotion, something like a eureka going off in my mind. "I'm so sorry to tell you this," I said to Andrew. "But your brother is here, and he's trying to talk to you."

Andrew had gone a little pale, a common reaction to my intuitive abilities. "He's really dead?" he asked me.

"Yes," I said, and reached up to squeeze his arm. "I feel he died shortly after he left home."

Andrew swayed slightly, and Steven jumped out of his seat. Pulling the chair out, he set Andrew down and handed him a glass of water. "Drink," he said firmly.

Andrew looked around, probably extremely self-conscious of where he was and what he was doing, but he took a small sip and thanked Steven. "My mother is going to freak," he said. "All these years she's held out hope that Richard was still alive."

There was a flurry of information going on in my head, and I had the distinct feeling that not only did Richard die shortly after he left home, but that he had been murdered. "Tell me about when he ran away," I said.

Andrew took another sip of water and said, "It was thirty years ago. I was seven and Richard was sixteen. He was my hero in a lot of ways. He had his own car, and he smoked pot, and he was supercool. And then one night he had a really bad fight with my dad and he left, just like that. No good-byes, no 'See ya later.' Just gone."

Richard was showing me a bunch of intense images, one of which involved a body of water. I felt the poor young man had drowned, and I knew he'd died at the hands of someone else. "Did Richard have any enemies?" I asked.

Andrew seemed to catch where I was going with this. "He was murdered?"

I nodded. "That's what he's telling me."

Andrew dropped his gaze to the tablecloth. "Richard was a pretty cocky kid," he said. "My family lives in Wheaton, and where I come from there's always someone out to get you."

"I don't understand," I said.

"Wheaton is about twenty miles from Lake Placid. It's blue-collar. Most of the service-industry people who work in Lake Placid live there. Wheaton's got its share of drugs and gangs and bad stuff. It wouldn't surprise me if Richard got into it with someone and came out on the losing end."

"Is there a lake or a pond in Wheaton?" I asked, as the image wouldn't leave my mind.

Andrew shook his head. "No. All the lakes and ponds are over on this side of the tracks. Is his body near water?"

I nodded. "Not so much near as in, I'm afraid. He's telling me he drowned."

Andrew's face fell. "You know, he was

101

always afraid of water. That's why he swore he'd never come to work around here."

Richard gave my mind a few more images, and I said, "Your brother is telling me that he's very proud of the fact that you're going back to school."

Andrew seemed to brighten. "He knows that?"

"Yep. You go back in the fall, right? And it's something to do with health care?"

"That's right!" he exclaimed. "I think thirty-seven is too old to still be a waiter, so I'm going to NYU in the fall to become an X-ray technician."

"Your brother says you'll do great," I said.

Just then a man in a dark business suit came by our table. "Excuse me, Andrew? Is everything all right?" he asked, looking pointedly at Andrew.

Steven stood up to his full height and said, "Everything is very good. Our waiter is participating in a little fun with us. He is a very good waiter. I think you should give him a raise."

Andrew stood up quickly, a flush coming over him. "I'm so sorry, Mr. Gearson," he said.

"Apologies are not necessary," said Steven sternly, looking sharply at what I assumed was Andrew's manager. "We insisted that you sit down, and you were merely doing what we asked."

Mr. Gearson smiled tightly. "Well," he said. "As long as everything is to your liking." With that he gave us a short bow and walked off.

"Thanks," Andrew said. "My manager's got a major stick up his butt."

Gilley giggled like he liked that idea, and I gave him a dirty look before reassuring Andrew. "Richard has pulled his energy back, but he wanted you to know that he meant to come back home, and he never would have left without saying good-bye to you."

Andrew nodded, and I saw his eyes grow moist. "Excuse me," he said, and hurried off.

"Are you going to try to cross this Richard over?" Steven asked, taking his seat.

I shook my head. "He's not a ghost. He's already on the other side."

"How can you tell when someone has made it over and someone else hasn't?" he said, passing the basket of rolls to me before taking one for himself.

I buttered my roll, thinking about it for a moment before I replied. "Basically I can tell the difference because the energies feel different."

"Different how?" Gil said.

"Well," I said, still trying to think of how to put it into words. "Earthbound energies — ghosts — feel lower."

"Lower?" Gil said.

"Yeah, like they hit me in a different way, sort of a thud in my solar plexus that then pulls down. Whereas energies that have already crossed over hit me in the stomach area too, but then their energy lifts up a little to float right around my head."

Steven and Gilley passed a look between them and then turned back to me. "We don't understand," Gil said.

I sighed. "I didn't say it was an easy thing to describe. It's more that I get a sense of lightness with energies who have crossed and a sense of being weighed down by energies who are stuck here. There's also the intensity of the energy. Ghosts are all about showing you the drama of what just happened to them. Spirits — or people who have crossed over — are much more into telling you about a loved one they want to connect with."

Gil's face seemed to register comprehension. "I get it," he said. "A ghost is all about the last moments of their death, and a spirit isn't as concerned with that so much as they are making contact, right?"

I smiled. "Exactly."

Andrew appeared next to us again, looking embarrassed. "I'm sorry," he said. "I forgot to get your order."

We ate our meal, which was one of the best I've had in a long time, and enjoyed some terrific service too. Andrew took excellent care of us, and even surprised us by presenting three delicious crème brûlées prepared especially for us by the chef. I thanked him for his attentiveness at the end of the meal, and that was when he shocked me with, "Did my brother mention who might have killed him?"

Gil and Steve stopped talking between them and gave their full attention to me. "No, Andrew, I'm so sorry. His sole purpose was making a connection to you."

Andrew smiled, but it didn't go anywhere near his eyes. "Yeah, I figured as much. Still, if he was murdered, I'd like to nail the bastard who did it."

At that moment Richard came lightly back into my energy, and the message I got from him was short and to the point. "Andrew," I began, feeling the message out. "Your brother is telling me that you may find out who killed him one of these days. He's saying that he promises to help reveal who it was and why."

Andrew brightened. "Thank you," he said kindly. "And your meal this evening is on me."

The three of us vehemently protested. The bill for our meal had to be in the three-hundred-dollar range, but Andrew would have none of it. "It's the least I can do," he insisted. "Please?"

Steven deferred to me, and I nodded reluctantly. "It's very kind of you, Andrew; we're very touched by your generosity."

He smiled. "Thank you," he said, and cleared our dessert plates. We chatted for another few minutes and then stood to leave. I noticed Steven reach for his wallet, and then he discreetly laid four one-hundred-dollar bills under his wineglass.

I gave him a huge grin and took his arm as we left the restaurant.

The next day Gil and I were up early, going over our plan of attack for the school and doing some last-minute equipment check-ing. Karen had sent me a text that she would call me as soon as the dean gave his okay, and by noon we still hadn't heard anything, so I went for a run.

When I got back Steven was in the kitchen sipping on some coffee. "Good morning," he said in his rich voice.

"Hey, there," I said, still breathing hard.

"Gilley is in the shower. He told me to tell you that Teeko has sent word; we can go to the school when you're ready."

"Great, let me just take a quick shower myself and we'll be on our way."

"Need any help with the back scrubbing?" he asked, looking at me over the brim of his mug with smoldering sensuality.

Thank God I was already red from my run, because I could feel my cheeks burn even hotter at the suggestion. "Nope," I said quickly, and hurried toward my bedroom. "Got it covered, thanks!"

"Next time, then," he called after me.

I hurried through my shower and met Gil and Steven back in the kitchen. "We ready?" I asked.

Gil saluted. "Van's loaded."

"Let's rocking roll!" Steven said.

I laughed and we left the lodge. We arrived back on the school's campus about ten minutes later and were met by an eerie quiet. The weather had improved a little — no rain, but thick black clouds threatened to unload some water if we even thought about walking around outside without an umbrella.

There hadn't been anyone walking around

on campus three days before, but it had still felt like it had a lot of activity going on. As we parked the van and each grabbed a duffel bag and some equipment, I looked at the landscape and frowned.

"What's wrong?" Steven asked me when he noticed I wasn't following after Gilley to the admin office.

"I'm not sure," I said. "But something wicked this way comes."

"I am not understanding this," Steven said.

I shivered a little and turned back to follow after Gilley. "It's nothing," I reassured him. "Just my radar picking up our ghost, I think."

We filed into the front door of the main building and made our way to the dean's office. No receptionist was there, but the lights were on. I rang a small bell on the counter, and a moment later Dean Habbernathy appeared. "Good afternoon," he said. "I was hoping you'd be by shortly. The last student has left campus for the summer, and I'm just about to close up here."

"We appreciate your cooperation on this, Dean," I said.

"Yes, well, Mr. Dodge and Miss O'Neal can be most persuasive."

Gil discreetly poked me in the ribs with

his elbow, but I ignored him.

"Mr. Dodge has convinced me to allow this . . . er . . . *procedure* to take place, and we've agreed to give you until Friday to complete whatever it is that you do. At that point Mr. Dodge's own construction company will be taking over the renovations on the new wing."

"How will we get in and out of the building?" I asked, noting that the dean had turned off the light to his office and was reaching for his coat.

"I will leave you a key," he said, and dug into his pocket. "It opens the door to that wing. The other buildings on the campus are off-limits, however."

Gilley took the key and said, "Thank you, Dean. We'll make sure to lock up after ourselves."

"I should hope so," he said. "Again, I must express that I really don't approve of this at all."

"Would you approve next year if half your students left because you hadn't taken care of the problem?" I snapped. This man's snobbery was getting on my last nerve.

The dean looked askance at me. "I don't believe there is a problem, Miss . . ."

"Holliday, and it's because of that attitude that one of your students had a mental breakdown once upon a time, am I right?"

The dean gasped, and Steven gave me a look that suggested I might have gone a little too far. "How did you know about that?" Habbernathy asked.

"I read it in the paper," I said, not backing down. "How many students does it take, Dean Habbernathy, for people like you to *want* to try something, *anything* that might help? I mean, I just don't understand all the resistance on your part."

The dean narrowed his electric blue eyes at me. I could tell he didn't like it when people stood up to him. "As I said, you have one week, Miss Holliday, to complete your ritual. Now, if you will excuse me." And with that he ushered us out into the front hall and hurried us out the door.

"Charming man," Gil said sarcastically as we watched the dean walk briskly to his car. "He must be a real hoot at parties."

"Come on," I groused, still put off by the dean's attitude. "Let's get on with this."

We carried our equipment over to the right of the main building. It was easy to tell where we were going, as a huge banner over the old elementary wing read, FUTURE SITE OF JOHN DODGE HALL.

Gilley pointed to the banner, "Subtle," he said. "I wonder how he got it up so fast?"

"Money talks, bulls walk," said Steven.

"Bullshit," I corrected.

"No, it is true," Steven insisted, misunderstanding me — again. "Money can motivate people sometimes better than bulls. Especially if they are walking bulls. You know, that saying really should be, 'Money talks like a charging bull.' It's better, no?"

I gave Gil a big wide-eyed stare. He could take this one. While Gil attempted to explain we arrived at the front door, and Gil set down his duffel bag to free up his hand and unlock the door. I glanced through the pane of glass into the dark hallway, and the hair stood up on the back of my neck exactly at the same time I saw a shadow pass from one classroom across the hall and into the opposite classroom. "Ohmigod!" I shouted.

"What?" Gil and Steven said together.

"Gil! Hurry! Open up the door!" I said, setting down my own duffel bag and grabbing at his hand for the key.

"M.J.!" Gil said with alarm. "What's going on?"

I snatched the key from him and shoved it into the lock, twisting and pulling at the same time. "It's Hatchet Jack!" I said, struggling with the door. "I just saw him in the hallway!"

Gilley laid his hand over mine and applied

pressure to the door with his free hand. He then turned the key and pulled, and the door swung open. I dashed inside and ran straight for the classroom where I'd seen the dark shadow pass. I pulled open that door and hurried inside. Nothing moved or looked amiss. "Crap!" I said.

Steven and Gilley came into the classroom then, and they too looked around. "Where is he?" Steven said.

I looked up and down the neat rows of small desks in perfect straight lines facing the chalkboard. "I swear I saw him duck in here."

"Maybe he —" Gil said, but was interrupted by a tremendous crash across the hall.

"What the . . . ?!" I shouted, and we ran out of that classroom and into the one across the hallway. The hair on my arms was now also standing on end, but in here as well everything looked orderly and neat. Desks were arranged in four long rows, perfectly angled to the teacher's desk in front of the chalkboard. "He's around," I said, and opened up my energy. "I can feel him."

Again another crash sounded, and we all jumped. It came from the classroom we'd just left, so we turned to head back across the hall when the classroom door smashed closed in our faces. Gil got the brunt of it, and the force that was used to close the door was so strong that it sent all three of us tumbling backward. "Bastard!" I swore, and jumped forward.

"Ohhhhh, my nose!" Gil moaned from the floor, holding his face while Steven tried to help him up.

"Shit!" I swore as I pushed at the knob on the door and threw my weight against it. "I think he locked us in here!" Stepping back, I swiveled slightly to an angle to the door and raised my foot. I'd been taking some Tae Bo lessons lately, and I was mad enough to kick that door into splinters. With a loud, "Ha!" I thrust my foot out as hard as I could . . . and fell flat on my face when the door swung open away from me and there was nothing to stop my momentum. To add to my humiliation, in my ear I distinctly heard the low, guttural laughing of something truly wicked.

"Ugh!" I said when I hit the ground rolling over to lie flat on my back.

"M.J.!" Steven said, leaving Gilley to come over to me. "Are you all right?"

"I'm fine!" I snapped, and got to my feet. Then I looked over at Gilley and took a deep breath. "How's Gil?"

"He's fine. Just a bruise."

"It hurts!" Gil whined in a nasal voice. "Why do they always attack *me?*" he added.

I moved back over to him. "Sorry, buddy. Do you want to go back to the van?"

Gilley nodded, still holding his nose. "Yes, please."

"Okay," I said, turning to Steven. "That leaves you and me to hunt this asshole down."

There was another crash from the classroom across the hall, and that door slammed shut too. "I believe I may know where he is at present," Steven said.

Gilley pushed off from the desk he was leaning on and dashed out of the classroom. I watched him run down the hallway without looking back and hurry outside to the van. "He is a brave man," Steven said as we watched Gilley run.

I broke into a grin. "Yeah, well, he's always telling us he likes to monitor things from the safety of the van."

Steven pointed to the other classroom. "Shall we?"

I set my shoulders and moved across the hallway to the closed door. Peering through the glass I saw a dark shadow disappear through the opposite wall, and the creepy feeling I'd had that made the hair on my neck and arms stand up vanished with him. I turned the handle on the door and pulled it open anyway and came up short. "Whoa," I said as I stepped into the classroom.

"Whoa," repeated Steven as he came in right behind me.

We were reacting to the perfect pyramid made up of every small desk in the room going up to the ceiling. "That is wild!" I said, crossing over to the desks.

Steven gasped. "Be careful, M.J.! The hatchet man could tip those over on you!"

"He's gone," I said calmly.

"Where?"

"Through there." And I pointed to the wall that faced the outside.

"Should we go after him?"

I thought about it for a moment before deciding. "Nah. He's long gone by now. My feeling is that he's got a pretty wide range, and he probably haunts this entire campus."

Steven glanced out at the parking lot, and I saw his eyes go wide with alarm. "Uh-oh," he said.

I turned and looked myself, and that was when I noticed Gilley being tugged back and forth on the sliding door of the van. Something had hold of either him or the van's door and was throwing him around like a puppet. *"Oh, shit!"* I yelled, and flew out of the classroom with Steven right behind me. We ran down the hall as fast as we could and bolted out the double doors. By this time Gilley was lying flat on the pavement, and my heart went straight to my throat. *"Gilley!"* I screamed, but he didn't move.

We got to him a moment later, and Steven knelt down by his head, placing his fingertips on Gil's neck for a pulse. I saw him breathe a sigh of relief and check carefully around Gilley's head for any signs of trauma. Finally he looked at me and said, "He's fainted."

I let go of the breath I'd been holding and pulled Gil close to me. "Oh, man! Gil, I'm so sorry!" I said to him. "I had no idea this thing was so strong and so mean!"

"Mwaha . . . ?" Gil said.

Steven was at Gil's feet, propping them up on the side of the van. "I think he's coming around," he said. "It might be a good idea to get him back to Karen's place."

"Right," I said, helping Steven pick Gilley up and lay him gently on the seat in the back of the van.

"Wha' happen . . . ?" Gil asked me in a woozy voice.

"Shhhh," I said gently. "I'm taking you back to rest."

"That thing!" Gilley said, his voice suddenly stronger. "It's out there!"

"No, Gil," I said. "It's gone away for the moment. You're okay, I promise." Looking at Steven I said, "Stay with him. I'm going back for our equipment and to lock up."

"I should go with you," he said.

I shook my head. "No, Steven. Please stay here with Gil. I promise I'll be right back, okay?"

I didn't wait for Steven to answer me, but hurried out of the van and back to the building, anger fueling my every step. "Okay, Jack," I said as I opened the front door. "You may have won this round, pal, but just so you know? This means war!"

Nothing answered my challenge, but something told me Jack had heard me. I moved back into the classroom and gathered up everyone's duffel bag. I was about to head back outside when something told me to check out the other classroom again.

I did, and my breath caught in my throat. The pyramid was gone, and all the desks had been arranged again in their neat rows. I shook my head. "This may be the mackdaddy of ghostbusts," I muttered, and hurried back to the van.

CHAPTER 4

We drove Gilley back to the ski lodge and helped him over to the couch. He'd said very little on the ride to base camp, but then, he'd become fully conscious only as we got close. He asked me what happened, and I'd explained that he'd had a nasty encounter with our resident poltergeist. He seemed to accept this rather well, or so I thought, until he sat down on the couch and said, "I'm quitting the business."

"You can't quit," I said, throwing an afghan over his legs while Steven went back out to the van to get our equipment.

"Yes, I can, M.J. I'm out."

"Gil," I said patiently, "we can work through this."

"Really?" he snapped, rubbing the back of his neck as if it ached. "And how do you propose I work through the fact that I've been *physically attacked* by the walking dead twice in two months?" Gilley had been pushed down the stairs by a confused and angry spirit at Steven's hunting lodge one month earlier.

I sighed and moved off the couch into the kitchen, which was directly across from the living room and allowed us to continue our conversation. While I filled the teakettle with water I said, "Gil, I understand where you're coming from, but we are partners in this, and you made a commitment to me to see this thing through way back when."

"Yes, M.J.!" Gil said, his voice rising with frustration. "I did agree to that, but I certainly didn't agree to needing disability insurance every time we go on a job!"

"Twice in eight months isn't all bad, Gil," I said, setting three cups on the counter.

"Oh? And how many times have *you* been attacked?"

I looked him smartly in the eye and started ticking off the physical encounters I'd had. "Let's start with Millie Kerkowski's place — you remember, the one with the teenager who liked to set things on fire? I've got a lovely little scar on my leg from where my pants started smoking. Then there was the Robinowitz job. Remember the patriot who liked to throw stones?" I asked, lifting up my bangs and pointing to a small scar I'd gotten when I'd been pelted with a rock.

"Or how about the Hudsons? Remember the ghost horse in their barn that liked to kick open stall doors? That bruise went all the way to the bone, Gil!"

"What is all this yelling?" Steven asked as he came in loaded down with duffel bags and heard our argument.

"Gilley wants to quit just because he has a little boo-boo," I snapped.

"You can't quit," Steven said.

I nodded my head vigorously. "See? I'm not the only one who thinks you're being a big baby."

"Oh, I do not think he is being a baby," said Steven. "If I were wearing his shoelaces, I would want to quit too."

"How is this helping?" I asked.

"I am just stating the truth of it," Steven replied.

"See?" Gil sneered at me. "Steven understands my pain!"

"Which is exactly why you must get back on the donkey again," said Steven.

"Horse," I said.

"Where?" Steven asked, looking out the windows. "I do not see a horse."

I put a tired hand up to my forehead and took several deep breaths before I said, "Steven's right, Gil. If you let this one incident define you as a quitter, then that's

120

what you'll always be. A quitter."

The teakettle started whistling, and I hurried to pour us some tea. "Do you think I want to quit?" Gilley asked me sharply. "M.J., it's not that I *want* to leave this job. I'm just finding it more and more dangerous."

"Dangerous or scary?" I asked bluntly, handing him a steaming cup of tea.

It was Gil's turn to sigh heavily. "I'm not like you," he admitted. "This stuff creeps me out, and every time I set foot out of the van I become the target."

"So, from now on, stay in the van," I suggested.

"I was halfway in the van when that . . . that . . . *thing* pulled me out and started swinging me around!"

"What if I made it safe for you?" I asked, getting an idea as my eye lit on Gilley's leather jacket. "What if I guarantee that no ghost will ever attack you again?"

"How can you do that?"

I set down my cup of tea and picked up the keys to the van. "I'll be back in a while. I've got an errand."

I got in the van and pointed it toward town. While I was driving my cell rang. "Hey, girlfriend," I said, noting the caller ID.

"Did the dean let you guys in?" Teeko asked.

"He did," I said. "Thanks for getting us on campus."

"How's it going so far?"

"It's tough," I admitted. "This Hatchet Jack guy is one nasty entity."

"What happened?" she asked, probably sensing that we'd already had a bad encounter.

"The thing attacked Gilley."

"Is he all right?"

"Physically, yes. Mentally, well, what can I say? He's always had the nerves of a frightened five-year-old girl."

"Are you on campus now?"

"No," I said. "We had to take Gil back to your place. I'm going to get some supplies to make him a nice suit of armor so that we can continue the job."

"Suit of armor?"

"An idea I had. Say, how's Paris?"

"It was rainy, same as New England, so we're in Italy now."

My eyebrows rose in surprise. "Sounds like you're getting the four-star treatment."

"When in Rome," Karen quipped.

"Should we be expecting you back this way anytime soon?"

"Probably not. John was able to literally

buy you five days, and then he needs you to clear out so his guys can get to work."

"I know," I said. "The dean has also made it perfectly clear that the clock is ticking."

"Now that you've encountered Jack, do you think that'll give you enough time?"

"I hope so," I said, trying not to sound too pessimistic. "I've got to try to figure out why this guy is here, I mean, what's with him and that building, anyway?"

"Can't you just find his hole or whatever it is that you call that thing and put those spikes in?"

"You mean his portal," I said. "Trust me, that's going to be my main mission. But it could be anywhere, Teek, and that school is a big place. Plus, if it's located in one of the other buildings I won't be able to get to it, because the dean has put everything but the old elementary wing off-limits to us."

"Well," she said, "do what you can, M.J."

"I will," I assured her. "I promise."

I got back to the ski lodge about two hours later, having taken longer than I expected to find what I'd need. Gilley was still on the couch, playing cards with Steven. "We were wondering what happened to you," Gil said.

I reached into one of the bags I was carrying and pulled out several thin black squares. "It took me a little extra time, but it should be worth it," I said.

"What are those?" Steven asked, pointing to the black squares in my hand.

"Magnets."

Gilley's eyebrows arched when I pulled out the sweatshirt and long-sleeved shirt I had purchased. "I don't get it," he said.

"You will in a little while," I said. "Now, if you'll excuse me, I'll be in my room for a bit. You two keep on with your game."

I headed into the bedroom and got to work with a glue gun. About an hour and a half later, just as I began to smell Gilley's efforts in the kitchen, I came out holding my creation. "Ta-da!" I said, holding up the garment I'd been working on.

Gilley turned from the stove and glanced at the sweatshirt I was holding up. "Cute," he said. "I like the color."

"I'm glad you do, my friend," I said, coming over to him and laying it across his shoulders. "Because this is your new suit of armor."

"It's heavy," he said, feeling the weight of it. "What's in it?"

"Magnets," I said.

"Oh, I see," said Steven, who was watching us from the couch. "So Gilley can wear

124

this and the ghost won't want to attack him."

Gil set the spoon he was stirring his spaghetti sauce with down on the counter and pulled the sweatshirt off his back. "How did you make this?" he asked me.

"I glued a bunch of those flat magnets I showed you earlier to a long-sleeved shirt, then sewed that to the inside of the sweat-shirt. Wear that, Gil, and no ghost will come near you."

"How does this work again?" asked Steven, who had gotten up to come over and feel the sweatshirt himself.

"Magnets play with the electromagnetic frequency that ghosts like to hover around. You put enough magnets in a room and a ghost won't want to go anywhere near it. That's why kitchens aren't usually haunted."

"Kitchens?" Steven asked me with a puzzled expression.

Gilley turned and pointed to the O'Neals' refrigerator. "Magnets on the fridge," he explained. Then he looked at me critically. "Are you sure I'll be safe in this thing?"

I nodded vigorously. "Absolutely!" I said. "But you'll have to stay in the van, because with that thing on you're sure to chase Hatchet Jack away, and I want to figure out why he's haunting the place and find his portal, not send him into hiding until we leave."

Gilley took a deep breath, like he was weighing his options carefully. "Okay, M.J., if you really need me on this bust, I suppose I can wear this thing and monitor from the van."

"You are the best, Gil," I said happily, and gave him a hug. "I promise, as long as you're wearing that thing you'll be the last person Jack wants to screw with."

Steven looked a bit concerned. "Perhaps I should also wear some of those," he said.

"Oh, no," I said with a laugh. "You, my friend, need to be completely open and vulnerable when we go back there."

"Why is this?" he asked me.

"Someone's got to act as bait," I said.

"I am thinking that I am not liking this bust very much," Steven said glumly.

"Relax," I said. "If it gets too dicey, I'll send you to the van with Gilley, okay?"

Steven didn't look convinced, but there was no way I was going to let him off easy. I had realized on the way into town that this job might be just a bit over my head, and I was going to need all the help I could get.

After dinner we packed the van again, making sure that Gilley had a direct link from the monitors in the van to all of our gadgets. "I love this new stuff," he confessed as we checked the equipment against what he could read on the three monitors he had set up. "This one records the feed from the night-vision video cameras. This one records the feed from the thermal imager. And this one records electrostatic readings from the two meters you are both carrying. I might even be able to tell you when there's a ghost around before you know it yourself."

"Glad you decided to rejoin the party," I said, and gave him a pat on his bulky back. "How uncomfortable is this thing, by the way?" I asked, looking at the sweatshirt he was wearing.

"It's not too bad," he said. "A little warm, but I can always crack the windows."

"Are we ready to bust?" Steven said, coming out with the last of our duffel bags.

"We're ready," I said, trying not to sound too excited. I love ghostbusting at night, and tonight promised to be extra good, with the damp chill in the air and a full moon. I could just feel the electrostatic energy charged with anticipation.

We drove back to the school and left Gilley in the van. "You going to be okay?" I asked him one last time.

"I will be as long as you promise nothing freaky is going to happen to me."

"It won't," I said, putting on the new headset that linked me to Gilley. "Sound check."

He placed a finger to his ear and said, "I can hear you loud and clear."

"Awesome," I said. "Me too." With that I closed the door to the van and hurried after Steven, who had already made it to the door of the elementary wing. He unlocked the door and held it open for me as I went inside, clicking on the flashlight I held in my hand.

"Remind me again why we don't just flip on the lights?" he whispered.

"Because surges in electricity can throw off our meters, and it makes it much harder to see ghosts. It's always better to do the baseline test and the investigation in total darkness."

"How will we be able to see?" Steven asked, squinting into the darkness of the hallway.

"Let your eyes adjust, Steven. There's a break in the clouds and a full moon out tonight, which should also help. If you get frustrated, switch on your flashlight."

I set my duffel down on the floor and pulled out our equipment, handing him one electrostatic meter, one thermal imager, and a night-vision camera. "I do not have enough hands," he said, trying to juggle all the gadgets.

"Click the electrostatic meter on and put that in your back pocket," I advised. "Hold the camera with one hand and the thermal imager with the other."

"How will I write down the measurements for the baseline?" he asked.

"I'll handle that," I said, retrieving a clipboard from the duffel, along with my own set of gadgets. "You just worry about pointing things in the right direction when I give you the cue."

"Where do we start?" he said.

"First we need to get some dimensions," I said. "While you and Gil were cleaning up the dinner dishes, I went ahead and sketched a rough outline of the building from what I remembered this afternoon. It looks like this hallway has six classrooms off it. Which makes sense, I guess, for grades one through six."

"I am thinking you are going to want to measure the hallway and the classrooms?"

"Yep," I said, handing him the end of the tape measure. "Hold this," I said, and moved down the hall. We got the length and width of the hallway and I recorded it on my diagram. "Okay, now let's hit the rooms."

We headed into the first of the classrooms, which happened to be the one where the desks had previously been arranged in a pyramid, and I made Steven hold the tape while I stretched it along the wall. In my ear I could hear Gilley singing a little ABBA. "How you doin' out there, Mamma Mia?" I asked him.

"Bored, bored, bored," he sang to the tune of "Dancing Queen."

I laughed. "How's the feed from our equipment?" I asked, motioning Steven over to the far corner of the room. He set down his thermal imager on one of the desks so he could hold the end of the tape measure while he wove around the desks to the corner of the room.

"Everything looks good," Gil said. "I've got a little spike in your electrostatic, though. Are you near an outlet?"

I looked down where I was standing by the window, and sure enough there was an outlet there. "Roger that on the outlet," I said. "I'll move over as soon as Steven gives me the measurement."

"Fourteen feet, two inches," Steven said, clicking off his flashlight.

"Uh . . . M.J.?" Gil said in my ear.

"Hold on, Gil; I gotta write that down." I held the tape measure awkwardly under my

130

arm while I scribbled on my clipboard.

"Er . . . this really can't wait," Gil said, alarm in his voice.

I stopped writing and pressed the headset to my ear. "What's up?"

"I don't want to frighten you," Gil said. "But is Steven's thermal imager facing you?"

I glanced across the room, and in the dim light I could just make out his meter on one of the desks. "Roger that," I said.

"Then you might want to turn around," he said.

"What's going on?" Steven asked, holding up his night-vision camera to navigate his way through the desks.

I didn't answer him right away. Instead I turned around and dropped my clipboard. On the other side of the window were two wide-eyed, frightened little faces staring into the classroom at me. I gasped, pointing at them while I backed up, and that was when one of the little boys disappeared. "Wait!" I called out to him, but he was gone.

"Whoa," Steven said as he spotted the other little boy through the camera. "I can see through him!"

"Gilley, are you getting the feed from the camera?" I asked, my eyes as wide as those of the other little boy on the far side of the glass.

"I am!"

Slowly I set down my clipboard, never breaking eye contact with the energy in front of me. "I'm M.J.," I said to him. "Did something happen to you here?"

The little boy nodded.

"What's your name, sweetheart?" I asked.

Eric, came into my head loud and clear.

"Hi, Eric," I said gently. "Can you tell me what happened to you?"

The hatchet man came. . . .

And just like that Eric's image disappeared. "He's gone!" Steven said, still recording through his camera.

"He's still here," I said. "I can sense him. Eric, if you're still with us, can you tap on something?"

Immediately there was a hard knock on the chalkboard. Steven swiveled and pointed his camera at the chalkboard. "Eric, were you hurt in this classroom?" I asked. Nothing happened, so I instructed, "If you were hurt in this classroom, please knock twice for yes, once for no."

Two knocks followed, and I could sense Eric's anxiety increasing. *He's coming!* I heard in my head, and just like that Eric's energy vanished.

132

I was about to call out for him when a scream loud enough to wake the dead ripped through the earpiece in my ear. "Ahh!" I yelled, tearing it out of my ear.

"Gilley!" Steven said, and ran out of the classroom. It took me only a moment to realize the scream was connected to my best friend out in the van.

Racing after Steven, I flew down the hallway and through the double doors while Gilley's frantic cries for help echoed across the school grounds. At the van we saw a large figure holding something clublike in his hands, and with it he hit the van. "Bastard!" Steven said next to me as we pounded the pavement.

"Stop it!" I screamed as we got closer. "Step away from him, you demonic son of a bitch!"

The figure backed up and looked at me, and that was when I realized he wasn't a ghost, but a real, live man with a bat. Steven must have realized it too, because he slammed on the brakes and pulled me protectively behind him. "Gilley," he called to my still-frantic partner. "Are you all right?"

"You can't be here!" the man with the bat said. "This is private property!"

"Put that thing down!" I snapped at him,

furious that he had attacked Gilley.

From inside the van we heard Gil yell one last time; then everything went quiet. "Gilley!" I shouted. "Are you hurt?"

"No," he said meekly, sticking his head out of the window closest to us. "I thought it was that Hatchet Jack guy."

"You can't be here!" the man said again, and it was then that I realized he looked just as scared as we did. It was also when I noticed that he was wearing a uniform that looked like it was made for a janitor. "Do you work here?" I demanded.

"I'm calling Owen!" he said. "He's going to come down, and then you're going to be in big trouble!"

"M.J.," Steven whispered over his shoulder. "He is suffering some mental-capacity issue."

I squinted at the man. His name tag said Nicholas. "We have permission from the dean to be here," I said calmly to him. "Dean Habbernathy told us we could be here."

This seemed to catch Nicholas off guard. "Oh, no, he didn't!" he insisted, much the way a stubborn child would respond. "You're liars and probably thieves! I'm calling Owen, and you're going to be in big trouble!"

"Who is this Owen?" Steven asked him, still eyeing the bat in Nicholas's hands.

"He's my brother," Nicholas said. "He's the dean."

"Nicholas," I said calmly. "We want you to call your brother. By all means, get him on the phone so that you can see we're not thieves or robbers or bad people, okay?"

In the distance there was the sound of sirens, and I realized the police were likely on their way. "He called the cops," Steven said.

"I called them," Gilley said, holding up his cell phone.

"You're in big trouble!" Nicholas said with a little bounce to his step. "The police are coming to arrest you!"

"They are not," I snapped, annoyed by this whole ordeal.

It turned out, however, that Nicholas was right on the money, as I found out a short time later, when I was handcuffed and furious in the backseat of a black-and-white. "This job blows," Gilley grumbled, squished in between Steven and me in the backseat.

"How do you tell the difference between blowing and sucking?" Steven asked. "I have heard you Americans use both; this thing or that sucks or it blows. Which is better?"

Gilley smiled wickedly and opened his mouth to answer, but I gave him a warning look and said, "Don't you dare," leaving Steven's question unanswered.

To my relief, at that moment another car pulled up next to ours in the parking lot. The cop who had thrown us in the backseat of the black-and-white called to his partner, who was currently inside our van digging around for any incriminating evidence. "The dean's here," I said.

"Great," Gilley grumbled as he fought with his handcuffs. "Maybe Mr. Happy Pants will cut us a break for a change."

We all watched as Nicholas hurried over to his brother's car and began pointing at us excitedly. One of the cops approached the car, and he and the dean spoke at length, with lots of glances in our direction.

Finally the cop came over to Gilley's side and opened the door. "You three," he said gruffly. "Step out of the car."

Gilley hurried to clamber out; Steven and I followed. The cop unlocked our handcuffs and said, "The dean here has vouched for you."

"Thank you, Dean Habbernathy!" Gilley said with a wave to the rather grumpy-looking man in the car.

"Try to stay outta trouble from now on,

okay?" the cop said.

"The season for false alarms at this place started early this year," grumbled his partner.

I looked sharply at him. "I'm sorry; what did you say?"

The cop I'd addressed seemed to realize he'd revealed more than he'd meant to, and tried to cover up with, "Nothing. We get called out here a lot, and it's always the same story."

"And what story is that?" asked Steven.

The cop adjusted his security belt, uncomfortable that we weren't letting him off the hook. "You're here to hunt Hatchet Jack, right?"

I gasped. "Yes!" I said. "What do you know about him?"

Again the cop seemed to fidget uncomfortably. "Only that through the years we get one or two calls, usually teenagers from around town who dare one another to go looking for Jack in the woods. They're always so surprised when they find him," he added with a snicker.

My eyes darted to Gilley, and an unspoken exchange passed between us. "You know what's funny?" I said to the cop. "We've been trying to dig up information on Jack online, and we've been coming up with zilch. You'd think that a legend like him would have a couple of Web sites devoted to him."

The cop gave me a snarky grin. "You gotta remember that Lake Placid is a tourist attraction. The last thing the locals want the tourists to read about is some ghost haunting their ski slopes. If you live here, you benefit in some way from tourism, and no one wants to jeopardize their bread and butter."

"Makes sense," Gil said to me. Before we could ask the cop any further questions the dean had come out of his car and approached us. "I'm sorry about Nicholas," he said with no real empathy in his voice, which was curt and annoyed. "He can be a bit too zealous about looking after things here at the school."

"We'll be on our way then," said the other cop. "Dean Habbernathy," he added, giving the dean a salute before motioning to his partner to leave.

I looked over the dean's shoulder at Nicholas, standing by his brother's car looking dejected and sad. "He was just doing his job," I said. "No harm done."

The dean sighed heavily, as if his brother were an unusually heavy burden. "I had, of course, informed Nicholas that you would be here, but I'm afraid his disability causes him to forget the more important things."

I scowled. I didn't like the dean, not one bit. I didn't like the look of irritation he gave Nicholas, and I certainly didn't like the way he talked about his own brother. "Again, Dean Habbernathy, there was no real damage done other than a little lost time."

"Very well," said the dean, but I could tell he was still irritated and embarrassed. "I shall leave you then to your investigation."

As he was about to turn away I called, "Hold on one moment, sir." When he turned back to me I said, "I'm interested in something we came across tonight in the elementary wing. In the school's history, did any of the children ever go missing or die while they were in attendance here?"

The dean looked shocked. "Of course not!" he said, completely indignant. "Northelm has *never* lost a child in attendance. Their safety and well-being is of our utmost concern!"

I was surprised by his reaction. It seemed overly severe. "I didn't mean to imply any negligence on your part, Dean Habbernathy. My apologies if that's how it came out."

The dean scowled in distaste and turned

away to deal with his brother, whom he ordered into his car, and the two drove over to the other side of the parking lot, where the dean parked, apparently so that they could talk in private. "Geez, M.J.," Gil said to me as the dean drove off. "Way to win him over."

"Oh, whatever," I said, completely annoyed. "Listen, about what the cop said —"

"I'll check the old blotters for any sightings on Hatchet Jack. Towns like these usually keep those down at the courthouse under the Freedom of Information act. I'll also recheck the local paper. Maybe we missed something in our initial online run-through."

"Good," I said.

"Are we going back in there tonight?" Steven said, motioning over his shoulder.

I glanced at my watch. It was past midnight, which was usually pretty good for hunting ghosties, but my sixth sense was telling me that all was quiet on the western front and we had probably gotten the most out of our first foray into the elementary wing. "I'd rather go back to Teeko's and analyze the footage from tonight. There's a larger puzzle here, and I want to try to get a handle on it."

Steven looked relieved, and Gilley was

already packing our stuff into the van. I had to hide a smile at his enthusiasm to leave.

We drove back to Teeko's, and I brewed some coffee while Steven and Gil set up the feed from the camera to the big-screen TV in the living room. When we'd all gotten our coffee and were sitting comfortably on the couch, Gil pressed the play button and we watched the film. "I reviewed the footage on the drive back here, and I've set it up so that you can see what's happening on the thermal imager and the night-vision camera at the same time," said Gil. "We'll start with this sequence first, though." Gil clicked a button on his remote control, and the window for the thermal imager expanded and filled the screen. "This is when you two first came into the classroom. See the windows?"

"They're blue," said Steven.

"Yep. Nothing giving off much heat there, but wait for it," Gil said, and a few moments later three little warmer green circles appeared very faintly against the blue outline of the window.

"Three?!" I gasped. "I thought there were only two!"

"Watch," said Gilley, and sure enough the third and faintest of the little circles faded into the blue background as the two others became clearer and more greenish yellow. Incredibly, we could also see that the circles that formed the boys' heads were now attached to little bodies as well.

"What happened to the third ghost?" Steven said.

"You'll see in a bit," said Gilley, clicking another button and reducing the picture from the thermal imager so that it coincided with the footage we'd gotten through the night-vision camera.

"Wow," I said, peering at the screen, which showed the two frightened boys looking at us through the window. As the boys faded away Gilley increased the thermal imager footage again, and I was amazed that both yellow outlines had clearly come through the wall and entered the classroom.

"This is where you start asking Eric questions," said Gil. "Watch what he does."

On the video feed you could hear me asking Eric to knock twice for yes and once for no. Eric's yellow outline was over at the chalkboard, and a little stick of yellow came away from the outline of his body and blazed orange as it knocked against the outline of the chalkboard. "That is freaking me out!" Steven said, and Gilley and I both gave him a smirk, but quickly glanced back at the screen.

"Did you sense that he was so close to you?" Gilley asked me.

I thought back, trying to remember the moment. "I wish I could say yes, but I honestly don't remember. I think I was just focusing on keeping the dialogue going."

Gilley nodded and pointed at the screen. "This is where it gets really scary. Go back to the window in the left-hand corner of the screen."

Our eyes followed his direction, and we all sucked in a breath as we watched a figure of blazing red appear out on the lawn and begin walking with purpose toward the window. "Jack," I said in a hushed voice.

"Yep, and this is when the boys sense him."

The two yellow outlines of the boys darted with amazing quickness out of the room through the window and were joined by the reappearance of the third little green energy. They darted across the lawn in the opposite direction of the approaching red image, then faded altogether into the woods. At that moment the imager began to shake violently, and the screen was too difficult to watch. "What's happening?" I asked.

"This is when I was attacked by Nicholas," Gil said with a hint of embarrassment.

"So what can you make of it?" Steven

asked me.

I shook my head. "I have no idea," I admitted. "We're clearly dealing with a psychopath," I said. "Hatchet Jack is one deranged son of a bitch, and the fact that we're now seeing evidence of three young boys who have become grounded on the school's property . . ." I let my voice trail off, not really knowing what conclusions I could draw.

"Well, it's obvious that whoever Jack was, he killed three little boys."

"The third one could have been a girl," Steven pointed out.

I nodded. "Yeah, that energy was so light even I didn't pick up on it. And I don't think we can assume too much here, guys."

Gil cocked his head. "What do you mean?"

"I mean that even though these energies are interacting with Jack, we can't automatically assume he murdered them."

"How else would they know about him?" Steven asked me. "Besides, don't you remember that Eric confirmed that he was hurt in the classroom by Hatchet Jack?"

"Grounded spirits can definitely interact with one another, and often their interactions aren't pleasant. A grounded spirit is already in a state of confusion, and when it encounters another spirit wandering around in what it considers its territory, there can be a confrontation. That's as often a cause for doors slamming or objects being tossed around as because we physical energies irritate the spirit."

"This ghost stuff is so complicated," Steven said with a sigh.

I smiled. "I know, I know. The first thing we need to do is work on the children," I said. "They're the ones I'm most concerned about."

"You want to cross them over before we tackle Jack?" Gil asked.

"Yep. I'm not comfortable knowing there are children running around the ether in terror. Plus, maybe we'll be able to get one of them to open up and tell us what happened. I'll do my best to try to find out the year or decade they died in, and we can focus our investigation from there."

Steven looked upset, and in a low voice he asked me, "Do you think they were students at the school?"

"I couldn't say for certain," I said. "And, again, I really don't want to jump to conclusions. The school has been in existence for only the past hundred years. These kids could have been on the grounds long before then."

"How do you think they died?" Gil wondered.

I shrugged. "It could have been anything, buddy. Disease, farming accident, some sort of natural disaster, fire, hunger. I mean, take your pick."

"Again we have more questions than answers," Steven said.

"Welcome to ghostbusting," I said flatly. Looking at Gil, I said, "I think your suggestion to check out the old police blotters is great. Tomorrow, let's see when the first of these calls started coming in to the Lake Placid police."

"Got it," Gil said.

Turning to Steven, I said, "You and I can go down to the library and dig through some of the old papers. Maybe we can find something that will point to what might have happened to the boys. Who knows, maybe we'll get lucky and stumble across an article that will tell us everything we need to know about them."

Steven frowned. "I am not feeling so lucky, M.J.," he said.

"We gotta start somewhere, honey," I said. "Now let's head to bed and get an early start. I have a feeling that tomorrow is going to be a bitch of a long day."

146

Little did I know — that wasn't even the half of it.

CHAPTER 5

Early the next morning I went for a quick run, keeping fairly close to Karen's place so as not to get lost. When I got back Steven was already up and making breakfast. "That smells good," I said cheerfully while I poured myself some coffee.

"I am making waffles," he said. "Do you like blueberry or strawberry compote?"

I gave him a good-morning kiss and whispered, "Surprise me." Steven set down his spoon and scooped me up in his arms. "Whoa!" I said. "What are you doing?"

"Are you surprised?" he said, and kissed me passionately before I could answer.

In the background we heard a cough. "If this is a bad time I can come back," Gil said.

Steven swiveled around, still holding me in his arms. "No, this is not a bad time. We were just saying good morning."

Gilley smiled and opened his arms wide. "Well, in that case, Doctor, may I say good morning too?"

I rolled my eyes. Gil made no attempt to hide his major crush on Dr. Delicious. "Ahem," I said into the uncomfortable silence that followed. "I think you're burning the waffles."

Steven set me down gently and turned back to the waffles. I gave Gil a pat on the head and swiveled him around to the table. "Killjoy," he muttered.

"Himbo," I replied with a giggle.

We gobbled down our breakfast and piled into the van to head into town, where we dropped Gil at the courthouse and cruised around until we found the library, a lovely, rather small structure with a beautiful view of Mirror Lake. Heading inside we realized that the size of the building was very deceptive. The library had four levels, the first of which, just off the street, led into the adult-fiction and circulation-desk area. Stopping at the circulation desk I asked one of the librarians where I might find older copies of the local newspapers.

"Right here," she said pleasantly. "We have copies of the *Daily Enterprise* dating back to the first edition in 1894, and the *Lake Placid News* from its beginning in 1905, all preserved on microfilm. What years were you interested in viewing?"

"We'd like to start at the beginning for both," I said, and Steven groaned. I ignored him and continued with, "Can we have a few years at a time?"

"Certainly," she said, turning around to a large group of cabinets behind her. "Let's see now," she said, placing a set of reading glasses on her nose while bending down to open the bottom drawer.

Pulling out a long, narrow box of film containers, she handed them to us and said, "Those are for the first five years of both papers. You can view them down on the next level. You'll see a microfilm machine next to the children's section."

Steven and I trooped down the stairs and found the microfilm machine. "There's only one?" he asked as he looked skeptically at it.

"Looks like it," I said, glancing around to be sure. "I'll look through these first and when I get tired I'll turn it over to you, okay?"

"Sure, sure," he said, and I could tell he was already bored.

"Why don't you go explore the library and I'll sift through this stuff."

Steven shrugged his shoulders and wandered off. I loaded the film into the machine and began skimming. What felt like eons later I took my eyes away from the print and rubbed them tiredly.

I'd learned a great deal about Lake Placid and its history, but nothing even hinting at the three boys we'd seen at the school.

The only article of interest had been regarding Northelm. The story was published in 1898 and indicated that land for the school had been purchased from the State of New York. "Which means it wasn't held privately," I muttered. I'd really been hoping that I'd find a link to a family name that I might be able to use with the boys, but the more I looked, the more I was convinced the boys did not live on the land prior to the school's opening. That meant they were associated in some way with the school. The question was when.

Leaning back in the chair I was sitting in, I glanced around and found a clock on the wall. I'd been looking through film for two hours, and Steven had never once come back to check on me.

I got up grumpily and strolled through the children's section. The good doctor wasn't anywhere to be seen. I glanced back up the stairs we'd come down and decided he might be up in the adult wing. I passed the librarian who had given us the microfilm on the stairs, and she asked me, "Are you having any luck in your search?"

"Not as much as I was hoping for," I said. "Listen, have you seen the gentleman I was with? I've lost track of him."

"He's upstairs in the adult wing, sitting with a group of teenagers."

That checked me. "He is?"

"Yes." She laughed. "I've had to tell them several times to keep their voices down. He seems to be entertaining them to no end."

"This I have to see," I said, thanking her and hurrying up the stairs.

I found Steven seated at a table sur-rounded by a group of kids in their late teens, many of whom were looking at him like he was the coolest thing on earth. One young girl had a rather dreamy look on her face as I caught Steven describing an inven-tion he'd developed with some other doc-tors in Germany before coming to the U.S. "It's a simple contraption, really," he said. "The first prototype was a ladle that we carved a square hole in and pressed over the area of the heart needing to be repaired. The heart was able to continue beating while keeping that section still and allowing us to operate. Many people are now able to avoid bypass surgery with our invention."

"That is too cool!" said the young teen.

I gave a soft, "Ahem," as I stopped at the table.

"M.J.!" Steven said, and everyone looked up at me.

"Hey, there," I said. "I came to recruit you for some microfilm time."

Steven ignored the hint that he should leave his adoring fans and come with me to the machine downstairs. "Everyone, this is M. J. Holliday. She is a ghostbuster."

Six sets of eyes swiveled with surprise to look at me. "Hi," I said with a small wave.

"Ghostbuster? For real?" asked one young man.

"For real," Steven said. "M.J., you might want to sit and talk with us. These young people have some interesting stories to tell."

I smiled tightly. "Actually, Steven, we're on a deadline here, and I really think we need to get back to our investigation."

"So she's the one you were telling us about? The one who can kill Hatchet Jack?" asked the same youth who had spoken before.

I scowled. What had Steven been feeding them? "I'm not out to kill Jack," I said moodily.

"Oh," three of them said in unison, and looked decidedly disappointed. "Then he's still going to be out there?"

I gave them all a curious look. "Have you seen him?" I asked.

Four heads nodded vigorously. One of the heads belonged to the girl who had looked so dreamily at Steven, and I saw that she shivered when I asked the question. "Beth saw him up close and personal," said one of the boys, motioning to the girl.

"It was, like, the worst thing that's ever happened to me," she whispered.

I pulled a chair from the neighboring table and sat down next to her. "Tell me," I said.

Beth glanced at Steven, who gave her an encouraging nod. "It was last summer, and I was like, hanging out with these guys, and Jeremy said we should all, like, go to the woods by that private school and look for Hatchet Jack."

"How did you know about him in the first place?" I asked, curious about Jack's reputation.

"Everyone knows about him," said the young man to her right. "My brother used to go to the woods every summer and try to see if he'd come out. Some kids say if he gets mad enough he'll chase you through the woods."

"How long have there been stories about Hatchet Jack?" I asked the group.

A few of the kids shrugged and looked at

one another to see who would answer. One boy with a bad case of acne and bright red hair said, "My mom told me about him when I was a little kid."

"Your mom knew about him?"

The youth shrugged again. "Yeah, I guess. She used to tell me that Hatchet Jack was going to get me if I didn't come home on time, and once she told me that when she was in high school she saw him in the woods up near Hole Pond."

I glanced at Steven meaningfully. "And how old is your mom?"

This got me another shrug. "I think she's, like, in her late thirties or something."

Steven smirked. "It is hard to judge anyone older than twenty when you are so young," he said.

"Hole Pond," I said. "That's near Northelm, isn't it?"

Everyone nodded. "Northelm owns half the pond; the other half belongs to the park. There's a really big oak tree on the park side," said Beth in a breathy whisper, her face slightly pale. "And you're supposed to go to that tree and close your eyes and say Jack's name ten times."

"And then what happens?" Steven asked when she didn't continue.

I looked around the group. All eyes were

on Beth, and one or two faces looked guilty. "He's supposed to show up and chase you with his hatchet."

"And he showed up for you?" I said, searching her haunted eyes.

Beth nodded.

"Tell me what happened," I said, laying a soothing hand on her arm.

Beth took a big breath. "Like I said, Jeremy dared me to do it." There was a bit of venom in her voice as she glanced at the boy across the table.

"I didn't know anything was going to happen, Beth!" he said, and I had a feeling he'd told her as much a hundred times before.

"Well, it did!" she spat at him.

"What happened?" I asked again, gently but firmly.

Beth turned her wide eyes to me. "I heard him before I'd said his name the full ten times. I thought it was just one of the guys trying to scare me, so I didn't scream or anything. But you're not supposed to open your eyes until you say his name all ten times, so I said his name again, and I heard this . . . this . . ."

"What?" I asked, completely absorbed in her story.

Beth shivered. "Laughter," she finally said. "He was laughing, but the sound was, like, right behind my ear!"

"He was behind you?" Steven asked, trying to picture it.

"That's what was so weird!" Beth said, her voice squeaky with fear. "I had my back to that tree. He couldn't have been right behind me. So, that's when I opened my eyes, and at first I didn't see anything, but then all of a sudden he, like, came at me out of the woods."

"Where were you all?" I asked, looking at the three boys sitting around the table.

"On the other side of the clearing," said the redheaded boy. "We didn't see Jack until he was halfway to Beth."

"What did you do?" Steven asked them, and I could tell he was irritated that they had put this wisp of a girl up to such a prank.

More shrugging from the boys, who looked at the tabletop before Jeremy finally mumbled, "We ran."

"You *ran?*" I gasped. "And left Beth at the tree?"

Beth was staring at the boys as if she'd like to punch their lights out. "That's right," she snapped. "They ran and left me there."

Steven was shaking his head reproachfully. "In my country, boys are more respectful to girls."

I put my attention back on Beth. "So you opened your eyes and saw him coming at you. How do you know for certain it was Hatchet Jack?"

"He was carrying a hatchet," she said. "And he had these crazy eyes, and he was running right at me with this hatchet over his head. I screamed and screamed and then I guess I closed my eyes again, 'cause the next thing I remember was this loud noise right next to my head."

"What kind of a loud noise?" I asked.

Beth took a moment to consider. Finally she said, "It was exactly like the sound of an ax hitting a tree. I must have opened my eyes then, and I know I was still screaming, but the weird thing was, Jack was gone. The only thing I remember as I took off was that this hatchet was sticking out of the tree right next to my head."

"And you didn't see any other sign of Jack?" I said, wanting to be sure that after he cut into the tree he had disappeared.

"Well, no," she said. "But I was pretty freaked out. I mean, I was screaming and running, and I don't remember a lot more after that."

I gave Steven a meaningful look and mouthed the word *portal* at him. He gave me a nod of understanding and said to the boys, "Take us to this tree."

All three boys snapped their heads up and looked at him, their faces completely pale. "No way, man," said Jeremy. "There's no freaking way I'm ever going near that place again."

Steven gave him a level look. "You will be perfectly safe," he said. "M.J. has much experience dealing with these types of things."

"No way," said the redheaded boy. "Nuh-uh."

I scowled at them. "Fine, then draw us a map."

Twenty minutes later, crude map in hand and microfilm returned to the front desk, Steven and I were driving to the county clerk's office to check on Gilley and let him know what we were up to. "So, you believe that the tree is this Hatchet Jack's portal?" Steven asked me as I navigated the traffic.

"Hope so," I said. "That may be why there's so much activity around the tree. He comes and goes through that portal."

"And what will you do if you find this portal, again?"

"Seal it up," I said. "If I drive some magnetic stakes into the heart of it, he won't be able to go back and forth between our plane and his lower plane."

"Why do they like to go back and forth?" Steven asked me.

"It's a little easier for them on the lower plane," I said. "They don't get as tired, and they can learn things from other nasty energies that exist down there."

"Learn things?"

I nodded solemnly. "Yep, they can learn how to scare people more effectively. Sometimes they can even grow more powerful, and that's when things can get dicey. You know how Jack stacked those desks up really quickly?"

Steven nodded. "That was creepy," he said.

"Well, that type of thing takes a tremendous amount of energy. He was showing off. Most nasty ghosts like him can only manage to move a few chairs around awkwardly. He stacked an entire classroom of desks in a very precise manner. He's one powerful SOB, I tell you."

"Do you think he is dangerous?" Steven asked.

"I do," I said. "Remember what he did to Gil out by the van? He's incredibly strong, and he might be growing stronger. We've got to shore him up as soon as possible."

"And once you find his portal, all we have to do is drive a few stakes into the tree and be done with it?"

I sighed tiredly. "Unfortunately not," I admitted. "I'll need to locate him out here first, then drive him through the portal. It does me no good to lock up his portal if he's out and about on this side. He may not be able to gain any more strength if he's locked out of that lower plane, but he's still powerful enough to scare the hell out of kids in the area. And he seems to like to attack them, as Beth can attest."

"What do you make of the fact that she says she saw a hatchet sticking out of the tree?"

"It's not unheard of," I said. "I remember a friend of mine, Eli Stinnet, one of the best ghostbusters in the South, telling me this amazing story of an investigation on Kolb's Farm in Georgia, which was the site of a Civil War battle in 1864. While Eli was out taking his baseline, a soldier in full Union garb and smelling like someone who hadn't bathed in a month walked right up to him and extended his hand out, like he wanted to give Eli something. Eli assumed it was some kind of prank, so he opened his hand, playing along, and the soldier dropped two bullets into his palm. He told Eli that he was almost out of ammo, and that was all he could spare. And then he vanished right in front of Eli's eyes."

"Whoa," said Steven.

"Whoa is right," I agreed. "Eli showed me the bullets. They've been authenticated by three experts as dating from the Civil War."

"How can ghosts carry real objects?"

I smiled ruefully. "We haven't figured that one out yet," I said. "Which, again, is why this Hatchet Jack character might be so dangerous. If he can wield an actual hatchet, and local kids are putting one another up to provoking him, then we owe it to this community to seal him up good."

By now we had pulled up in front of the county clerk's office, and we parked and went in to track down Gil. We found him without a lot of trouble in one of the small reading rooms available for people researching records. "Hey," he said when he saw us. "I was wondering how you guys were making out."

"I tried calling you from the van. Your phone is turned off," I said.

Gil pointed to a sign in the hallway that indicated in big bold ink that all cell phones be turned off within the clerk's area. "They're pretty grumpy about that," Gil said, and I had a feeling his had gone off and he'd been put in his place by one of the employees.

"Ah," I said, smiling at him. "So, did you find anything?" I asked, changing topics.

Gilley nodded. "Actually," he said, "I did find a few police reports that give us a tiny insight into Jack's comings and goings. The reports go back about thirty years, and of the handful that I've come across, they all describe the same thing, namely, a man in the woods near Northelm wielding a hatchet and chasing after local kids. The first report came into the police station in July of 1976, and the cops back then were pretty freaked out about it. The city had just won the rights to host the Olympics in 1980, and no one wanted some crazed psycho running around to spoil the friendliness of the place. Bad for publicity and all."

"So, what did the police do?"

"Well, the cops conducted a very private but thorough investigation but couldn't find a shred of evidence that anything unusual had occurred. No dead bodies, no missing person fitting the description of either the victim or the guy with the hatchet, so there wasn't really anything to go on. Two summers later the next report came in of a man running across the water at Hole Pond with a hatchet chasing a kid, and the cops responded, but the witness was a homeless guy, and the whole running-over-water thing made them think he might be a little lulu. But then not three weeks later they got another report, this time by a young couple walking near the pond, and they claimed they were chased through the woods by a guy with a hatchet."

"How did the cops react to that report?"

"They covered it up," Gil said. "No one wanted this type of story to hit the local papers and cause a panic, so it looks like there was a lot of covert investigating going on."

"That's why we haven't been able to find anything online, even under our public-records search," I said. "I'm thinking these reports are only kept here and on paper — that they're not part of the public online record?"

"You'd be thinking right. But that's not all that unusual. It's really expensive to go back through decades of data and digitally scan them into the database. Usually only the larger, wealthier communities can afford to do that. Places like this would rather focus on putting their tax dollars to better use."

"Were any of the reports filed from students at the school?"

"Only a few that I've hit on so far. Twenty years ago a young kid who went to Northelm was chased on one of the running trails near the school. Another witness from Northelm called in a report fifteen years ago — a teacher named Martin Ballsach. He was a math teacher who lived in town, and he said that he been at the school grading papers after final exams when he'd heard a noise outside his classroom. When he went to investigate he saw a man with a hatchet running through the halls, chasing a young boy into one of the opposite classrooms. Ballsach ran to the aid of the student, but when he got to the doorway of the classroom, there was no hatchet man and no young boy."

"Might be one of the three boys we saw last night," said Steven.

I nodded. "Those have been the only reports associated with the school?" I asked.

Gil glanced at the notepad he'd been scribbling on. "Yep. That is, until ten years ago, when a seventh grader claimed he was cornered in one of the old classrooms by a man with a hatchet, but he had a nervous breakdown very shortly thereafter, and the police were never able to get any more from him."

"That's the incident we read about in the school's newspaper," I said.

Gilley nodded. "And before you ask, I've

already checked into possible disappearances of students at Northelm from all the previous years, and there are none. No student at Northelm has ever gone missing or been killed, as far as I can tell."

I frowned. "Crap. That makes it harder to identify who these boys are and why Jack keeps chasing them."

"Well, at least I might have one bit of good news. I think I know why there are so few reports of sightings of Jack in and around the school."

"Why?"

"The sightings always start during the third or fourth week of June. Northelm usually lets out the second week of June, but this year there was a nasty ice storm, and most of the teachers couldn't get to the school to teach for a full week. That forced the school to extend the school year out one week. The same thing happened five years ago, when Ballsach reported his sighting. The school had to shut down that year due to a pipe bursting in the main building. School was extended that year too."

"That's curious," I said, thinking about the implications.

"Why is it curious?" Steven asked.

"Jack has a pattern. He becomes active the week after Northelm usually lets out.

That might tie him to the school in some way." Following that thought I asked Gil, "You said that these reports always come in during the summer, starting from about thirty years ago?" Gilley nodded. "Are there any reports at all during the school year, or around the holidays?"

Gil looked down at his notes again. "Nope," he said. "They begin the third week in June and stop the middle of August."

"When does the school year start?"

Gil swiveled over to the laptop sharing space with the other courthouse books on his table and typed quickly on the keyboard. "Northelm begins its school year the Wednesday after Labor Day."

I sighed. "I think Jack was connected to the school in some way. There has to be a reason why he's beginning his haunts when there's no one around at the school to see him."

"Like how do you think he's connected?" Gil asked me.

I shrugged. "Not sure. Gilley, dig around in Northelm's records if you can. See if you can find anyone working at the school who died in 1975 or 1976. Since 1976 is the year that the activity began, it's likely he died sometime within two years of that date."

"That could be a pretty tall order," Gil

167

said with a hint of a whine. "Unless the old records are kept on a computer that's networked to the Internet, I'm not going to be able to find much of anything."

"Well, do your best and see what you can come up with," I said. "Then look through the obituaries. Who knows? Maybe we'll get lucky." Thinking of something else, I said, "Is there an address listed for that teacher . . . what was his name?"

"Martin Ballsach," Gil offered. "And yes, I have his address here. Did you want to interview him?"

I nodded. "Might be a good idea if we can't find Jack's portal by the tree at Hole Pond." Gil gave me a quizzical look, and I filled him in on what the kids at the library told us.

"Is that where you two are headed?" Gil asked.

"Yep," I said. "We just wanted to bring you up to date and see what you'd uncovered."

"Okay. I'll keep digging through this stuff until you get back. If I'm not here when you two finish at the pond, I'll be next door at that sandwich shop getting something to eat."

We took our leave of Gilley and went back to the van. I took out the map the teenagers

168

had given us and gave it to Steven. "Let's go find ourselves a tree," I said enthusiastically.

"You're looking forward to this?" Steven said, giving me a sideways glance.

"Yep," I said. "I like sealing up nasties like Jack once and for all."

"You are like the ghost police."

I grinned. "If the shoe fits," I said, and we pulled out into traffic.

It took us a little while to find the tree the kids had told us about. After parking in a small clearing on the park side of Hole Pond we tried to follow the map they had drawn for us, which indicated that we should follow a trail by an old garbage can. Trouble was, there were no old garbage cans — only new ones here and there around the pond. Steven and I were forced to follow every trail we could find and see if it came to a dead end near a big old tree at the edge of the pond.

As we followed our third trail we came to a small rise. In the distance we could see Northelm's main building. "How far away do you think we are from the school?" Steven asked as he squinted into the distance.

I glanced at the building up ahead. "Probably a quarter mile or so," I said.

"Seems like a lot of terrain for a ghost to cover," he said.

"Not really," I said. "Lots of ghosts are known to haunt more than one location. Abraham Lincoln, in fact, is supposed to haunt three buildings in three different states."

"Really?"

"Yep. He's famous for haunting one of the bedrooms in the White House, but he's also been seen at his desk in the Illinois State Legislature, along with his childhood home, which has been moved to Greenfield Village in Michigan."

"Impressive," Steven said. "The man gets around."

"It's a pretty common occurrence," I said, "which is why I'm really hoping we find Jack's portal here. Otherwise it could be anywhere out here, and we'll be hard-pressed to find it."

The trail in front of us dipped again, and we entered some thick foliage that made keeping an eye on the trail difficult. "This can't be it," Steven complained as he pushed against the small branches from trees on either side of him to make his way through the narrow passage.

"All the same," I said, pushing on my own

branches, "we'd better make sure before we give up and look for another trail."

At that moment the branch gave way and the trail widened and became more distinct. We emerged from the woods and came to a clearing, and fifty yards in front of us was a gigantic oak tree on the edge of the western side of the pond. "Bingo," I said, pointing to it.

"Well, I'll be uncle to the monkey," Steven said. "You were right."

I smirked a little at his constant misattempts at American colloquialisms. "Come on; let's check it out."

Steven and I approached the tree cautiously. My senses were open and alert as I felt the energy surrounding the tree for any sign of nastiness. I was somewhat surprised as we approached that there was no apparent negative energy that I could pick up on. Instead a feather of something touched the edge of my radar, and as I tried to pull it closer we came to a stop at the front of the tree.

"Are you sensing anything?" Steven wanted to know.

"I'm picking up far less than I thought I would," I admitted. Then I noticed the tree and my breath caught. "Would you look at that!" I said, reaching up to touch a deep

171

scar in the trunk of the tree.

"There's one there, too," said Steven, and he pointed to another scar to the left of where I was looking.

"Over here too," I said, seeing another.

"There must be half a dozen of them," Steven said, edging his way around the trunk. "Nope, make that a full dozen, at least."

As Steven walked the circumference of the tree, I stepped back and opened up my radar completely. I could still sense that feather of energy — it felt gentle and nonthreatening — but there was something about it that made me want to scratch my head. Something about that energy was tickling my mind with a puzzle that I couldn't quite figure out. Momentarily frustrated, I pushed that aside and focused on trying to find Jack's portal.

I scanned the tree, letting my eyes go unfocused, and looked for that little circle of vapor that indicated a portal was there. Nothing appeared to me, and I felt my shoulders sag. "Damn," I muttered.

"Fifteen," Steven said as he came up beside me again after having gone around the tree. "There are fifteen slashes in the trunk."

"Hatchet Jack," I said distastefully. "I'd

bet you anything that they were all made by him."

"Some look newer than others," Steven commented. "And there are quite a few on the other side, but they're lower down."

This got my attention. "Lower?"

"Yes, about this high," he said, indicating a spot about midway up his chest. "And they are the ones that look the oldest."

"Let me see," I said, following him around to the other side of the tree. Sure enough there were several old cut marks in the trunk of the ancient gnarled tree that were decidedly lower than those on the opposite side. "That's weird," I said when the whisper of energy that had been tugging at me suddenly came on fast and strong. I stepped back away from the tree and looked at the ground, shocked by the imagery playing out in my head. "Steven," I said breathlessly.

"What's the matter?"

"Do you have your cell phone on you?"

"Yes."

"Call nine-one-one."

There was a pause, and then he said, "What is the emergency?"

"Tell them there's been a murder."

"What?!" Steven gasped.

I looked up at him, feeling a well of sadness form in my chest. "A little boy named Eric. His body is buried under my feet."

CHAPTER 6

The police were quick to respond. They were equally quick to judge. "You mean to tell me that you called us out here to investigate a ghost?" said Detective Muckleroy, a portly man in his fifties with a close-shaved head and a bulbous nose.

"No," I snapped, irritated that I'd wasted twenty-five minutes of my time trying to convince him that a young boy had been murdered and buried at the base of the tree we were standing around. "That's my job. Your job is to take a shovel and dig where I tell you to!"

Muckleroy narrowed his eyes at me. "I'd watch that attitude if I were you," he said evenly.

I narrowed my eyes, completely unperturbed. "Or what? You'll arrest me for being snippy?"

"No, I'll arrest you for reporting a false crime," he growled.

Behind Muckleroy stood two cops, both with arms crossed and expressions that could carve granite. No one, it seemed, was giving me the benefit of the doubt about this. "What have you got to lose?" I asked. "Seriously, Detective, if I'm wrong then you can take me away in handcuffs. And if I'm right then you'll make the local news. It's a win-win situation."

The detective snickered. "The way I look at it, lady, there's a mountain of paperwork either way. Hardly sounds appealing to me."

I looked back to the spot in the dirt I'd marked with a large stick. "Then do it for the family," I said. "They've waited a long time for closure. It's your day to be their hero."

Muckleroy sighed heavily and considered me for a long moment before he said to the cop over his shoulder, "Davis, get a shovel."

I smiled wide. "That's the spirit!"

He eyed me critically, and when Davis returned with the shovel Muckleroy took it from him and handed it to me. "You've got ten minutes to dig up a body or I'm haulin' you in."

My jaw dropped. *"Me?!"*

Muckleroy nodded. "You think I'm gonna break a sweat over this?" he said, glancing at his watch. "Nine minutes, fifty seconds."

I swore under my breath and snatched the shovel. Walking over to the stick marker I pushed the shovel into the ground, gritting my teeth as I thought about how I might be destroying evidence because some fat excuse for a cop was more interested in avoiding paperwork than in a possible murder investigation. My shovel of dirt revealed nothing. "Eight minutes, fifty-nine seconds," Muckleroy said.

I glared at him, then dug in again, this time going deeper. My shovel hit something, and for a moment I got excited that I might unearth some bone, but as I pulled up on the shovel only a bit of tree root came up. There was a snort of laughter from one of the cops, and I felt my face growing hot. Suddenly there was a presence at my side, and strong hands gripped the handle of the shovel. "Let me," Steven said.

I smiled at him and gave the shovel over. Steven jammed it into the small hole I'd dug and pushed hard with his foot. He pulled up a large chunk of dirt and swung it to one side, dropping it into a pile. "Dig through that with a stick while I keep going," he instructed.

I nodded and grabbed one of the markers, pawing through the pile of dirt he'd made. "Six minutes, twenty seconds," the detective said.

I ignored him, and Steven dropped another pile at my side. We worked like that for five more minutes. Steven had broken into a good sweat as he dug deeper and wider, pulling up huge shovelfuls of dirt while I poked around with my stick. "One minute!" Muckleroy said happily, and out of the corner of my eye I saw him rocking back and forth on his feet, enjoying the show.

That was when my stick poked into something hard, and I quickly scraped at the dirt, then jumped back like I'd been bitten. "What is it?" the detective said with a laugh. "Find a worm in the dirt?"

I snarled at him as I put a hand out to stop Steven from shoveling. "No," I said slowly as I pulled my sleeve down over my hand and reached into the dirt. Pulling up gently, I lifted out a small skeletal hand.

"Shit!" Muckleroy said, all sense of mirth gone.

I set the hand down. "I suggest you call your CSI team before we do any more damage to the grave site," I said. "Unless, of course, you want me to report to the local news how the town's police department is forcing its tourists to dig up dead bodies because they're too lazy to do it themselves."

Muckleroy pulled his cell phone from the clip at his belt and began punching numbers into the keypad. Steven handed the shovel back to one of the cops, who was standing slack-jawed and staring at the hand lying on top of the dirt mound where I'd set it.

I walked over to my duffel bag, which I'd brought up from the van when we called the police, and searched inside for something to wipe my grubby hands on. "That was impressive," Steven said, mopping his own brow with his sleeve. "How did you know the body was buried there?"

"Eric spoke to me when I went around that side of the tree. He kept drawing a cross on the ground, and I knew he'd been buried there."

"Poor little boy. Do you think Jack murdered him?"

I nodded, absolutely positive now that Jack wasn't just chasing the boys in spirit; he was repeating something that had happened in real life. "I will so enjoy locking up that son of a bitch," I said with a shudder.

"Where do you think the other two boys are buried?" Steven asked, reminding me of the boys we'd seen at the classroom.

I frowned. "I don't know," I said, scanning the ether for any hint of their energy

179

but coming up empty.

Just then Muckleroy approached us looking decidedly less mocking. "I've got the coroner and some techs on the way. You mind answering a few questions before you head back to town?"

His tone indicated that he wasn't so much asking as stating that I wasn't going anywhere for a while. I gave Steven a rueful smile and said, "Why don't you head to town and let Gil know what's going on and get something to eat while I talk with the detective."

"Can I bring you back something?" he asked.

I glanced at the hard look on the detective's face and said, "A club sandwich with a side of scotch might be just the ticket."

Steven smiled, then looked warily at Muckleroy. "Call me if they give you too much problems," he whispered into my ear.

"Will do," I said, and gave him a gentle squeeze on the arm.

Steven stepped onto the path leading back to the van and quickly disappeared into the thick brush. Turning to the detective I gave a wave of my hand and said, "Fire when ready, Detective."

Muckleroy already had a small notebook out to take notes on our conversation. "Tell me again how you knew there were skeletal remains buried there."

I resisted the urge to sigh. "Dealing with the dead is my specialty," I said. "As I've already told you, I'm a professional medium who specializes in dealing with spiritual energies that refuse to leave our plane of existence."

"Can I please have that in English, Miss Holliday?" Muckleroy said with a pained expression.

I smiled tightly. "I'm a ghostbuster. And I've been hired by the family of a girl who attends Northelm to look into the spiritual activity at the school. While on that investigation my colleagues and I came across three young male energies."

Muckleroy cocked his head. I didn't think he was quite following. "Come again?"

"Three little-boy ghosts are haunting the school," I explained as informally as I could. "One of them identified himself to me. He said his name was Eric and that he and his friends were running from a man carrying a hatchet."

At this, Muckleroy's expression seemed to light up. "Hatchet Jack?" he asked.

"You've heard of him?"

"Everyone in the department's heard of him," he said, scratching his chin thoughtfully. "A summer doesn't go by around these parts without a couple of calls coming in about him chasing kids around here."

"And what is the department's view of these reports?" I asked, feeling a little pissed off that Muckleroy had been so dismissive of my claim that there was a body by a tree known to be active with sightings of a ghost wielding a hatchet.

Muckleroy shrugged. "No one in the department's ever seen him, so we all thought it was one of those urban legends that the local kids were keeping up."

I scowled. "So typical," I said, crossing my arms.

"Listen," he said, becoming defensive. "I'm not the only one who don't believe in ghosts, Miss Holliday. You fortune-tellers are all a bunch of con artists to me."

I narrowed my eyes at him. "Really?" I said. "Con artists?"

"Yeah," he said, caring not one whit that he had obviously insulted me. "I mean, I believe in science, and there's no evidence that this stuff exists."

My back went ramrod straight. "On the contrary, Detective," I snapped. "In the past fifteen years there have been over a thousand intensive and comprehensive experiments conducted and published in all sorts of scientific journals that *clearly* point to the fact that paranormal activity doesn't merely exist, but *can,* in fact, be quantifiably measured."

Muckleroy wasn't so easily swayed. "Like what kind of journals?" he asked.

"I have a list of them on my computer. Leave me your e-mail address and I will send them to you, along with some of the better findings."

It was Muckleroy's turn to narrow his eyes. "Whatever," he said dismissively. "You're not going to convince me. You'll just have to consider me a skeptic."

Now, someone like me can't hear something like that without taking it as a personal challenge. The switch I used to turn on my communication link with the other side flipped itself on, and I immediately welcomed a lovely older female into my energy. "I see," I said. "Well, your grandmother on your father's side, Martha, thinks that you shouldn't be so closed-minded. She says that she's disappointed that you don't make time in your schedule to get up north to visit your dad as often as you should, and she really doesn't like the new wallpaper you've put into your bathroom. She says the paint was a better color in there."

Muckleroy's jaw fell open so far I could

see his tonsils. I smiled and continued on. "And your mom agrees," I said. "Carol, but with the middle initial A, for Anne, right? She's telling me she crossed over due to something that happened in her brain. It was sudden, like an embolism, correct?"

Muckleroy's expression turned from dumbfounded to downright stupid. "How . . . ?"

I ignored his question and plugged along. "She's grateful at least that you put fresh flowers on her grave site last weekend, but next time she'd prefer tulips to carnations."

And then something occurred that had never happened in all the years of my giving away my impressions. Muckleroy fainted.

He went down hard and fast, thumping to the ground like a huge sack of potatoes. The two cops who had been over by the burial site setting up crime-scene tape stopped and snapped their heads in our direction as they heard the loud *whump* of Muckleroy's body hitting the dirt.

Dropping the roll of tape, both cops were quick to react as they ran to the detective's aid. "What'd you do?" one shouted as the other pulled his gun and leveled it at me.

My hands shot straight in the air. "Nothing!" I insisted. "He just fainted!"

The first cop got down on the ground

beside Muckleroy and rolled him gently over onto his back, looking for any signs of a wound. The other closed in on me and whipped me around so fast I nearly fell myself. "On the ground!" he screamed in my ear.

I obeyed quickly and dropped to the dirt, resisting the urge to pee my pants as I felt the gun press itself against my back. The cop patted me down while the other one said, "I can't find a wound!"

"What'd you use?" the other growled in my ear. "Stun gun?"

"I swear to God," I said, grimacing as the cop felt his way in between my legs. "The guy fainted. I had nothing to do with it." Okay, so that was a lie, but I wasn't exactly thinking it was a good idea to tell these two that I'd prompted Muckleroy's reaction.

"He's breathing, and his pulse is normal," said the cop behind us. I heard some faint slapping sounds and the cop said, "Detective! Bob! Come on, man, wake up!"

The cop over me finished patting me down and placed his foot on my back to prevent me from moving. I heard him shout into his walkie-talkie for an ambulance and add something about, "Officer down!"

"This is ridiculous!" I shouted over my shoulder. "Guys, he *fainted!* You're overreacting here!" The foot on my back pressed itself with unnecessary force, and I felt the air whoosh out of my lungs.

"Shut up!" the cop over me yelled. "You don't talk until I *tell* you to talk!"

I gritted my teeth and swallowed my frustration. From behind me came a moan. "Mom?" I heard Muckleroy say woozily.

"He's comin' around!" said the cop at his side. "Bob? Can you hear me?"

"Wha . . . ?" Muckleroy said. "Where am I?"

"Lie still," said the cop firmly. "We've called for an ambulance."

There was an irritated grunt, and I imagined Muckleroy pushing the cop away as he sat up. "What the hell is she doing on the ground?" he demanded.

"She hit you with something," said the cop over me.

"No, she didn't!" Muckleroy snapped. "Larry, get the hell off her!"

The foot lifted off my back and I inhaled deeply. "Help her up!" the detective yelled.

Rough hands scooped under my arms and lifted me straight up off the ground. "What happened to you?" said the cop by Muckleroy's side.

Muckleroy's face went from slightly pale to deep red. "I fainted," he admitted. "I remember her talking about my mom, and then the world just spun and I went down."

"So she did hit you with something?" the cop next to me said, shooting an accusing look in my direction.

"No," said Muckleroy with a small laugh as he too got to his feet. "Just the truth. Jesus, Mary, and Joseph, Miss Holliday, how the hell do you *do* that?"

"It's a gift," I said woodenly, looking at the cop next to me with venom in my eyes. He stepped away a few feet and gave me back my personal space.

"I never would have believed you," he said. "But no one knew I went to my mom's grave last week. I didn't even tell my wife, and those flowers I got last-minute at a gas station."

"She prefers tulips," I said quietly.

Muckleroy laughed so hard he doubled over. The other two cops broke into grins and looked at each other quizzically, unsure what was so humorous. Finally Muckleroy stood again and said, "Mom's favorite flower was the tulip. Her front lawn used to be covered with them. My dad always got it wrong. Over the years he would bring her roses or daisies or carnations, and she would always say thank-you, but that she preferred tulips. It was kind of the joke in the family, and I didn't even remember it until you mentioned it."

I nodded and shrugged my shoulders. What else could I say? To my left the cop pulled his walkie-talkie off his shoulder and called into his dispatch to cancel the ambulance and report that the detective was okay.

Smoothing back his hair and wiping off his dirty trousers, Muckleroy cocked an eye at me. "Okay, so you've obviously made a believer out of me. Now tell me more about this little boy over there."

An hour later the area around the giant oak tree was teeming with crime techs and police. Muckleroy was over by the grave site, hovering next to the coroner, who had the area marked off with a grid of twine and pegs while she carefully scooped up dirt and placed it into a screen that one of the techs was holding.

The coroner, a woman in her forties with round features and mousy brown hair, lifted something round out of the dirt as I watched and peered closely at it while she dusted it with a small brush. I realized that she was holding a skull and felt a great sadness in my chest that such a young boy had died so tragically.

"How is it going?" I heard a familiar voice

say from just behind me.

"It goes," I said wearily, turning to face Steven. Gil was standing next to him holding up a brown sack in one hand and a Styrofoam cup in the other. "Club sandwich and a Coke, as ordered," he said with a cheerful smile.

I took the food gratefully and gave a long pull on the soft drink. Flashing Gil a smile, I said, "Awww. You added lemon. Thanks, buddy."

Gil beamed at me and placed a friendly arm around my shoulders. "You look beat, pumpkin."

"I am," I said, and motioned over to the coroner. "They've been here for about an hour, and they just found the skull."

"Maybe dental records will help identify who the boy was?" Gil said hopefully.

"Let's just hope the kid had some cavities and that his dentist is still alive," I said.

"Any sign of the other two we saw in the classroom?" Gil asked.

I shook my head. "Nope. And Eric has been woefully quiet ever since we started digging around his grave."

"How is it that a ghost knows where his grave is?" Steven asked. "I thought that ghosts didn't know they *were* dead."

"Many don't," I said, taking the sandwich

out of the bag while Gil held my Coke. "But I've always found with child ghosts that they're more likely to accept that they've died."

Steven scrunched his face up in a confusion. "Then how can he be a ghost? Wouldn't he have 'crossed over,' as you say?"

I took a huge bite out of the sandwich and moaned. It was delicious. I waited to chew the food before answering. "Not necessarily," I said. "Children will accept the death of their bodies, but often they haven't truly absorbed the concept of heaven. They may be frightened of moving on, and they'll stick to this plane like glue out of fear of the unknown."

"That is so sad," Steven said as he thought about it. "He should not be afraid to go to heaven."

"I agree," I said, munching on another bite. "That's why we've got to work our tails off to help him and the others, and lock up Jack forever."

"I'm afraid I wasn't a lot of help today," said Gilley. "I looked through all the local obits, M.J., and came up empty for anyone fitting Jack's description."

"Crap," I said, wadding up the wrapping that came around the sandwich. "I was really hoping for a solid lead there."

Gil looked dejected. "Sorry," he said.

I was quick to reassure him. "Buddy," I said gently, "it's not your fault. This one's just going to give us a run for our money."

"What do we do now?" Steven asked.

I stretched and yawned tiredly. "Now I could use a nap," I said. "There's not a lot I can do here if Eric won't talk to me right now. We should probably head back to the ski lodge and chill out until tonight; then we'll go back to the classroom and try it again."

I noticed as I was speaking that Muckleroy had gotten up and was coming over toward us. We fell silent as he approached, waiting to see if he'd tell us anything about what the coroner had found in the dirt. "Looks like you're right on more than a few fronts, M.J.," he said, now addressing me by my first name, as if we were fast friends.

"Do tell," I encouraged.

"Coroner says that the skull appears to be of a young adolescent between ten and fourteen years old."

I dug into my memory of what I'd gotten off Eric. "He was thirteen," I said confidently.

Muckleroy cocked his head quizzically, but didn't jump on the comment. "She says there is one cut mark on the back of the skull, and we've found a rib bone with some of the same marks."

"Like those made by a hatchet," Steven said.

Muckleroy nodded. "Too soon to tell definitively, but I wouldn't rule it out."

"Anything else so far?" I asked.

"Yeah. From the surrounding soil and the condition of the bones, the coroner is estimating the body to have been buried there for at least the last twenty to thirty years. That also fits with what you got off the boy's spirit."

"And it fits with the timing of the first sightings of Hatchet Jack," said Gilley.

"The question of the day, then, gentlemen, is how did Hatchet Jack die?" Everyone looked blankly at me, so I elaborated. "I think it's every bit as important as who this maniac was. Based on the ghost sightings, he must have died shortly after Eric. Every description I've heard describes a thin male in his late thirties to early forties with black hair who chases young people through classrooms and the woods. I'd be hard-pressed to believe someone that young and that vital died of natural causes."

"Could have committed suicide," Gil said reasonably. "I heard once that a lot of serial killers commit suicide because the guilt eventually catches up to them."

I shook my head. "I'm not buying it in this case, Gil. That lunatic got off on what he did. He wasn't the type to feel one ounce of remorse."

"I'll check through the county records," said Muckleroy. "Maybe I can come up with a death certificate."

"I already looked through the obits," said Gil. "Got nothing."

"Not all deaths are reported to the paper," said Muckleroy. "If this guy had no family or close friends, then his death would likely go unreported."

"Great," I said to Muckleroy. "In the meantime we'll try to find the other boys."

"That's right," he said thoughtfully. "You said there were two other ghosts at the school. Did you get names for them?"

"Not yet," I said. "But we're going to work on that tonight. We'll call you if we get anything."

"I'll work the missing persons for Eric too," added Muckleroy. "Maybe we'll catch a break and find his family."

"I'll keep my fingers crossed," I said, handing him one of my business cards. "Call the cell number for me if you need us. Otherwise, we'll be in touch."

■ ■ ■ ■

We drove back to Karen's without a lot of chatter. It seemed I wasn't the only one worn out by the long day and night. "What time do you want to head back to the school?" Gil asked me.

"Midnight," I said.

"Of course," he said with a grin.

I yawned again and stared blearily at the road passing under our van. "I am plumb tuckered," I said. "I did a reading for Muck-leroy while you guys were in town, and it wore me out."

"He asked you for a reading?" Gil said, surprised.

"Not exactly," I said with a sneaky grin.

"Don't tell me; let me guess," Gil said with a knowing glance at me. "He was spewing skepticism and you gave him the old medium one-two punch. Am I right?"

I laughed. "You know me too well."

"How'd he take it?"

"Lights-out in two rounds," I said, and giggled at my own wickedness.

"Will they ever learn?" Gil said with an exaggerated sigh.

We filed into the O'Neals' ski lodge, and I went immediately to my bedroom, where I fed Doc, then plopped onto the bed and took a nice nap. I had the most delicious dream in which I was lying next to Steven, and his nearness was filling my senses with his smell, his heat, and his passion. I began kissing him in the dream; his lips were soft at first, but soon became hungry. He moaned and I wiggled closer to him, pressing my body into his.

His hands found their way under my nightgown, and my skin felt electric where he touched me. I felt a moan form deep in my throat, my heart seemed to be hammering in my chest, and my fingers clawed at his back. In the back of my mind I thought about the amazing vividness of the dream. It all seemed so real, including the hot breath I felt on my neck as Steven whispered my name.

Dream me felt completely uninhibited. If I were awake I'd be far more conservative; after all, Gilley was in the same house, and who knew how much noise carried through these walls? But here in my dream I could throw caution to the wind and follow my passions without fear of consequence. I gave dream Steven a few nudges with my pelvis, encouraging the imagery that came to mind, and his passion rose to the occasion — literally. "I want you," dream me whispered. "I

195

want you right now!"

"M.J.," he said, his voice thick and rich.

Deedle-deedle-do! came a noise that dream me seemed to recognize, but not place. *Deedle-deedle-do!* it came again.

Dream me glanced up, and a bird sat in a branch above our heads singing, *Deedle-deedle-do!*

Dream Steven growled and, reaching up, he slapped the bird, sending it sprawling across the grass. I was horrified as the bird began to speak. "Hello? Hello? M.J.?" And then the bird turned into Karen.

"Hellooooo?" she said from her prone position on the grass. It was then that my eyes fluttered open and I realized I was half-naked and semientwined with the real Steven Sable.

"What's happening?" I gasped, trying to clear my foggy brain.

"M.J.?" I heard faintly from the floor. "Is that you?"

I shook my head and twisted in Steven's arms to reach for the phone. "Hello?" I said quickly.

"Hey, girl," Karen said, her voice happy and light. "What's going on?"

"Nothing!" I nearly shouted, then realized Teeko had no idea I was currently sprawled in a very compromising position with a gorgeous man still nibbling at my neck and feeling his way up and down my torso.

"Okay, okay," she said, somewhat taken aback. "I was just asking."

I slapped at Steven's hands and sat up, pulling a pillow across my chest. I was quick to reassure her. "I'm sorry, Teek; I was having a weird dream when you called, and I must have knocked the phone off the nightstand."

"No worries," she said easily. "I only wanted to check in and see how you guys were doing."

"We're doing all right," I said, shooting Steven a glaring look and placing a finger to my lips for quiet. He sighed and laid his head back on the pillows, apparently willing to cooperate while I talked to Teeko. "We've made some progress, in fact."

"Tell me."

"We found the body of one of the boys murdered at the school."

"Whoa, back up here. *What* boy murdered at the school?"

I remembered then that Teeko wasn't exactly up to speed with all that had happened between last night and tonight. I filled her in on everything I knew, and finished with, "So we're heading back to the school tonight to see if we can make contact with Eric. I want to try to get a surname if I can, which might help police locate his family."

"You're positive this Hatchet Jack character murdered him?"

"Yes," I said firmly. "I think we're dealing with the ghost of a serial killer."

"But why hasn't anyone ever heard of him?" Teeko asked. "I mean, M.J., if this guy murdered Eric and the others only thirty years ago, hell, my family would probably have heard of it. We spent a lot of time at Lake Placid as a kid. Maybe I was too young to remember, but my brother or my parents definitely would have mentioned it over the years."

"It wasn't in the news, Karen," I said. "Somehow this guy was able to kill these boys without anyone knowing about it."

"How is that possible?"

I swept a hand through my hair. "I don't honestly know."

There was a long pause before Karen spoke again. "What can I do to help?"

I smiled. "Nothing, kiddo. Enjoy Italy for now —"

"London," she said. "We're in London today."

"Okay, then enjoy *Europe*. I'll fill you in tomorrow." I clicked off and placed the phone back on the nightstand, then turned an accusing look at Steven, who was lying back with a rather confident smile on his lips. "*What* do you think you're doing in my bed, exactly?" I demanded.

The smile on Steven's face broadened. "I thought I was rather obvious," he said, snaking an arm around my middle. "But maybe I need to give another demonstration?"

I pushed at him. "Will you stop!" I said, then looked around the room in alarm. "Where's Doc?"

"I snuck him into Gilley's room."

"Why is Doc with Gilley?"

"So that I could be with you without worry of being dive-bombed."

I scowled and pushed again at the arms that kept trying to encircle me. "We have to get up," I said reasonably.

"Mmmm," Steven replied, snuggling closer.

"It's eleven thirty," I said.

"Mmmm," Steven repeated.

With a great push I wiggled away from Steven and hopped off the bed, still clinging to the pillow. "I'm serious."

Steven sighed and propped his head on his hand to consider me. "That is the problem," he said. "You are always so serious."

"We're on a job," I said.

"We are not allowed get-down time?" he asked.

I looked blankly at him for about two beats before I said, "It's downtime, not get-down time, and yes, we are allowed some downtime, but not in the way you're thinking."

"So I am not understanding this . . ." he said, struggling to find the words, "this thing that is between us."

I sighed heavily, trying to think of a way I could explain how I felt without bruising his ego, but just then there was a knock on my door, and Gilley opened it without waiting for me to respond. He came halfway into the room before his jaw fell open when he spotted Steven on my bed and me standing there with a pillow to my chest. "Sorry!" he said, and wheeled around as fast as he'd entered. "I just wanted to ask when we were leaving."

"It's not how it looks!" I called after him, feeling heat sear my cheeks.

Steven laughed and got up as well. "You Americans," he said. "So up tightly. You should learn to take things with strides. You know, like, to relax?"

I gave him a level look, and he wisely chose to leave my bedroom without further ado. I quickly changed my clothes and splashed some cool water on my face. Looking reproachfully at my reflection in the mirror, I muttered, "Stupid subconscious."

By the time I was finished freshening up, Gil and Steven had packed the van and were ready to roll. Gil made sure to let me know how "rested" I looked and that I had a certain "bounce" in my step. I ignored him and we piled into the van without further delay.

We arrived at the school, and I had to admit the place had a certain eerie quality about it at night. Lights illuminated the parking lot and the front of the elementary wing, while a cool mist spread across the lawn. "This is good ghost-hunting weather," said Gil, pulling up under one of the streetlights.

"Let's just hope they're in the mood to come out and play," I said. While Gil moved to the back of the van and began flipping on the monitors, Steven and I grabbed our duffel bags and equipment and went through our microphone sound checks.

"Mine's not working," said Steven as Gil shook his head no when Steven spoke into it.

"Do we have a backup?" I asked Gil.

Gilley got off the seat he'd been perched

on and rummaged around in one of the side compartments, finally coming up with a replacement microphone. "Try to be careful with this one," he advised, handing it to Steven. "It's our only spare."

Once we had tested the equipment and were sure the cameras were feeding directly to Gil's monitors, we closed the van door and began walking over to the school.

"About what happened back at the ski lodge," I began, a little uncomfortable with the topic.

"It was nice, wasn't it?" Steven said, bumping me with his hip.

I gave him a tight smile. "I really think we should focus on the job at hand, Steven."

He gave me a coy smile. "I'm good with a hand job," he said.

"I'm serious. You know it takes a lot of energy for me to communicate with these spirits, and I need time to recoup. If you and I are . . . er . . . carrying on, then I might not have the energy to do what I have to do."

Steven looked a bit dejected. "Are you giving me the sweep off?"

"It's brush-off, and no, I'm not giving that to you. Listen," I said, placing one hand on his arm. "I don't want to push you away, but when I'm on a job I need all of my attention, energy, and strength to go into busting the ghost. This Hatchet Jack is one hell of a challenge, and if I'm going to bust his ass to the lower planes in the next few days, I've got to be on top of my game."

"So I cannot be on top of your game?" Steven asked, but the sneaky grin he flashed me let me know he knew exactly what he was saying.

"All I'm proposing," I said with a giggle, "is for you to give me some room and some space until we finish this job. And then . . ."

"And then?"

"When we get back home we can see about developing our . . ." I paused, trying to think of exactly what word could best describe where Steven and I stood. Finally I said, "Interest in each other."

"Interest," Steven repeated.

"Yes."

"You are interested in me," he said, and it wasn't a question.

I felt the corner of my mouth lift. "I suppose so."

"This is good," Steven said. "This is very good. All right, M.J.," he said to me. "No panky in the hanky until we're done with this job."

I had to laugh. Sometimes the things that came out of his mouth sounded so ridiculous, they were too funny to ignore. "Thanks for understanding."

"But when we get back to Boston, it will be a different thing."

"Really?" I asked. "You think so, huh?"

Steven nodded vigorously. "I know so."

We had reached the building by then, and I fished around in my pocket for the key. After unlocking the door we moved inside and stood for a moment in the hallway. "Where will we set up the campsite?" he asked.

I glanced at all the classroom doors and finally decided to go back to the most active site we'd been in. "That one," I said, motioning to my left where we'd first seen Eric and the other little boys. "If they've been there once, they're likely to come back again."

"Do you feel them here now?" he asked, glancing up and down the hallway.

"No," I said, a little disappointed. "But then, it's still early and we've got all night."

We set up our equipment in the classroom, and I noticed all the desks were in their original order of five neat rows of four. Steven pointed one of our cameras directly at the window, where Gilley could monitor it from the van for movement. He set the thermal imager up next to the camera too, in case the video wasn't sensitive enough to capture any spirits who might show up.

Steven held the other camera and I had the second thermal imager. I sat down on the large desk at the front of the classroom and closed my eyes, concentrating on feeling out the room and the surroundings for any hint of a disturbance in the ether.

Nothing rippled along my senses, so there was nothing to do but wait. The minutes ticked along mostly in silence, until I finally heard Gilley say into my ear, "I've got absolutely nothing registering on any of the equipment, M.J. How're you doing?"

"Coming up empty," I said with a sigh. "There doesn't seem to be anything in the ether tonight."

"What do you want to do?"

"How long have we been here?" I asked.

"Almost an hour."

"We'll stay put for a while longer," I said. "If nothing shows up we'll try something else."

We waited another hour and a half, and still nothing disturbed the quiet peacefulness of the evening. I opened my eyes and stretched out from the crouched position I'd been holding. From the light coming in from outside I could see Steven sitting at one of the small desks, fast asleep.

I walked over to him and slid his earpiece out of his ear, placing it in his pocket, and took the camera out of his hand. Easing out of the classroom I said quietly, "Gil, you still with me?"

"I'm here."

"Steven's asleep."

"I saw him nod off about forty minutes ago," Gil said. "You seem to have tired him out."

I ignored that comment. "I'm going out on the grounds."

"Alone?"

"Unless you'd like to accompany me?" I said, knowing what his answer would be.

"Uh . . . er . . . maybe I should just monitor you from here."

"Good call," I said with a chuckle.

"Do you think there's activity out on the lawn?"

"I'm not sure," I said. "But it's weird that we got so much activity last night, but tonight things are quiet."

"I was thinking the same thing," he said. "What do you make of it?"

"Not sure. It's odd, I'll admit, but then, Jack and the others did display a lot of activity last night. Maybe they're recuperating."

I opened the front door and walked down the steps. Pointing the camera in front of me so that Gil could track my progress I cut to the right of the parking lot and headed out to the front lawn, my senses still open and on high alert. Nothing moved in the stillness of the evening, so I used my ears. Auditory phenomena are far more prevalent than any other type exhibited by earthbound energies. I was hoping to hear footsteps or knocks or even voices, but nothing at all came to my ears or my radar.

"All monitors still clear of activity," Gil said into my ear.

"And I'm not picking up anything either," I said. "Crap, Gil. This is perfect ghost-hunting weather. I was really hoping to get a hit."

"What about the back of the school?" Gil asked. "Maybe there's something around the other side?"

I moved away from the lawn and made my way to the back of the building. It was darker here, so I flipped on my flashlight and walked carefully along the grass. As I rounded the corner I could see a light on in one of the other buildings. Curious, I headed toward it. "Where ya goin'?" Gil asked.

"There's a light on in the other building," I said.

"Not unusual," Gil reasoned. "Someone

probably forgot to turn it off."

"Uh-huh," I said, but I was drawn toward the light. It seemed to be coming from the ground floor, and as I got close to the building I noticed that the window the light was emanating from was slightly submerged under the ground level. A shadow passed in front of the light, and immediately I flipped off my flashlight and whispered, "Gil! There's someone inside the school!"

"Who?"

I crept closer. "Hold on; I'll tell you in a second." I hurried to the side of the window, not wanting to approach it directly, and eased my head out to take a peek inside. I gazed down a few feet and realized that I was looking into a room in the building's basement. In a chair in the middle of the room sat Nicholas, the janitor, completely absorbed in a video game. Around him was a playroom any kid would envy. Shelves on one wall were loaded to the gills with games and action figures. Model airplanes hung from hooks in the ceiling, and posters of comic-book heroes adorned the walls.

"Whoa," said Gilley. "Lookit all that." And I realized I'd been pointing the camera straight at the window I was peeking through.

Before I could agree the ether I'd been

silently monitoring all night seemed to tingle, and I recognized Eric's familiar energy. I focused immediately on the direction it was coming from, and gasped when I realized it was emanating from inside Nicholas's room.

Nicholas looked over to the exact location I felt Eric's energy and smiled before he said, "Hi, Eric!"

My eyes widened. "He can see him!" I whispered into the microphone.

"Who?" Gil asked. "M.J., are you okay?"

I didn't answer. I was too wrapped up in the scene happening in the room just below me. Intuitively I had a vision of Eric as he sat in the chair next to Nicholas and pointed to the TV screen where the video game had paused. Nicholas pumped his head up and down and said, "I know! I made it to level four!" Nicholas turned back to the game to continue playing.

I realized I'd stopped breathing. It was incredibly rare for a child ghost to interact with an adult, even one who was mentally challenged. I felt Eric's energy quiver, and I realized he was laughing at Nicholas, whose video game player had just gotten tromped on by a gargoyle-looking thing.

"Awww! You made me lose my concentration!" Nicholas complained. And the two seemed to carry on for several more minutes, like best friends from middle school.

I eased away from the window, amazed at their interaction and wanting time to think about it. "Hello?" Gil said. "Come in, M.J."

"I'm here," I said quietly. "Give me a minute, 'kay, Gil?"

Gil was quiet, and I walked with purpose back to the elementary wing, where I roused Steven from his slumped position in the chair. "Rise and shine," I said brightly.

"I'm awake!" he said, jerking upright.

"Sure you are," I said with a laugh. "Come on; we're heading back home."

"No activity?"

"I'll tell you about it in the van."

We loaded our equipment and got into the van. Gil turned his head to look at me from the front seat and said, "Dish," before turning the key in the ignition and pulling out of the lot.

"Eric and Nicholas interact," I said.

Steven looked back at me, his eyes showing his surprise. "The dean's brother?"

"The very one," I said. "I think he may live in the basement of the main building. He was playing a video game, and I saw him interact with Eric."

"The little-boy ghost?"

"Yep."

"It's like my grandfather and Willis," Steven said, referring to the chess game his ghostly grandfather played each day with his retired groundskeeper. We'd encountered them six weeks earlier, when Steven had first hired me to help his grandfather cross over after he'd fallen off a roof at the family hunting lodge.

"Yes, it's like that," I admitted, "but this is on a level I've never seen before. Willis and your grandfather didn't speak. Their interaction was limited to a few chess moves. These two actually engage each other like two living people."

"What were they talking about?" Gil asked.

"A video game," I said, shaking my head. "Which means that Eric has an awareness of his surroundings that is incredibly unusual for a ghost. The fact that he can see things as they really are and not as they appeared thirty years ago says that he's evolved and amazingly well adjusted for such a young spirit."

"I am not understanding this," said Steven.

I took a breath, thinking how best to explain. "Most ghosts don't fully see the environment they're in as it changes over time. They will act and react to things that they knew existed in their own time. So, to give you an example, say you're a ghost from the eighteen hundreds and your main mode of transportation is the horse and buggy. You will move around as if you're still in your horse and buggy, and you'll see cars not as they are, but as other horses and buggies."

"Why?" Steven asked. "Why not see things as they are?"

"Because most of these grounded spirits are in a state of confusion. Often they're in denial about their own mortality, so to cope they imprint their thoughts over the images they see. Sometimes they become aware that things aren't as they should be. Like if a door they liked to keep closed is kept open by the current tenants, they'll work hard to constantly keep the door closed. That's why construction is so unsettling to them. They don't like having to work so hard to imprint their thoughts over the changing images in their environment."

"Eric's a pretty special ghostie then," said Gil.

"Only two percent of recorded grounded spirits ever interact on an active level with an individual," I said, quoting my research. "And that tells us something about Nicholas too."

"He's a medium too?" Steven said.

"Highly likely," I said. "And if he's as gifted as I think he is, able to have an entire conversation with Eric, then it's also likely that he's seen other things as well."

"The other boys," said Gil.

"And Hatchet Jack," I said.

"Explain to me, then, why we're driving home," Gil said.

I sat back in my seat wearily. "Because Eric wasn't interested in me tonight," I said. "He wanted to hang out with his friend. The poor kid died an awful death, and he gets chased on a regular basis by this freakazoid Jack. I figured he deserved a little downtime with Nicholas. Besides, we can head back there tomorrow and try to talk to Nicholas ourselves. He might know a whole lot about this little boy. Who knows how many details they've shared between them?"

"That could cut our investigation time way down," said Gil.

"Exactly," I said. "I'll call the dean in the morning and clear it with him. With any luck we'll be able to identify Eric and gain some ground on these other boys too."

We pulled into the O'Neal ski lodge then, and everyone got out of the van. As we walked to the front door Gil asked me, "Is

Doc staying with me the rest of the trip?"

I caught the hopeful little look Steven sent my way, but said to Gil, "No. I'll take him back. Thanks, though."

Gil turned to Steven. "Sorry, man. I tried."

I pushed past them and went into the lodge, where I gently picked up Doc's cage from Gil's room and trucked him back to mine. Before turning out the light I groaned when I saw that the clock read three thirty a.m. It was turning out to be a long week, and I had a feeling the toughest part of this bust was yet to come.

CHAPTER 7

It was after ten, and light was pouring into my room when I pulled myself groggily out of sleep and sat up. Doc was whistling from his perch, entertaining himself by mimicking the birds outside. Right now he had a sparrow from just outside the window completely confused.

"Morning, sailor," I said to him.

He stopped whistling and turned around to me. With a bob of his head he said, "Nice bum, where you from?"

I laughed. It'd been a while since I'd heard that one. "Valdosta," I said, referring to our hometown in Georgia.

"Gonna cost ya!" he said, remembering the banter I'd taught him when I was a kid. I'd had Doc since I was twelve, and every once in a while he took me down memory lane.

"You hungry?" I asked him.

Doc gave me several more head bobs. I

threw back the covers and grabbed my robe off a chair in the corner. Opening his cage I took him into the kitchen where Steven was reading a newspaper and sipping some coffee. "Good morning," he said when he saw us.

"Nice bum, where you from?" Doc asked him.

"Argentina," Steven said.

Doc cocked his head, and rolled his tongue around. After a moment he said in an almost perfect mimic of Steven's voice, "Argentina."

Steven laughed. "That is a smart bird you have there, M.J."

"He's a keeper," I said, and gave Doc a kiss on the top of his head, then placed him on the counter while I reached for a banana and some blueberries to cut up for him.

I heard shuffling from behind me. "Is that coffee?" Gil said, his voice croaky.

"Fresh pot," said Steven.

"Pour me a cup, would you?" I said to Gil while I worked to cut up Doc's breakfast.

Gil poured me a cup of black coffee before getting his own and heading over to sit across from Steven. "Your detective called here at eight a.m.," he said moodily.

I looked up from the bowl I was filling with fruit. "Muckleroy?"

Gil nodded and gave a tremendous yawn. "He called my number instead of yours." Because Gil took care of booking all of our jobs, his cell was listed on my business card as the main number for our ghostbusting business.

"Sorry," I said, carrying Doc on my shoulder as I carefully maneuvered the coffee and fruit over to the table. "What'd he want?"

Gilley yawned again. The poor guy looked like a wreck without his usual ten hours of beauty sleep. "He said that none of the teeth in the skull they found at the pond had dental work."

"So there won't be any dental records to compare them to," I said.

"He asked if you'd call him when you woke up."

"Do you know why?"

"He thinks maybe you can give a description of Eric's ghost. He wants to compare it to the files he's pulled of missing children from the seventies and eighties."

"That's a great idea," I said. "I'll call him after I shower."

"Don't forget the dean's brother," said Steven, reminding me that I still needed to talk with Nicholas.

"Looks like there's no time for a run," I

moaned, glancing at the clock on the wall.

"And you wanted to interview that teacher, too," Gil reminded me.

I looked to him and Steven, a little annoyed that the bulk of the work kept falling on my shoulders. "Why don't you two go interview him?" I suggested. "That way I can meet with the police and give them a description, then head over to the school and pick Nicholas's brain."

"You do not want me to come with you?" Steven asked, and I realized I'd been pushing him away but good the last few days.

"I can go this one alone," I said gently. "You and I can hang out later, okay?"

He nodded and I got up to shower, making quick work of it, as I wanted to call Muckleroy sooner rather than later.

With my hair still damp I called the number Gilley had written on a piece of scrap paper for me. Muckleroy's demeanor had done a one-eighty from our first encounter, and I found him to be pleasant and courteous on the phone. "We've got a great sketch artist here in town," he was saying. "I was hoping you could give her a general description of this little boy and maybe we'd get lucky."

"How many missing boys do you have to compare it to?" I asked.

"Four boys fit the age range from this county," he said. "But they're spaced pretty far apart, from 1966 to 1985, and only two actually still have the photos attached to the files. I figure I can take the sketch from your sit-down with our artist and show it to the families of the boys — see if they recognize it."

"Were any of your four reported missing around 1976?" I asked.

"Only one," he said. "But your name, Eric, doesn't fit."

"Were any of the other boys named Eric?"

"No."

I frowned. I knew that was the boy's name. He'd said it clearly several times, and Nicholas had even confirmed that was the name the boy went by. Then again, maybe it was his middle name or a nickname. "What time would you like me to drop by?" I asked.

"Can you come now?"

"I can," I said, and got directions. I then looked through the notes and found the number for Dean Habbernathy. I got a general voice mail, so I left a rather urgent message and crossed my fingers that he'd get back to me. I knew I could always go back to the school and knock on Nicholas's window, but something told me that Nicholas wasn't the type to warm up to strangers. I'd need his brother to make him feel at ease about talking to us.

I met Gil and Steven back in the kitchen. I let them have the van while I took the keys to Karen's Mercedes. Friendship has its privileges.

I followed behind Gil and Steven until we hit downtown, and, going by my directions, I turned left onto Saranac Avenue while they continued down Old Military Road.

I arrived at the police station and fed the meter with enough quarters for two hours, hoping that would be plenty. I made my way inside and gave my name to the dispatcher. She told me to wait in the lobby. I took a seat and waited only a minute or two before a door opened and Muckleroy motioned me over. "Thanks for coming so quickly," he said. "Our sketch artist works for us part-time, and she has only a couple of hours this morning before her next appointment."

"No worries," I said, following him through the door down a brilliantly white hallway to an office at the back. "In here," he said, and allowed me through the door first. I went in, and a woman of about sixty, with lovely silver hair and deep brown eyes, rose to meet me. "Hello, M.J.," she said warmly, extending her hand. "I'm Amelia Myers."

"Hi," I said, shaking her hand. She pointed to the other side of the table and I took a seat.

Muckleroy said from the doorway, "I'll leave you to it. Amelia, call me when you two are through and we can sort through the photos I've got upstairs."

He left the room, and Amelia said, "Bob tells me you're quite the talent."

I smiled crookedly. "He's downplaying it."

She laughed. "Well, you've got a fan in him for life."

"He likes my spirit." I giggled. Somebody stop me.

Amelia laughed again; then she sobered and pulled out her sketch pad. "All right, M.J., why don't you start by telling me the basic shape of this boy's face as you saw it?"

We worked together for nearly two hours, and I was glad that I had fed the meter appropriately. Finally, with ten minutes to spare before I'd have to bolt out of there to put more quarters in, she turned her sketch pad around, and the face staring out at me was unmistakable. "That's him," I said sadly. There was something so tragic about seeing that face on the pad. Eric seemed so alive and vibrant, even in spirit.

Amelia turned the pad back around. "He's

a good-looking young man," she remarked. "And you're sure his hair is red?"

"Yes. He's got a little of that Opie look to him. All red hair and freckles."

Amelia made a *tsk*ing noise. "I can't imagine anyone wanting to hurt such a lovely young man," she said.

"I agree, which is why I'm on a mission to hunt Hatchet Jack down and put an end to his nightmare once and for all."

"Bob tells me you believe there were other victims?"

"Yes," I said. "I think there were at least two more boys who were murdered."

"I've lived here all my life," she said. "And I never remember anything the likes of which you describe."

"Again why I'm so anxious to solve this riddle," I said. "Essentially we're talking about no less than four deaths happening within this city's borders that were never reported. You'd think that someone alive today would know *something*."

"You know who you should talk to?" she said. "You should talk to my nephew, Lance. He attended Northelm in the late seventies, and if memory serves me he was one of the first boys to report seeing that ghost they call Hatchet Jack."

My eyebrows shot up. "Really?" I said.

"Will you write down his number for me?"

"Certainly," she said, and fished out one of her business cards. After scribbling Lance's name and number on the back of her card, she gave it to me. "He owns a liquor store on McKinley, and he's there most afternoons."

I thanked her, then glanced at the clock. "Sorry, Amelia, but the meter where my car is parked is just about out of time."

"Oh, by all means," she said, making a small wave of her hand. "Go on then. The meter woman here is an unforgiving soul."

There was a tiny smile on her face as she said that, and I gave her a pat on her arm as I got up and began to edge out of the room. "Have Detective Muckleroy call me if he gets a hit from that sketch."

"Will do," she said.

I hurried out of the station and made it to my car just as the last minute was ticking down. To my chagrin, a meter maid stood about ten yards away, her ticket pad out and her pen at the ready. Amelia wasn't kidding; I'd barely escaped a ticket.

I got in Karen's car and turned the key in the ignition, but before pulling out of the lot I checked my phone for messages. I had none. "Crap," I said. The dean never called me back.

As I pulled out onto Main Street I called Gilley. "Yo!" he said when he answered. "What's the word?"

"The sketch turned out great," I said. "I'm pretty confident that if the police have a photo from the missing persons list they've complied, they'll find a match."

"That's great. We didn't have as much luck."

"Tell me."

"Ballsach is an asshole."

My eyes widened. Gilley was usually more circumspect. "Wow," I said. "Seems like you two really hit it off."

"Seriously, M.J., the man is an idiot. Completely uncooperative. Wouldn't even let me ask him a few simple questions. The moment we mentioned Hatchet Jack he became totally unreasonable."

"Gil," I said, "I'm sure he wasn't all that bad. Did you tell him to think about it and maybe you could talk to him later?"

"He slammed the door in our faces," Gil said. "I think that ship has sailed."

"What the heck is *with* these people, anyway?" I said. "Don't they get that talking about it might make it better?"

"Thank you, Dear Abby," Gil said moodily. I knew that because of his genteel Southern upbringing, rudeness from strangers always threw him.

"Hey," I said. "It's okay, Gil. I may have a lead that might pan out for us."

"Did the dean call you back?"

"No," I said. "Can you do me a favor and call him again for me? Explain what we've uncovered and let him know that I believe his brother may be able to shed some light for us."

"Got it. What's his number?"

"It's on my notepad in the bedroom. Are you guys back at the ski lodge?"

"Uh, not exactly," Gil admitted, and it was then that I heard music in the background.

"Where are you?"

"Er . . ."

"Gil?" I said in an insistent tone. "Tell me where you are."

"At the Mirror Lake Spa."

"You mean I'm working my ass off while you two are goofing off?!" I shouted, completely irritated.

"It was Steven's idea!" Gil said hurriedly.

I counted to ten and took a few deep breaths, but wasn't having any luck calming down. "Guess what?" I said.

"What?" Gil squeaked.

"Playtime is over."

"Steven," Gil said, his voice pulling away from the receiver. "We've got to go."

"But I'm in the middle of my pedicure," I heard Steven say.

"You two are *ridiculous!*" I shouted, and I was so mad that I hung up on Gilley and threw my phone on the seat beside me.

A minute later my phone rang. Caller ID said it was Steven. I didn't answer. Instead I made my way over to McKinley Street and found Lance's Liquor. I parked just down the street and walked back to the door, working hard to check the frustration that was welling up inside of me. I was quickly becoming sick of pulling all the weight on this job while Gil and Steven looked for every excuse to get out of working.

When I pulled open the door and stepped inside I found the store nearly empty. Behind the counter and up a ladder was the store's only occupant. "Good afternoon," a man said pleasantly while turning awkwardly on his ladder in my direction.

My heart skipped a beat. The guy was beautiful. He had a square jaw, thin nose, full lips, and beautiful blue eyes. "Hi," I said.

"Can I help you with something?" he asked.

For a moment I completely forgot why I'd come into the store. "Um . . ." I said, swiveling in a small arc as I looked around the store. "I need wine."

"We've got plenty," he said, coming down the ladder. He was dressed in a white button-down shirt and great ass-hugging jeans. He was tall, with slightly olive skin and blond hair. "Over here," he said, moving past me to the back of the store.

I followed dumbly behind, the way a dog will follow anybody with a big, juicy bone. He stopped in front of a large wall and looked back at me. "Red or white?"

"Huh?" I said. Sometimes I am *so* sophisticated.

"Wine," he said. "Do you drink red or white?"

I blinked rapidly. "Red," I said.

"Dry or sweet?"

"Little of both."

"We have this great Shiraz," he said, moving over to a rack near the bottom of the shelving. "Comes from this little orchard in Australia."

"I'll take it," I said quickly.

He gave me a startled look. "Okay," he said, and pulled the bottle from the rack. "Did you only want the one bottle?"

About then the fog of endorphins the sight of him had invoked lifted and I said, "One bottle should be fine. But the other thing I need is a little information."

"About what?" he asked.

227

I crossed my fingers, really hoping that when I asked him this next question he didn't react the way everyone else in this town had. "I need to know about Hatchet Jack."

His head pulled back in surprise. "Was there another sighting?" And even before I could respond he followed up with, "Yeah, it's June. That bastard always shows up around now."

I let go of the little breath I'd been holding and followed him back to the counter, where he began wrapping my wine. "My name is M. J. Holliday," I explained. "Your aunt Amelia sent me and I've been hired by the family of a girl who was chased by him last week. My expertise is getting rid of . . . well, things like Jack."

Lance gave me another curious look. "You're a ghostbuster?"

I smiled, relieved he seemed so open to the idea. "Yes," I said. "I've got a pretty good practice going in Boston."

"You don't say?" he said, leaning back against the wall behind him and crossing his arms. "Are you a medium or a techie?"

It was my turn to be surprised. "A medium. My partner is the techie."

Lance nodded. "I've been on a few ghost hunts myself."

"You're kidding," I said.

"No, it's true," Lance said, rubbing his chin thoughtfully. "I had an encounter with Jack when I was fifteen, and it nearly did me in. I was scared outta my mind for years after that. I couldn't sleep without a light on, and every little noise made me jump. Finally my mom suggested that I either get therapy or look for a way to overcome my fear.

"I had a college girlfriend who was really intuitive; she could sense stuff that other people couldn't. Her grandmother lived in this haunted house, and one night we spent the night over there. We heard noises, and a door closed right next to us, but I survived the evening. After that I wasn't so afraid of things that went bump in the night."

"Tell me what happened with Jack," I said.

Lance paused, collecting the memory before he spoke. "I was a sophomore at Northelm. I was on the cross-country team, J.V., and I really wanted to make the varsity team, so the week after school let out I ran the trails around the school every morning and every evening. The fourth day of this routine I kept feeling like someone was running along behind me, but when I looked back there was nobody there.

"About a quarter mile into the run I swore

I heard something like a scream or someone yelling. I stopped and looked back and I heard these footsteps running straight at me, even though there was no one on the path but me. There was this sense of fear that hit me like a fist right in the chest. I started running as fast as I could, and the footsteps behind me got closer and closer."

Lance paused again, and I could tell all these years later it was still a difficult memory for him to recall. "Then what happened?" I asked.

He took a breath and continued. "I glanced over my shoulder, and ten feet behind me was a man with this crazy, wild look in his eyes. I'll never forget it," he said, shaking his head. "He was holding a bloody hatchet over his head, and I knew he was going to kill me. I screamed and probably ran faster than I'd ever run before — or since."

"How long after you saw him did you notice he was no longer following you?"

"About the time I passed Hole Pond," Lance said. "I was nearly completely out of breath by then — like I said, I'm a long-distance man, not a sprinter — and I looked over my shoulder and he was just gone."

"And you reported that to the police?"

Lance nodded. "Yeah. They were really

great at first, and they sent a big patrol out there to search the area, but there was no trace of him. He just vanished."

"Do you remember any specifics, Lance, like the day of the week and the time this happened?"

"It was Friday evening around six. Why?"

"If we know when Jack becomes active, we can try and pinpoint his location."

"Makes sense," he said with a nod.

"And what year was this?"

"The summer of 1978."

Mentally I did a little arithmetic, and I had to admit I was mighty impressed at how trim and fit and damned good-looking Lance was for someone in his midforties.

"You just did the math, didn't you?" he said, breaking into a grin.

I felt my cheeks grow hot. "No," I said quickly.

"Sure, sure," he said with a look that said he wasn't buying it. "I look young for my age."

I cleared my throat and searched for a way out of the embarrassing moment. "When the police didn't find any evidence of Jack, what happened next?"

"Nothing much," Lance said bitterly. "I mean, when they went to the cross-country trail to investigate, they only found my footprints. No one else's."

"No one else's on a running path?" I asked, amazed that only one set of footprints was found.

"It had rained that morning," Lance explained. "The path was still a little soggy, and it had washed away any prior footprints. I showed the police exactly where I'd first heard someone chasing me; then I showed them the point where I'd looked back and seen him almost on top of me, waving the hatchet."

"So they didn't believe you," I said, more statement than question.

"Nope. My aunt did a sketch anyway, and it was a great rendition, but no one came forward to claim knowing him."

"Does she still have the sketch?" I asked.

Lance rubbed his chin. "Probably. You can ask her; she rarely throws them away."

"I will, thanks," I said, making a mental note. "Can you tell me if you know of any other sightings of Jack in the area?"

Lance scratched his head thoughtfully. "I learned through my aunt that these sightings started a little earlier. She had a good friend who worked as the police dispatcher, and she told Aunt Amelia that an anonymous call came into the station late one night, and the caller said that they had seen a guy running after a kid near Hole Pond. The caller said she thought the guy was waving some kind of weapon while he was chasing the kid. The cop who responded said he couldn't find anything suspicious, and no calls of missing or injured children followed. The cops assumed it was some local dad who'd caught his kid up to no good and was chasing him home, so it was dropped."

A chill ran down my spine as I remembered Gilley's recounting of the police blotters. "That was, what, 1977 then?"

"No," said Lance. "That was July of 1976."

"Great. Listen, could you show me where this cross-country trail is around North-elm?"

Lance shuffled his feet and looked uncomfortable for the first time since I'd started talking to him. "I can't, M.J.," he said softly.

"Why not?"

Lance looked up at me, and his eyes were haunted. "I may have overcome a lot of my fears since that encounter with Jack, but risking another one with him is not a demon I'm willing to conquer."

I smiled reassuringly. "I get it," I said. "How about drawing me a map, then?"

I left the liquor store a little later with a

detailed map and the beginnings of a plan forming in my head. I drove back over to the station and told the receptionist that I needed to speak to Detective Muckleroy as soon as possible. He came to get me from the lobby a bit later. "I'm glad you came back," he said soberly. "I'm afraid we've come up with a dead end on this kid Eric."

"His picture didn't match?"

"No," the detective said. "The red hair is the clincher. None of the kids reported missing had red hair."

"Can I see the pictures?" I asked as we walked back down the long corridor I'd come down earlier.

Muckleroy brightened. "Sure, if you think it will help."

He directed me into a small office just off the main hallway and into a chair in front of a grossly overcluttered desk. "Sorry about the mess," he said, scooping Styrofoam cups and plastic wrappers into a waste can before handing me a folder.

I opened the folder and pulled out the pages, sorting through them one by one. Midway through I stopped on the face of a young boy with black hair, dark eyes, and a great big smile. The name on the page read, *Hernando Rodriguez,* and it gave a birth date of 1964. I sucked in a breath as I read the date he'd gone missing: July ninth, 1976.

"Did you find something?" Muckleroy said, looking intently at me.

I swiveled the paper around and showed him the photo. "I'm pretty sure this is one of the young ghosts I saw in the classroom at Northelm," I said. "He was with Eric the first night I encountered them."

Muckleroy took the paper and studied it himself. Then he turned around to his computer and began typing into it. "Says here Hernando was last seen by his father when he returned him from his weekend visitation with him. José Rodriguez says he dropped Hernando on the front porch of his mother's home the evening of July ninth, 1976. Mother and father were having a bitter custody dispute. Hernando's mother believed strongly that her ex-husband kidnapped their son and smuggled him back home to Brazil."

"What was the father's story?"

Muckleroy was quiet for a moment as he read the report. "Says here that police took a preliminary interview, and when the son failed to show up, the father disappeared too. They assumed he also went back to Brazil."

"Is the mother still alive?"

"Not sure," said Muckleroy. "I can try and

hunt her down if you'd like."

I nodded. "See if she ever heard from either of them again," I said.

"You think this Hatchet Jack guy killed the boy?"

I felt a tingle of energy in the ether, and something hit my consciousness like a bolt of lightning. "Detective," I said urgently. "Lance Myers told me about the very first sighting of Hatchet Jack. He said an anonymous call had come into the station about a man chasing a little boy near Hole Pond. Can you look up the exact date of that incident?"

The detective turned to another file on his desktop. He rummaged through a few papers, and as I watched I saw his face drain of color. "Holy shit," he said softly. "That call came in around eleven thirty p.m. on July ninth, 1976."

I wasn't so surprised. "It was no ghost that night running along the pond," I said. "That was the real deal."

Muckleroy wiped a beefy hand down his face, then sat back in his chair to regard me. "How the hell did we miss this?" he said.

"Were you on the force back then?"

He shook his head. "No, I didn't come on board till the mideighties. Still, I knew a lot of the guys who would have been on patrol back then, and they weren't likely to miss something big like this. I mean, you said you saw three little boys, right?"

"Yes. If you're asking for my opinion, it's that Jack murdered at least three."

"Why can't we find any word about the other two?"

"I don't know, Detective. Maybe their parents never reported them missing."

Muckleroy scowled at that thought. "They'd have to be really shitty parents," he said. "Besides, wouldn't neighbors or relatives or friends or teachers say something? I mean, it's just so odd."

I held up my hands in surrender. "I'm afraid I don't have the answers."

"Okay," Muckleroy said, sitting forward again and grabbing a piece of blank paper and a pencil. "Let's break this down into known and unknown. What do we know so far?"

"Do you want to include my intuitive information as known or unknown?" I asked, testing him a little.

"No, I trust you," he said to me with an encouraging smile. "You've definitely proven your abilities, M.J. I'm willing to take the info you give me as fact."

"In that case, we know that sometime

between the years of 1976 and 1977 a child serial killer was loose here in Lake Placid. He preyed upon young boys and involved them in some sort of psycho game of tag, but if he tagged you, he did it with a hatchet."

"Sick bastard," Muckleroy mumbled as he wrote my thoughts down.

I continued on. "We know that Hernando might very well have been one of his last victims."

"How do we know that?" Muckleroy asked.

"Because two years later Lance Myers was chased by the ghost of Hatchet Jack, not the real thing."

"Still, two years is a long time. There could have been more victims in that time."

I sat with that for a moment, feeling it out intuitively. Finally I shook my head and said, "Detective, you'll have to trust me on this. I know Jack died the same summer as Hernando."

"Do you think he was a local?" he asked, pushing me a little.

"That I don't know," I said. "But he seems so connected to the property around North-elm and Hole Pond that I'd say he probably lived here, at least for a period of time."

"Wish I knew how to identify him," Muckleroy said. "Might help a lot to solve this riddle."

"There may be a way," I said. "According to Lance, Amelia drew a sketch of Jack shortly after Lance was chased by Jack's ghost. Maybe we could pull that from the files and compare it to any criminals in the area from the seventies."

"Good idea," Muckleroy said, jotting that down. "I'll give her a call and see if she's still got the sketch. Maybe I can also post it around town, and someone might recognize him."

"Terrific," I said.

"Are you going to try to make contact with this Eric kid again?"

"Yes," I said, glancing at the clock on the wall. "In fact, I may have an in on that front."

"An in?"

"There's a janitor who works at Northelm who might be the key to finding out more about what happened all those years ago," I said.

Muckleroy looked at me in surprise. "You mean Nicky?" he said. "How could Nicky know anything about this?" I told him about what I'd seen and sensed the night before. His look of surprise never wavered. "Wow," he said when I'd finished. "I had no idea

Nicky could do what you do. He's so shy, and usually scared of his own shadow."

"Well, he must not have been too scared," I said, recalling when he'd all but attacked Gilley in the van. "He can wield a bat when he has to."

Muckleroy laughed. "Yeah, I heard about that. That was rare for Nicky. Usually he leaves stuff like that to his brother." I noticed a tiny hint of sourness in the way Muckleroy mentioned the dean.

"What's up with Dean Habbernathy?" I asked carefully. "He seems pretty uptight about all this."

Muckleroy sighed. "You could say that," he said. "Owen's not a bad guy. He's just a bit rigid. Except, of course, when it comes to his brother. I will say that about the man — he's made sure to look out for Nicky all these years."

"But he forces Nicholas to live in the basement of the school," I pointed out. "I would think the least he could do would be to find a proper home for him."

"Oh, he tried," Muckleroy said. "But Nicky has lived on that property ever since he was adopted by their father and the former dean of Northelm, Winston Habbernathy."

"The boys are adopted?"

"Yeah, although Owen would never admit to it. I only know because my wife was the estate attorney for Winston when he passed away."

"Are Owen and Nicholas even blood related?" I asked.

Muckleroy shrugged. "Not sure," he said. "Word has it that the old man wanted to pass on his family's legacy, and since he didn't have children of his own and wasn't likely to produce any . . . if you get my drift," he said, looking carefully at me.

I cocked my head, trying to follow. "Sorry?" I said.

Muckleroy shuffled some papers around on his desk and mumbled, "Winston was a bit . . . er . . . light in his loafers."

"Ah," I said. "He was gay."

Muckleroy cleared his throat. "That was the rumor. Anyway, he adopted the two boys around the same time and brought them up on the school grounds. That was before Winston bought his new house on Church Pond."

"There sure are a lot of ponds and lakes around here," I remarked.

Muckleroy grinned. "Church Pond is a stone's throw from Hole Pond and the school. And yes, there is a lot of water around here."

"Does the family still own that home?" I asked.

Muckleroy nodded. "Owen lives there now."

I took another glance at the clock. "Well, I think I've taken up enough of your time, Detective."

"Will you stop with the formalities?" he said warmly. "It's Bob, okay?"

I smiled. "Got it. Thanks, Bob. I'll let you know if I get any more info."

"In the meantime I'll circulate Jack's sketch and check the older files. Let's plan on talking tomorrow to bring each other up to speed."

Muckleroy walked me out, and as I headed to Karen's Mercedes my cell phone rang. "What's the word, Gil?" I asked when I answered.

"That Dean Habbernathy is one hell of a cranky man," he said, his voice telling me he was completely aggravated.

"What happened?"

"Well, I called the number by your bed and got nowhere, so I did a little searching around on my computer and found his residential number."

"Was it listed?"

"Of course not," said Gil.

"I'm going to go out on a limb here and

guess that he was not happy that you had found his home phone number."

"It's not like I'm some sort of telemarketer!" Gil exclaimed. "Geez! The guy gave me the third degree. How *dare* I call him at home!"

"I'm guessing he wasn't open to our request to speak to his brother, then, huh?"

"The only thing he was receptive to was hanging up on me," he said.

I sighed as I got into Karen's car. "Okay," I said. "Then we'll have to proceed without his consent and try to talk to Nicholas on our own."

"Are you heading back here?"

"I was thinking maybe you guys could head this way and we could eat in town."

"I'm all for it," said Gil. "But I'm afraid it's just going to be the two of us."

"Is Steven tired from his day at the spa?" I asked sarcastically.

"No," Gil said, then paused.

"What's up?" I asked.

"Steven flew back to Boston about an hour ago."

"What?" I said, a little too loudly. "Why would he do that?"

"Two reasons: The university called him — the plumbing problem's been fixed and his class is back on schedule. And two . . ."

"Yes?"

"He thinks you don't want him around."

"What? Why would he think that?"

"He may have overheard you say something about us being ridiculous this afternoon."

"Hey," I snapped. "You two *were* being ridiculous! I mean, Gil, I've been the one doing the bulk of the work on this case, and you two have been doing a lot of goofing off."

"I have *not* been goofing off, M.J.!" Gilley said defensively. "Who spent all day yesterday in a tiny little room at the county clerk's, huh? Who?!"

I drew in a deep breath. Gilley was right. He had been pretty good this trip. Steven had been the main detraction. "Maybe it's for the best that Steven's gone home," I said.

"Listen," Gilley tried, using his calm voice. "I think all Steven really needs is a little direction. He didn't come to us with a load of experience, and he's taking a lot of his cues from you. And you'll have to admit that he's been playing a lot of third wheel on this job."

I sat at a traffic light and stared blankly out the windshield. Gilley had a solid point. "Fine," I said at last. "I'll call him tomorrow and try to smooth things over."

"Whether or not you want to admit it, we need him around, toots," said Gil. "If for nothing else than to help us overcome all those financial obstacles that keep us constantly in the red."

"I get it, I get it," I said, really wanting to move on. "Meet me at Goldberries Restaurant on Main Street," I said, pulling into the restaurant's parking lot, "and we can discuss our next move."

CHAPTER 8

"So, let me get this straight," Gil said as he cut into his fried chicken. "Tonight your plan is to head to the school and just knock on Nicholas's window and hope that he won't come out swinging his bat at you?"

"Do you have a better plan?" I said, leveling a look at him.

Gilley chewed thoughtfully on his food for a moment. "Nope," he said finally. "As long as I get to stay in the van, then I'm jiggy with whatever you come up with."

I cut my eyes to my plate, afraid Gil would see the guilty look I had plastered there. If all else failed I had an idea about how to draw out Jack, but with Steven gone I would need Gil's help, and my plan didn't include him sitting idly by in the van.

"If Nicholas isn't the fountain of information that we're hoping for, I've come up with a name that might be of some assistance," Gil said, seeming to take no note of how I was avoiding his eyes.

"Oh, yeah?" I asked. "Who's that?"

"William Skolaris," he said smugly.

I gave Gil a quizzical look. "Who?"

"Bill Skolaris lives two blocks from here. He's been teaching at Northelm for a whopping thirty-three years."

"You think he might know about Hatchet Jack?"

"I'm sure of it," Gil said.

"How can you be?"

"Because he's the supervising editor of the school's newspaper. Remember that article that was pulled off the Web so quickly? That man's gotta know somethin' 'bout somethin'."

"Good job, Gil," I said, patting his hand. "We'll try to hit Nicholas up for info tonight when we go to the school for another vigil, and tomorrow we'll drop by Skolaris's and see if he's willing to talk to us."

After dinner Gilley and I drove back to the ski lodge for a power nap before our planned stakeout at the school. I had to admit that I was hoping I would catch a break and Jack would show up without a lot of prompting. If I could follow his energy back to his portal, I knew I could put that particular demon to rest, at least. Helping the boys to

247

cross over would be far easier if he was out of the way.

The lodge felt quiet without Steven, even though Gilley and Doc made enough noise for four people. I thought about what Gilley had said as I lay down on my bed, and figured I owed the good doctor an apology at the very least. Gil and I had been doing this so long that it came as second nature to us, and I forgot that someone just coming into it might not know what to do with such a difficult case.

My alarm went off at ten thirty, and I rolled over on the bed still feeling tired and out of sorts. My internal clock was starting to rebel against the crazy hours we were keeping, and I really hoped that this pace wouldn't continue much longer.

I got Gilley up, albeit with some difficulty, and we packed our duffel bags and got into the van.

Gil drove blearily along toward Northelm, and I handed him the traveler's cup of coffee I'd made him before we left Karen's place. "Thanks," he said. "I hope it's strong."

"It is," I said, giggling when he made a face after taking a sip.

"Good lord, M.J.!" he said, setting the cup

in the cup holder. "That tastes like Mama Dell's."

Mama Dell's was a coffee shop within walking distance of our office. The owner was a spunky little Southern gal who made coffee thick enough to patch pavement. Her shop flourished because of the pastries and sandwiches she sold, and her glorious personality. Mama Dell patrons were a loyal brood. "Thought you might be homesick," I said.

"Blach," Gil said, then picked up the cup and took another swig. "You're just lucky I'm really, really tired."

We arrived at the school, and after we went through our sound and video-feed checks I moved off to the elementary wing. "Remember," Gil warned, before I closed the van door, "since Steven's not here, you'll have to work the camera and the thermal imager for me so that I can monitor."

"I used to manage just fine before he came along, ya know," I said moodily. I was still a little sensitive about Steven's departure, and I was thankful Gilley let it drop at that.

After unlocking the door I made my way inside the dark school and stood still for a few seconds, getting a bead on the energy in the building. "I'm getting a little blip on the electrostatic gauge," Gilley said in my ear. "Are you near an outlet?"

I looked around. "No," I said into my headset, while pulling out the small gadget from my back pocket. Sure enough it was spiking in little blips.

"It's too faint for me to be sure it's spiritual," said Gilley. "How's your radar working?"

I opened up my senses and felt the energy around me. There was the smallest of tugs down the hallway, and I eagerly followed it. "I think I've got something," I whispered.

I moved into a classroom at the very end of the hallway, near the back door of the building and off to the right. As I opened the door it creaked loudly, cutting through the silence and causing me to wince. "Hello?" I said out loud. "Is there an energy here that wishes to communicate with me?"

Out of the corner of my eye I caught a flash of shadow, and my eyes darted quickly over in that direction. Nothing noticeable moved. Then there was just the barest hint of energy that tugged at my solar plexus. It felt male, and it felt young, but I knew it wasn't Eric. "Hernando?" I said, taking a chance.

There was a gasp by my left ear, and it was so unexpected that I jumped and turned around. I could feel the energy building in the room, and I waited to see what would happen next. "What's going on?" Gilley said softly. "I've got electrostatic energy registering, but you've got the camera pointed down and I can't see anything."

I picked the camera up quickly and pointed it around the room, feeling the very air as I tried to get a placement for Hernando. "Hernando?" I said again. "I'm here to help you, sweetheart. It's okay; I swear I'm not going to hurt you."

Again I saw a flash of shadow out of the corner of my eye, and I pointed the camera around to where I thought I'd seen it. "Who's Hernando?" Gilley whispered.

"Shhhh!" I hissed. He was ruining my concentration.

"Sorry!" he whispered. "I'll be quiet from now on. I promise. Just tell me when you're ready. I'll continue to monitor the screens. But if I get something I'll try to let you know quietly."

I clenched my free fist, irritated that he wasn't shutting up. "Gilley, please be quiet," I whispered.

"Sorry!"

I took a deep breath and focused on feeling out the little boy with the skittish energy. "Hernando Rodriguez," I said calmly. "I know you're here with me. And I want you to know that if you choose to communicate with me, I will be able to hear you."

I want my mom! his little voice said inside my head.

That tiny plea broke my heart. "I know, sweetheart," I said. "I'm sure she's been really worried about you. And your dad too."

I can't find them! he said to me. *I keep looking, but I can't find them!*

"I can help you with that, Hernando," I said.

There was another gasp, this time from across the room, and I felt Hernando's energy fill with fear. *He's coming!* he said. *The bad man is coming!*

"Damn it!" I said under my breath.

"Electrostatic is spiking off the charts, M.J.!" Gilley whispered urgently.

"Jack's coming," I said, then focused back on the little boy. "Hernando!" I commanded. "If you want to get away from the bad man you've got to listen to me. I need you to look up toward the ceiling!"

He's coming! He's coming!

"Focus, Hernando!" I yelled across the room. "Look up at the ceiling! Do you see a bright white light?"

There was a short pause as I felt Hernando hesitate. I knew he was struggling with his own confusion and fear, and he was torn between doing what he'd done every night for the past thirty years — bolting out of the classroom and trying to outrun Hatchet Jack — or listening to me and altering his pattern. It was very, very difficult for a grounded spirit to break out of their pattern once they'd adopted it.

"Please, Hernando! I swear if you listen to me you will never, ever have to deal with that horrible man out there again."

I see the light! his little voice echoed across my intuition.

I let go of the breath I'd been holding. "Perfect. Now, we don't have much time, so please listen carefully. I want you to pull that light down from the ceiling. You can do that by just thinking about it coming lower and lower and surrounding you in its glow."

It's coming down!

"Thank God," I said. "Now, we only have a second or two. Hernando, when it surrounds you I need for you to let yourself go into it. It will feel like it's pulling you somewhere, and it is. It's pulling you home. Let it take you, Hernando. Let it take you home."

My mom and dad! he said.

"I'll tell them you're okay!" I promised,

and in the very next instant Hernando was gone.

"M.J.!" Gilley shouted directly into my ear, and the noise made me double over.

"What?!" I shouted back as I worked to lower the volume on my earpiece.

"He's in the room!" Gilley squealed in full-blown panic. *"Hatchet Jack is in the room!"*

"Where?" And before Gilley could even answer me three of the desks jerked and tumbled as if they'd been picked up and thrown. I staggered backward, trying to get my defenses up, but I was hit in the chest so hard by an unseen force that I flew backward and hit the wall, my head snapping back with a loud thud as it connected with the concrete.

"Get out of there!" Gilley begged. "M.J., get out of there!"

My head lolled on my neck, and the room swam. I felt another blast of energy come right at my head again, and I tried to get my arms up to shield myself, but I was too late. White-hot heat exploded at my hairline, and I yelled out in pain.

"M.J.?!" Gilley screamed into my earpiece, and the sound was like a lightning bolt searing through my mind.

Suddenly I was lifted in the air, and the

room swam again as I felt myself floating up off the ground. My impulse was to kick and thrash, but my head hurt so much that the move was little more than a feeble effort.

"M.J.?!" Gilley screamed again. "Talk to me!"

There were crashing sounds but they felt far away, and the floating sensation continued. I tried to pick my head up, but that just made things worse, and then my vision began to close in and darken and I was in too much pain to fight it.

"Set her down over here," I heard Gilley say, his voice pitched high, like he was excited or upset. "I've brought the first-aid kit," he added. "Jesus, there's a lot of blood."

"We should call the ambulance!" someone else said. "I should call the nine-one-one people!"

"No!" Gil said. "Not yet. Let me look at her in the light first, and then we'll talk about ambulances." A bright light switched on as I was laid down on a soft cushion. I moaned and put my hand up to shield my eyes.

"M.J.?" Gilley said as he began gently slapping my face.

"Stooooooop," I wailed as one hell of a

headache throbbed against my temples.

"Oh, thank you, God!" Gilley cried.

"Should I call the ambulance?" the other voice in the room asked.

"No, Nicholas," Gilley said gently. "But thank you."

My eyelids fluttered as I tried to open them. "The light," I complained, pushing my hand toward it.

Gilley adjusted the light above my head so that it didn't glare in my eyes so much. "How's that?"

"Better," I said. "What happened?"

"Hatchet Jack," Nicholas said. "You made him maaaaad!"

I blinked several times as I tried to focus on Nicholas. Vaguely I realized that I recognized the room we were in. It was Nicholas's apartment in the main building of the school. Gilley had opened the first-aid kit and was soaking several gauze strips with a small bottle of peroxide before gently easing them over my forehead. "Ouch!" I yelped as he stroked close to my hairline.

"You've got one hell of a nasty cut, there, girlfriend," he said. My hand flew up to my head, but Gilley batted it away easily. "Don't touch," he snapped.

I winced for another five minutes as Gil worked on the wound. "In all the years we've been doing this, I've never seen a ghost actually inflict a wound like this," he said.

"Jack was maaaaaad!" Nicholas repeated, and he rocked back and forth on his heels.

My eyes cut to him. "Did you see him, Nicholas?" I asked. "Did you see Hatchet Jack?"

"He was maaaaaad!"

Gilley and I shared a look, and I took a deep breath. "Yes, he was. And you were very brave to rescue me."

"You help Hernando," Nicholas said easily. "I help you."

Gilley and I shared another look. "Hernando is safe from now on," I said. "Jack will never be able to hurt him again."

Nicholas nodded vigorously. "I know. That's why Jack was so maaaaaad!"

I sat up a little so that I could get a better look around.

"How many fingers am I holding up?" Gilley said, playing nurse for all he was worth.

"Twelve," I said sarcastically.

"Correct," Gilley said, undaunted. "And what day is it?"

"Easter Sunday."

"Correct. And what year is it?"

"It's 1776."

Nicholas was watching our byplay intently,

257

and he let out a loud laugh. "It is not!" he said, pointing at us. "It's Thursday!"

I grinned at him. The guy was like a big teddy bear. "You know, Nicholas? I think you're right. It is Thursday!"

"It's Thursday *morning,*" Nicholas said, pointing to a clock on the wall that read twelve a.m.

"You are a smart guy, my friend," I said. "And thank you again for coming to my rescue."

"You help Hernando. I help you," he replied.

I scooted back on the couch cushion I'd been resting on and sat all the way up, closing my eyes for a moment as the world gave a teeny spin.

"You okay?" Gil said, and his voice had not a hint of mirth in it.

"Fine, fine," I said, reaching out to place a hand on his arm. "But do you have any aspirin?"

I could hear Gilley rummaging around in the first-aid kit. After a moment he said, "No, but I have something much better!"

I opened my eyes and saw that Gilley was holding up a comb and some hair spray. "Girlfriend, you look a mess!" he said, and came at me with the comb.

It was my turn to swat his hand away.

"You mean to tell me you have a comb and hair spray but no pain medication?!"

Gilley looked pained. "There wasn't room in the kit," he explained. "Something had to go."

I let out a long, heavy sigh and waited a moment to speak. "Okay, Gil," I finally said. "But I think I'll sport the bad-hair day in lieu of getting some aspirin."

"Sorry, M.J.," Gilley said, slipping the comb and spray back into the kit.

I softened a bit. Reaching out to squeeze his hand I said, "Thank you, Gilley. I appreciate your trying to take care of me." Gil smiled brightly and leaned in again to mop at my head wound. "It's fine," I said, pulling back.

"It is not," he said. "I think you need stitches, but if I know you as well as I think I do, you will flatly refuse to get them."

"Can't you just put a Band-Aid on it and call it even?"

Gilley sighed dramatically. "I can try," he said, digging around in the first-aid kit again.

While Gilley worked to patch me up I made small talk with Nicholas, pointing out several things in his room and asking him to tell me about them. We started with the model airplanes and moved on to the comic-book posters. Finally, just as Gilley had placed the last bandage on my forehead, I pointed to Nicholas's PlayStation and said, "That is so cool, Nicholas! I bet you love playing that."

Nicholas gave me a vigorous nod again and shuffled over to his PlayStation to hold it up proudly. "I've been all the way to level four!"

Gilley whistled. "That's amazing!" he said. "You must be really good."

Nicholas pumped his head up and down. "I am! I am really, really, really, really, really good!"

I smiled. His enthusiasm was infectious. "I bet you like to play with your friends," I said easily.

"Some friends," he said, and pointed to a wall where there was a bulletin board filled with pictures of students hugging Nicholas. "The kids that go here during the school year like to play with me."

"I'll bet. And in the summer you have Eric to play with."

Nicholas pumped his head, then seemed to catch himself. "How do you know about Eric?" he asked, but his tone was curious, not accusatory.

"I met Eric at the school the first night we were here," I said. "But I've forgotten his last name; what was it again?" I said, and turned to Gilley as if he might have the answer.

"Foster!" Nicholas said. "His name is Eric Foster!"

"Yes, yes," I said, snapping my fingers. "I remember. Eric Foster. He's such a nice young man."

"He used to help Hernando," he said. "But Hernando always ran into Jack. Eric tried and tried to get him to come here, where it's safe, but Hernando always got scared."

"And there's another little boy, right?"

"Mark," Nicholas said, but he pulled his face down in a frown. "He won't talk to me. Eric says he's a chicken."

"Yes, Mark!" I said brightly. "I thought I knew his last name too, but I've forgotten it. . . ."

"Foster!" Nicholas said brightly. "Mark Foster!"

Gilley's eyes slid sideways to lock with mine. *Uh-oh,* they seemed to say. "Eric and Mark are brothers, then?" I asked.

Nicholas laughed like I'd said something really funny. "Naaaaaah!" he said. "They're not brothers! Me and Owen are brothers!"

"Yes, you are," I said, making sure I smiled brightly at him. "Listen, Nicholas, do you

261

should go home and let you get your sleep, okay?"

"Okay. It's safe now anyhow. Jack is gone away again."

"I wished I'd known when he was going to show up," I said. "Maybe I could have been prepared."

"Jack comes around on Mondays, Wednesdays, Fridays, and Saturdays," he said. "Never on Tuesdays or Thursdays. And never on Sundays."

"Why never on those days?" I asked.

Nicholas shrugged his shoulders. "I dunno."

"Okay," I said. "Thanks for the info, Nicholas. Is it all right if we come back and talk with you again?"

Nicholas gave another shrug. "I guess," he said.

"Let's get you home," said Gilley, and I could tell by the intense look he was giving me that I looked pretty bad.

Nicholas escorted us to the van, and we waved at him as we left. "He's such a sweetheart," I said as I watched him in the side-view mirror.

"You're just lucky he got to you in time," said Gilley. "What the hell happened in there, M.J.? I've never seen a ghost attack like that before."

I moved my hand up to my forehead, feeling along the bandaged cut. "That guy is one powerful piece of poltergiest, Gil. Those kids have no business being housed anywhere near that energy. I could see him seriously hurting someone."

"He's already seriously injured someone," Gil said, swiveling a look at me.

"Yeah, yeah," I said. "I'm tough; I can take it."

"Don't you think this case might be a little too much for us?" Gilley asked.

"What do you mean?"

"I mean, M.J., that if Hatchet Jack can knock you on your keister once and put a gash like that in your head, there's no telling what else he's capable of."

I leaned my head back and closed my eyes. My head hurt like nobody's business, and I really wished I had an aspirin handy. "Believe it or not I think that's the worst that Jack can possibly throw at me."

"Yippee," Gil said woodenly.

"I'm serious," I insisted. "He was really pissed off that I took Hernando away from him. All that rage came flying out, and this was the most he could do."

"I'm not seeing the bright side of this," said Gil.

"Other than a pretty good scratch and a

bump on the head, I'm fine. That means that as long as I take a few precautions, we should still be able to tackle him."

"You have something in mind, do you?"

"I do," I said. "I just need to find out where his portal is and lock him down. In the meantime we'll continue looking into who he was and who these kids are."

"At least we have a last name for Eric," Gil said.

I gave him a sardonic smile. "Eric Foster. Mark Foster. But the two weren't brothers. That doesn't make a lot of sense."

"They could have been cousins," Gil said reasonably.

He had me there. "I'll turn it over to Muckleroy," I said, closing my eyes again.

"How's your head feel?"

"Fabulous!"

"Sorry about the aspirin bottle, M.J.," Gil said guiltily.

I sighed. "Don't worry about it, Gil. We're almost home, right?"

I felt the van make a left turn and come to a stop. "Better," Gilley said. "We're already here."

Gilley helped me inside, then went straight to the medicine cabinet, where he found a lovely giant bottle of ibuprofen. I sucked down four of those suckers and shuffled my way to bed, where I waited for the pain relief to take effect and drifted off into a fitful sleep.

The ibuprofen had worn off by morning, which was what finally motivated me to get out of bed. Gilley met me in the kitchen again and was quick to pull out a chair for me and bring me coffee. "Need ibuprofen," I mumbled in pain, holding my head in my hands.

"You need to put something in your stomach first," Gilley said. "Here," he offered as he set down a bowl and a box of cereal in front of me.

"Not hungry," I muttered irritably. "Need painkiller!"

Gilley gave me a look that said he wasn't having any of it. "Eat first," he insisted. "Ibuprofen should never be taken on an empty stomach. And you haven't eaten anything since last night."

I gave a terrific sigh as I opened the cereal box. Then, with a dramatic hand motion, I lifted the box and poured some cereal into my mouth, then began crunching loudly. That was the wrong thing to do, because it just made my head ache more. "Owwwwww," I moaned.

"That'll teach you," Gil said. Taking the

box out of my hand he poured a small helping of cereal into the bowl and layered that
in milk. "Let it soak for a minute and it
won't be so crunchy."

I glared hard at him. "Seriously," I said
with ice in my voice. "Give. Me. The. Pills."

Gilley tapped his foot, holding on to the
bottle and not giving it up. "You will feel
better if you do it my way, M.J."

My mother died when I was twelve, and
she'd been very ill for the three years before
her death, so I'd learned early on to take
care of myself. That was why, once I became
an adult, Gilley's attempts to mother me
often went . . . well . . . unappreciated, to
say the least. "Gilley, I swear to God if you
don't give me those damn pills I'm gonna
—"

"What?" Gil snapped. "Jump up and
chase me around the table? You can barely
hold your head up, much less take me on."
Just then there was a knock on the front
door, and Gil pointed to my cereal bowl.
"You eat while I go see who's at the door."

I really hoped he'd set the bottle of ibuprofen down, but he took it with him, and
with a, "Humph!" I pulled the stupid cereal
bowl toward me, stabbing angrily at the
kernels of wheat or corn or whole grain in
the bowl.

I heard Gilley open the door and a man's voice echoed into the hall. It sounded familiar, but my head hurt so much that my thinking cap wasn't on straight. A moment later I didn't have to try to place the mysterious voice, because Gilley came into the kitchen leading Detective Muckleroy.

The moment the detective saw me he sucked in a breath and said, "Jesus, what happened to you?"

"She had a little run-in with Hatchet Jack," Gilley answered for me.

"A *ghost* did that?" Muckleroy's voice was loud, and I winced as the pain throbbing in my head intensified.

Gilley seemed to take pity on me, because he quickly opened up the ibuprofen he'd been holding hostage and doled out two tablets to me.

"Four," I said. "Give me four."

Gilley gave a pointed look at my cereal bowl. He knew damned well I hadn't taken a single bite, but he didn't argue in front of the detective, and he pumped out only one more tablet, setting it on the table next to my coffee.

I wolfed down the tablets, chasing them with a big swig of coffee. While I was popping the pills Gilley explained, "We went to the school last night to try to lure Jack out into the open. If M.J. can find out where he comes from, she'll be able to lock him up tight. While she was waiting for him that little boy Hernando appeared. M.J. was able to send him over to the other side just as Jack showed up. He was not at all pleased that M.J. had helped Hernando, and he attacked her."

"With *what?*" Muckleroy asked, still looking at me in a state of complete shock.

"His hatchet," I said simply.

Muckleroy blinked, standing there stupefied. Meanwhile, Gilley — being the ever vigilant host — had poured him a cup of coffee and was pointing to a chair at the table. Muckleroy sat down heavily and took a sip of the brew. "You mean this ghost carries a *real* hatchet?" he said after he'd found his voice again.

"No," I said, thinking about how to explain it to him. "Ghosts don't usually carry real objects. But they can manifest the energy of something so intensely that it can feel real to a live person."

"Huh?" Muckleroy said.

I rubbed my temples, starting to feel the tiniest bit of relief from either the coffee or the ibuprofen. "Jack believes so intensely that he is still alive, and still swinging his hatchet, that when he really puts his mind

270

to it he can physically harm someone as if he's cut them with it."

Muckleroy looked dumbfounded. "So he cut you with his *mind?*"

I nodded. "Yes."

"Jesus," Muckleroy repeated. "This is bad!"

"Yes, it is," I said. "I personally have never encountered such a dangerous energy as this Hatchet Jack. It's imperative that we not leave him to prey upon Northelm's students when the elementary wing gets turned into a dorm."

Muckleroy's face was now a mixture of fear and worry. "What do we do?"

"Well," I said, gathering my thoughts, "there are a few things we can do. So far I only know where Jack comes to; I don't know where he goes. What I forgot was that, statistically speaking, most nasty energies like Jack will create their portal at or very near the site where they died. I've felt out the elementary wing of the school. His portal isn't there, so I know he didn't die there. I've also felt out that tree on the other side of Hole Pond, and the portal isn't there either.

"Something is telling me that Jack died violently. It could have been a car crash or a fall or something, but I also think he died near the school. His presence there is just too intense for it to be otherwise. Therefore, what you can do, Detective, is to work hard to identify this guy. He lived nearby — I just know it — and if I can find out where, then I might be able to track down where he died, and then I've got him."

"I was going to look through those old death-certificate records for you," Muckleroy said. "I'll do that today."

"Also, we might want to put up pictures of Jack and see if anyone can recognize him. Did you get the sketch from Amelia?"

Muckleroy nodded, but his face looked grim. "I don't think we'll want to put this up around town," he said, reaching into a large leather briefcase and pulling out a sketch. The drawing was terrifying. It showed a man with wild eyes and an evil look on his face, holding a hatchet up over his head. "If I put this up, I'll either be the laughingstock of town or people will get completely creeped out."

"You're right," I said, pushing the sketch away. "Do me a favor, Detective —"

"Bob," he reminded me.

"Sorry," I said. "See if you can't get Amelia to rework this sketch. Maybe there's a way to retain Jack's overall facial structure and tone it down a bit. Just make it look like it's your everyday mug shot."

"Good idea," he said, tucking the sketch away. "I'll have her get right on it. Anything else?"

"Remember the Fosters?" Gilley reminded me.

I smiled warmly at my partner, which was a whole lot easier to do now that my headache was subsiding. "Yep, thanks, Gil. Bob, we learned last night that Eric's last name might be Foster. The other little boy's name is Mark, and his name also might be Foster."

"Brothers?" Muckleroy said, making the same assumption I had.

I shook my head. "We don't think so. They might be cousins, or it could just be a huge coincidence. See if you can get any hits on them."

"Will do," he said, finishing off his coffee. "What are you two going to do?"

"We're going to work a few other angles," I said. "Gil's been able to track down one of the teachers who's been at Northelm since the seventies."

"Who?"

"William Skolaris," said Gilley.

Muckleroy made a dismissive sound. "That ol' geezer's not going to give you much," he said.

"Why not?" I asked.

"He's kind of a crank," Muckleroy said. "Has a reputation for being one difficult bastard. Most folks don't know why Habbernathy's kept him on all these years, but Skolaris and Habbernathy's dad go way back. He's even living in the old Habbernathy home."

"What old home?" I asked.

Muckleroy explained, "Back in the day the Habbernathys were some of the landed gentry around here. That is, until Winston fell into debt and the school almost went under. He was forced to sell his family home just to keep the school going, and it was Skolaris who put up the cash for it."

"Ironic that the employee is bailing out the employer," I said.

"No one knows where Skolaris came up with so much cash. That house is a gorgeous old thing, and Habbernathy probably sold it for a lot less than it was worth just to get out from underneath it."

"So that's when Winston moved back onto the campus of the school?"

Muckleroy nodded. "Yeah. His school limped along financially for a few years, until the Olympics came to town and he gave tours of the school to all the rich parents who came here with their kids to watch the games. His school was saved that year; otherwise, I think he'd have gone under."

For the second time that morning there was a knock on our door. Gil and I exchanged a curious look, and he got up to see who it was. "Expecting company?" Muckleroy asked.

"No," I replied. "But it's just my luck to have company come over when I'm looking so pretty."

Muckleroy smiled sympathetically at me. "It's not too bad," he said. "Maybe if you got a hat it wouldn't be so noticeable."

Again a male voice I thought I recognized echoed along with Gilley's through the front hallway, and that was when Gilley appeared, leading none other than Dean Habbernathy, looking a bit disheveled and deeply concerned. "Oh, my," the dean said when he saw me. "Nicholas said that you had been injured last evening, and I wanted to come by and see how you are."

"I'm fine, sir," I said, forcing a smile. "Please have a seat."

It was then that he seemed to notice Detective Muckleroy, and as I watched the mixture of emotions flash across his face the dean said, "Good morning, Bob. I'm surprised to see you're getting involved in this."

"Owen, good to see you," said Muckleroy. "And I usually get involved in cases that involve murder."

The dean seemed to fall heavily into the chair at the table, his face draining of color. "Mur-murder?" he stammered. "Who's been murdered?"

"As far as we can tell, three young boys so far. One of them we dug up just off school property, at Hole Pond."

If it was possible for Habbernathy's face to lose any more color, it did at that moment, and I couldn't help noticing that the dean thought about his response very carefully before speaking. "That's tragic," he said finally. "The boy's parents must be beside themselves."

Detective Muckleroy was also studying the dean closely, and I'd have bet the farm that he felt like I did that the dean knew something about the skeleton that we'd just dug up. "Talk to me about this Hatchet Jack character," said the detective.

The dean scrunched his face and cocked his head. "Who?" he said.

I wanted to laugh, it was *so* obvious that the dean knew exactly what we were talking about. "The ghost we've been investigating," I said flatly. "You know, the crazy spirit chasing *your* students around the aban-

276

doned hallways of Northelm?"

The dean made a sound like laughter, but it fell very short of the real thing. "That again," he said dismissively. "As I told you earlier, Miss Holliday, I don't believe in ghosts."

"Then how do you explain this?" I asked, pointing to the cut on my head.

The dean blinked at me several times, apparently confused. "Nicholas told me you had fallen last night in one of the classrooms," he said. "Is that not how you hurt your head?"

Gilley was standing off to one side, leaning against the counter. He gave an exaggerated sigh and rolled his eyes. "Oh, please, Dean Habbernathy. Give us a break, would you?"

"I'm afraid I don't understand what you're talking about," said the dean, working his way into a good huff. "The older students at Northelm have been telling the younger students ghost stories for decades now. I'm afraid that even after all our efforts to discourage such talk, it is a tradition that has continued. There is no such thing as Hatchet Jack. He is a figment of the imagination."

"Nicholas told us you believe otherwise," I said, baiting the dean.

Color returned in a flash to the dean's cheeks, and he flushed red. "My brother is mentally handicapped. He could no more relate my true thoughts than he could comprehend long division." With that the dean stood up, and I could tell he was trying to get a handle on his emotions. "Now, I just wanted to come by and see that you were all right," said the dean. "But I really do believe that your injury has clarified for me that it would be unwise to allow you to continue your investigation at the school. I cannot subject Northelm to any further liability."

"Would you like me to relate that to Mr. Dodge?" I asked, getting up myself to challenge the dean. "I mean, it seems to me that it was part of the deal you arranged with him when you discussed the new wing. Me and my team were to have a week to investigate without restriction."

The look he gave me was murderous. He knew I had him by the short hairs. "I'm sure Mr. Dodge will understand that I am risking a lawsuit by allowing you to continue on as you have," he said.

"She could sign a waiver," said the detective helpfully. "Right, M.J.? Just sign a waiver releasing Northelm of any physical liability during your investigation. Your insurance company would be okay with that, wouldn't they, Owen?"

"I'll draft one up immediately," said Gilley. I smiled at him, because we actually had a boilerplate waiver on hand for people who were nervous about us tramping around in the dark on their property.

The dean huffed and he stammered and finally he said, "Very well. But you have only one more day, Miss Holliday, before your agreement is at an end. As I said before, your so-called *investigation* is limited to the elementary wing of the school. Not to the school grounds or other buildings. And you are to stay away from Nicholas. I do not want him frightened by your ghost tales and nonsense. He's got a fragile mind, and he's quite impressionable."

"Leave me your fax number, Dean, and I'll send over the waiver," I said evenly.

The dean scribbled his number down and handed it to Gilley. "I shall expect the waiver before you make your way back to school property."

Gilley gave him a level stare. "No problem," he said. "Allow me to show you out."

With that the dean was gone. "Interesting reaction," I said, after we heard the door close.

"It was, wasn't it?" said Muckleroy.

Gilley came back into the kitchen. "I don't like that man," he said distastefully.

"He knows something," I said.

"Or he's just trying to protect the school's reputation," said Muckleroy. "If word got out that Northelm housed the ghost of a child serial killer, well, let's just say that more than a few parents might consider sending their kids to a different boarding school."

"That's a good point," I conceded. "But I still think he knows more than he's letting on." With that I got up from the table. "Now, if you'll excuse me, I'm going to take a much-needed shower, and after that Gil and I are going to chase down a few of the leads on our end."

The detective got up too. "Roger that," he said. "I'll call you two later and we can catch one another up."

Gil and I were in the van forty minutes later and heading toward town. I was just finishing up my phone call with Teeko, filling her in on our progress and begging for a little more time. "I really wish there was something I could do," she was saying. "But John's construction crew is on a really tight time line. It was just luck that they had a few weeks off before their next project, M.J.

I don't think I can win you any extra time."

I sighed. "Okay, Teeko, I get it. I'll do my very best, I promise you, but this Jack guy is one nasty poltergeist. If I can't lock him down before we run out of time, then I'm recommending you talk Leanne out of sending Evie back to Northelm."

"You think it's really that dangerous for her?" I hadn't mentioned the attack from the night before to Karen because I knew she wouldn't just worry; she'd likely come back from her European romance and try to lend a hand, and I didn't want anyone untrained near this psycho ghost.

"Trust me," I said. "Hatchet Jack is not for the timid."

"Okay, just keep me posted, and please be careful."

"On it," I said, and we clicked off.

"How's the head?" Gilley asked as I put the phone away.

"It's tolerable," I said honestly. "Still, it might be better to be a little more prepared next time. Do me a favor before we hit Skolaris's. See if you can find a hardware store."

We were lucky enough to find a Home Depot not far away, and I went immediately to the plumbing section. There I gathered three one-foot sections of lead pipe and some caps to put on the ends. Gilley looked at me curiously until I explained in the checkout line: "I can put the magnetic spikes in here, and not pull them out until I get close to Jack."

Gil's face lit up. "It would be like setting off a grenade in his energy field," he said. "Clever thinking, M.J."

"It would only be as a last resort," I said. "Let's just hope it doesn't come to that."

After leaving the store we got back in the van, and Gilley followed the crude map he'd drawn that led the way to Skolaris's. We found the old Habbernathy house at the end of a cul-de-sac just off Frog Lane near Upper Saranac Lake. Gilley whistled as the house came into view. "Nice digs," he said.

The house was a three-story Victorian painted a blueberry blue with black shutters and a black slate roof. An iron gate surrounded the grounds, which were well manicured and lovingly tended.

Hydrangeas lined the paved winding walkway up to the oak door with its stained-glass window. A bird feeder and birdbath were to the right of the lawn, just feet from one of the large windows that overlooked the front lawn.

Gil parked on the street and cut the engine. "How do you want to play this?" he asked me.

I was looking out my window at the huge house that was so well cared for. I could guess that Skolaris was all about appearances, and perhaps flattery could get us places direct lines of questioning couldn't. "Follow my lead," I said.

We hopped out of the van and strolled up the walkway. "I hope he's home, at least," Gil said.

"I have a feeling he is," I said as we stepped onto the front porch. After ringing the doorbell and waiting several seconds, we could hear footsteps coming across wood flooring from inside. There was a pause behind the door, and I guessed that Skolaris might be peeking at us through the peephole just under the stained-glass window. "Who is it?" he asked from the other side of the door.

"Hello, Mr. Skolaris," I said, putting some enthusiasm into my voice. "I'm M. J. Holliday, and this is my partner, Gilley Gillespie. If you have just a moment, we'd like to talk with you."

"No solicitation!" Skolaris yelled from the other side of the door.

I gave a big toothy grin to the peephole. "We're not here to sell you anything, Mr. Skolaris. We're here to ask you about your lovely house."

There was a click on the other side of the door just before it opened a crack. A smoky gray eye looked out at me. "What do you want to know?"

I glanced behind me at the lawn. "It's the most beautiful house on this block, and we were wondering about its history."

The door opened wider, and a lean man in his mid- to late sixties with a scruffy chin and silver hair stood there, assessing us. "I've lived here for nearly thirty years," he said. "Done a lot of improvements along the way."

"How old is the house?" I asked.

Skolaris scratched his chin. "I believe it was built in the eighteen sixties."

"I see," I said. "Was it handed down to you by family?"

Skolaris smiled crookedly. "In a way," he said. "But more like friends of the family."

"Well, it sure is beautiful," I said again. "It must have cost a fortune, even thirty years ago."

I might have pushed it a little too far, because Skolaris's face immediately turned suspicious again. "Who did you two say you were, again?"

"I'm M. J. Holliday," I said, extending my hand. Skolaris let it hang there without taking it, so I finally lowered it. "And this is my partner, Gilley Gillespie."

Skolaris gave a curt nod, then asked, "You two Realtors?"

I let go a light laugh. "Oh, no, nothing like that," I said. "Actually, we're here on behalf of John Dodge."

"John Dodge?" he said, and I could tell the name sounded familiar to him.

"Yes," I said. "John Dodge is a new patron of Northelm. He will be funding the renovation of the elementary wing."

"Ah, yes," said Skolaris. "But I still don't understand what that has to do with my house."

"Nothing directly, sir. Gilley and I were merely scouting out the location and we came across some troubling rumors about the elementary wing. Of course, you can imagine that someone of Mr. Dodge's reputation would not be pleased if such rumors were linked back to a project that he had direct control over."

Skolaris's brows had knotted together tightly. He seemed to be having a great deal of trouble following my train of thought, and, truth be told, by the expression Gilley was wearing, he wasn't the only one. I decided it was time to give up the ruse about being interested in Skolaris's house and get to the real reason why we'd come. "You see, Mr. Skolaris, there is this talk about the elementary wing being haunted."

Light seemed to dawn on Skolaris's face. "Oh, that's just nonsense," he said with a dismissive wave of his hand. "Juvenile nonsense."

"Is it?" I asked carefully. "It seems to be an incredibly persistent rumor, even making the Northelm newspaper, after all."

"That story was pulled as soon as I caught wind of it," Skolaris said. "Again, this business of ghosts and men with hatchets is just urban myth. Mr. Dodge can rest assured that no such thing exists."

"Lance Myers would disagree," I said.

Skolaris narrowed his eyes at me. "Lance Myers owns a *liquor* store, miss. He's probably been sampling too much of his own inventory."

"And yet he recalls a time back when he was a teenager attending Northelm when he had a very real encounter with this supposed ghost."

Skolaris was losing patience with me. He crossed his arms and kept those gray eyes narrowed. "Now, you listen here. I've been a teacher at that school for close to thirty-five years, with many a late night grading papers and such, and I have *never* seen this

Hatchet Jack character on or around the school grounds. It's a campfire story made up long ago that has continued to scare the students unnecessarily."

Something in the man's eyes told me he was a big fat liar. "I see," I said.

"No, you don't *see*," he snapped. "Every year it's the same thing. New students complaining about every little thing that goes bump in the night, and the older students convinced of a cover-up. It's ludicrous, ridiculous, and not worth the breath expended to dispel the story!"

"But why do you think the story is so lasting, Mr. Skolaris?" I asked. "I mean, I'm a firm believer that where there's smoke, there's fire. And this story seems to be a red hot inferno. It's lingered for thirty years, after all. That seems an awfully long time for something with little merit behind it to stay so topical."

"Who knows why these things continue to be talked about?" Skolaris said. "It certainly isn't because the teaching staff hasn't tried everything to squelch it."

"Wouldn't it be more prudent to show the students that you take them seriously?" I asked. "I mean, if the school conducted a thorough investigation, allowed, say, the student body to report on the rumor and follow the story to a resolution, wouldn't that help dispel a lot of this supposed myth?"

"On the contrary," said Skolaris. "We at Northelm want to promote ethical reporting. Having the children follow such nonsense would be like suggesting that tabloid journalism is credible."

"What the heck are you teachers afraid of?" I asked, feeling myself becoming defensive in spite of my efforts to remain calm. "Seriously, are you more afraid that there's actual truth to the story, or that the truth will lead back to something that happened at the school, say, oh, thirty years ago that maybe you people didn't investigate when you had the chance?"

Skolaris balled his hands into fists, and his face turned ugly. "Get off my property," he said evenly.

"But we just wanted to —"

"I said, get off my property!" Skolaris yelled, slamming the door in our faces, before adding, "Or I will call the police and have you removed!"

Gilley elbowed me and said, "Maybe we'd better go now."

I gritted my teeth and turned with him back down the walkway. When we were in the van again Gil started the engine and glanced sideways at me. "Smooth," he said. "Way to play it."

"Oh, come on, Gilley!" I roared. "That old geezer has *no* business teaching journalism to anyone, much less some impressionable, bright-minded students!"

"Probably not, M.J.," Gil said reasonably. "But did you really have to throw that fact in his face? After all, weren't you the one who suggested that the way to work Skolaris was through flattery?"

I pouted in my seat for a while, knowing full well that Gilley was right. I knew I'd started out okay with him, but my finish left a lot to be desired, and it had done the opposite of what I'd intended, which was to make someone with a long history at Northelm completely shut us out. "I blew it," I admitted after a bit.

"Yes, but at least it was entertaining," Gilley said with a grin. "I was definitely entertained."

"Glad to be of service," I said flatly.

"Pray tell, brave leader," Gil said with a snicker. "Who can we go intimidate next?"

I sighed heavily, thinking about it before I answered. "I think we should try another teacher," I said.

"Yes, that tactic seems to be working well for us so far."

Ignoring Gilley's running commentary I said, "Evie seemed to think highly of her science teacher. Maybe we could try one of the younger teachers and see what they know, instead of one of these old curmudgeons."

"What was the name of her science teacher, again?" Gil said as he found a spot to pull over and reached into a side compartment to pull out his laptop.

"Some guy named Vesnick," I said. "Not a real common name. See if there are any listings in the area for someone like that."

Gil hit pay dirt about ten minutes later. "I think I found him," he said. "Ray Vesnick, former address is in New York City. Employment record has him at Royce High School in Brooklyn, but his current address lists a place near here in Wheaton — remember?" he said to me when I gave him a blank look. "That's the town our waiter at the View was from."

I nodded, "Oh, yeah," I said. "And I'll bet it's the same Vesnick. Evie said that this was his first year here. Maybe his employment record hasn't caught up to him yet."

"That's a definite possibility. Employment records are usually the least reliable because they're so slow to update," Gil agreed.

"Should we pay him a visit then and see if

it's our guy?"

"We can be there in twenty minutes," Gil said, putting away the laptop and shifting the van into gear.

"Let's go," I said.

We arrived at the address Gilley had pulled off the Internet, and I looked skeptically up at the storefront apartment that appeared to be Vesnick's residence. If there was a seedy part of Lake Placid, this area seemed to be it. "Homey," Gil said sarcastically.

"Are you sure this is the place?" I asked for the third time.

"Yes, M.J., I'm sure."

"Well, then, let's get this over with." We got out of the van and scoped the street, which was littered with garbage. A party store was on the corner of the large building taking up most of the block. Vesnick's place was right above a tattoo parlor. A bar was next to that. We crossed the street, and I noticed that several young men hanging out in front of the bar were giving Gilley and me the once-over. I stole a glance at Gilley and noticed that he was doing his best impression of a straight man, as his walk had lost its usual swishy cadence. In any other circumstance I would have laughed out loud, but here and now I was actually grateful he wasn't inviting any extra attention.

At the doorway that marked the entrance to the apartments upstairs there was a list of four names on a nameplate and dingy, yellowed buzzers next to each name. Gilley depressed the one for apartment two, marked in faded black ink with R. VESNICK. After a moment a scratchy male voice responded through the speaker box, "Yes?"

"Mr. Vesnick?" Gil asked.

"Speaking," he said.

"Hi! It's Gilley Gillespie!"

"Who?"

"Ohmigod! I can't believe you don't remember me! I was in your science class at Royce!" There was no response to Gilley's claim, and he gave me an apologetic look that seemed to say, *Sorry, I tried,* when the buzzer on the door sounded and we both jumped. I grabbed the handle and pulled it open and we headed up the stairs.

From the top of the landing looking down at us was a man in his early thirties with wire-rimmed glasses and long, sandy blond hair. He had a square jaw and a Roman nose, and I could see immediately why Ellie had liked him. He was cute in a bookish sort of way. "Hello?" Vesnick said as we climbed the stairs.

We both waved at him and continued to climb. Gil had taken the unspoken lead on this one, as I'd had so much luck with the last teacher, so I let him go up the stairs to greet Vesnick first. When he crested the landing Vesnick's face became confused. Gilley was clearly too old to have been in his class. "Hello, Mr. Vesnick," Gilley said, extending his hand.

Vesnick took his hand and shook it. "Hello," he said. "I'm really sorry, but I don't recognize you."

Gilley smiled warmly. "I know, and I'm sorry. I may have tricked you a little down there with that bit about being in your class at Royce. We've actually been hired by the parents of one of your students, Evie O'Neal."

Vesnick's face turned immediately to worry. "Hired by Evie's parents?" he asked cautiously. "What for?"

"Do you remember an incident that happened last week during your final examination?" Gilley said.

"I never told Evie to go into that wing," Vesnick said, and there was something close to panic on his face. "I swear to God, I never told any of the students to go in there!"

Gilley seemed to be confused about

Vesnick's reaction. He hadn't thought through how accusatory his introduction had been. "Hello, Mr. Vesnick," I said, jumping in before Gilley completely botched it. "I'm M. J. Holliday, and I want to assure you that we're not here to point fingers. We're not the authorities, or attorneys."

"Then who are you?" Vesnick said, and his body language was still stiff and edgy.

"We're ghostbusters," I said, going for the God's honest truth.

Vesnick stared at us for a few seconds as if he were waiting to hear the punch line. "Seriously," he said. "What is this about?"

I reached into my coat and pulled out my business card. Handing it to him I said, "We really are ghostbusters. We've done dozens of paranormal investigations, and we've helped give relief to many families troubled by poltergeist activity."

Vesnick looked from my card to me, still wearing that *Is this a joke?* look. "And Evie's parents hired you to what? Get rid of Hatchet Jack?"

Gil and I both nodded vigorously. Finally, a teacher who got it. "Yes, that's exactly what they hired us to do."

"Okay," he said cautiously. "What do I have to do with this?"

At that moment a woman came out of the apartment next to Vesnick's and gave the three of us a pointed look. "I'm trying to watch my shows, Ray," she complained. "I can't listen if you threes are out here gabbing it up."

"Sorry, Adeline," he said to her. Turning back to us he said, "Won't you come in?"

We followed behind Vesnick out of the hall and into his cramped and cluttered apartment. The entry fed directly into his kitchen, which was strewn with Styrofoam containers and empty Chinese take-out cartons. "Sorry about the mess," he said as he scooped up several of the containers and emptied them into his trash. I was immediately reminded of Muckleroy and his cluttered office. "It's fine," I said, pointing to a chair with a silent *May I sit there?* expression.

"Sure," he said, and pulled out his own chair. Gilley sat next to me and was quiet. He'd let me take the lead back.

"As I was saying," I said to Vesnick. "We're investigating the paranormal activity at the school. Unfortunately, all the staff members we've spoken to so far haven't been very helpful."

"Who've you spoken to?" Vesnick wanted to know.

Hatchet Jack firsthand," Vesnick said, and I caught the smallest of shivers traveling up his spine.

"You've seen him," I said, more statement than question.

Vesnick gave me a level look. "I have," he admitted. "Once, last summer before the student body had returned. I was setting up my classroom late one evening when I heard a child calling for help out on the lawn. I raced outside and saw a young boy and a man running along the back edge of the property, the young boy still screaming for help.

"I ran after them and managed to almost catch up to them. That's when the man threw something at the boy, and I saw it was a hatchet. I even heard it strike the boy, and he went down to the ground immediately."

"What happened next?" Gilley asked with large, captivated eyes when Vesnick paused.

"They vanished," Vesnick said, wringing his hands. "Both of them. Just vanished."

"What day of the week was it?" I asked.

Vesnick gave me a startled look. I'm sure he thought it was an odd question. "Um . . ." he said, thinking. "It was a Friday."

"Do you remember the time?"

Vesnick thought for a moment and subconsciously glanced at the clock. "It was just after six p.m."

"And the boy," I pressed. "Do you remember what his hair color was?"

"It was red," he said. "He had red hair, like Opie."

Gil and I exchanged a look before I asked, "And the other teachers — have any of them had similar sightings?"

"Only one other that I know of, Cathy Wingerman. She taught Spanish at the school."

"Did you tell the dean about your encounter?" I said.

"Yes," Vesnick said, and his look turned spiteful.

"What was his reaction?"

"Adverse," Vesnick said. "He didn't want to hear it and he ordered me not to discuss it with anyone, especially the students."

"And did you?" Gilley said. "Did you talk with anyone else about it?"

"Besides Cathy, no, and I only did that because she brought it up to me. Cathy was let go just after midwinter break. She e-mailed me later to say that she never got a real answer from the dean about why he was firing her, but she suspected it was because she'd been overheard by some of the other teachers talking to some of the kids about

Hatchet Jack. See, there's an unwritten rule at Northelm that anyone who talks about Jack risks either getting fired or expelled, and, like I said, I need this job." He seemed to realize at that moment that he'd been doing exactly what could get him fired, and he looked nervously at us. "Uh, hey, you're not going to tell the dean what I said, are you?"

"Absolutely not," Gil assured him. "No one will know we were here."

"Thanks," Vesnick said, looking relieved.

"You've been most helpful," I said, getting up. "We'll do our best to get rid of Jack and make sure he doesn't scare anyone ever again."

We took our leave of Vesnick and made our way back to the van. Once inside Gilley asked, "What do you make of it?"

I shook my head. "Hell if I know," I said. "I mean, it's one thing to try to institute some rumor control so that you don't risk driving away the students who are your bread and butter. But it's a completely different game when you're talking about firing teachers and expelling said bread and butter merely for discussing a couple of ghost sightings."

"The question is: What is the dean really afraid of?"

"Or who?"

"Huh?" Gil asked.

"Who is the dean really afraid of?"

"Most people would be afraid of the ghost," Gilley said. "But Dean Habbernathy didn't strike me that way."

"No, he didn't," I agreed. "There's more to this than just a violent poltergeist, Gil."

"How do we find out what that is?" he asked.

"I don't know," I said wearily. "But let's start by swinging by the police station and seeing if Muckleroy has come up with anything."

CHAPTER 9

Since it was close to lunchtime by the time Gilley and I arrived back in Lake Placid, we opted to eat first, talk grisly murder scenarios second. As it happened, right around the time we'd placed our orders my cell phone beeped, and one glance at the caller ID told me it was Muckleroy. "Where are you guys?" he asked, getting right to the point.

"At the sandwich shop across the street from you," I said. "Why? Has something happened?"

"Sit tight," he said without further explanation. "I'll be right there."

"Something happening?" Gilley asked when I'd tucked my cell back into my pocket.

"Not sure," I said. "But Muckleroy sounded excited."

A few minutes later we saw the detective hurrying across the street, a folder tucked under one arm. He came into the diner, and Gilley and I waved. Sitting down next to me he flipped open his folder and slapped a photo on the table. "Recognize him?" he asked of the boy smiling out at me from the page.

"That's Eric!" I exclaimed, picking up the black-and-white photo to examine it.

"You found him?" Gilley asked.

Muckleroy nodded, but before he could fill us in the waitress came by to ask if he would like to order some lunch. "I'll take the grilled chicken club," he said. "And a side salad." After the waitress left he picked up where he left off by digging back into his folder and pulling out another photo. "How about this young man?" he asked.

"Ohmigod!" I said, picking up that black-and-white and looking at the little face I'd seen only in my mind's eye. "This is Mark!"

"These are the Foster boys, right?" Gil asked.

Muckleroy gave a wry smile and said, "Of sorts."

"Huh?" Gil and I said together.

"Foster isn't their last name," he said. "It's their status. They were both foster kids."

"Whoa," Gil said. "Why didn't we think of that?"

"It wasn't an immediate leap for me

303

either," Muckleroy said. "And Eric's description never popped out at me because, M.J., you and the coroner had me looking for a thirteen-year-old. Eric wasn't reported missing by his foster mother until 1980 — he would have been seventeen then, and too old for the body we found."

"Why would she lie?" I gasped, horrified that a child could go missing four years earlier and the woman assigned and paid to protect him hadn't reported it until it was far too late to find or help him.

Muckleroy's face was grim. "Unfortunately, like most counties, we're strapped for cash and resources. The social worker assigned to Eric was involved in a huge scandal some twenty-five years ago. Apparently she was overwhelmed with case files and had lost track of quite a few of the kids assigned to her. She was supposed to do physical check-ins once every six months for each child, but the state didn't find out that she'd actually stopped doing any kind of check-ins for many years before she was fired.

"The state assigned a couple of new social workers to take over her cases, and by all accounts they also botched the job. We think that dozens of kids simply fell through the cracks and either ran away and were never reported missing, or were reported missing long after they'd disappeared."

"So Eric's foster parents were able to continue claiming the money without notice until the new social workers came by?" I asked, still horrified.

"Looks that way. From the legwork I've already come up with, Eric Hinnely entered the foster care system when he was eight years old. He was bounced around from home to home for a few years and finally ended up with Maude Clayburn. She had a large house and said yes to every kid who came her way — apparently she needed the dough."

"Have you spoken to her?" I asked as our sandwiches arrived. "She belongs in jail."

"That's between her and her maker now," Muckleroy said. "Maude died in 1992."

"What's the story with Mark?" Gilley wanted to know.

Muckleroy took a bite of his sandwich and said, "He was in the same foster home with Eric and was reported missing at the same time. Maude claimed back then that the boys had run off together."

"They were abducted," I said. "Hatchet Jack took them."

"It seems so," said Muckleroy.

I'd pretty much lost my appetite, and I

305

pushed my plate away, completely disgusted with the lack of care given to two young innocents. "Have you been able to track down any of the next of kin?"

"Mark Dobb's mother died of a drug overdose shortly after he came into foster care," said Muckleroy. "His father was listed as unknown on his birth certificate. Eric's mother still lives in Wheaton. I have a call in to her residence, and I'd planned on going over there as soon as I hear from her."

"Those poor boys," I said. "I can't imagine anything sadder than no one to note your passing."

"At least this should help you get the boys to the other side, M.J.," Gil said, trying to cheer me up a little.

"How does that help?" Muckleroy asked.

"If you know a grounded spirit's backstory, they feel you are connecting with them. They tend to trust you more, and they'll accept that you're trying to help them rather than trick them."

"That's good," said Muckleroy. "Now that I know this stuff is real, I want to do all I can to help you help those two boys."

"Can we come with you to interview Eric's mother?" I asked. "I have a feeling Eric is going to give me the most trouble about crossing over. He seems to have implanted himself pretty firmly in his grounded-spirit status."

"Absolutely," said Muckleroy, polishing off the last of his side salad. "Say," he said, switching topics. "Did you two come up with anything?"

"Not really," I said. "Skolaris was a complete waste of time. He wanted nothing to do with us. But one of the other teachers, a Mr. Vesnick, was very cooperative."

"What'd he say?"

I pulled out my wallet as the waitress collected our plates. "He said he had actually had an encounter at the beginning of the school year with Hatchet Jack."

"You don't say?" said Muckleroy. "What happened?"

"He saw the replay of Eric's death," I said. "It's as I suspected: Jack would bring the boys to the school grounds, knowing there was no one around to witness or help the boys, and then he would chase them in some awful game of cat and mouse."

"What did Vesnick think of all this?"

I shrugged. "I suspect he was pretty rattled by it. He said two things that were curious to me, though."

"What?"

"He said that Habbernathy had given him strict orders not to discuss the incident or anything to do with Hatchet Jack, and he said that he was working at Northelm for peanuts."

Muckleroy grunted. "I'm not surprised," he said, "on either count."

"Really?" Gilley said.

"Really," Muckleroy said. "Owen has a reputation for being a tightwad. If he can get you for less, he will."

"Vesnick seemed to believe that wasn't the case with Skolaris," I said. "He said that Skolaris was being well paid."

"Well, that seems to be true," said Muckleroy. "But then, Skolaris never could be bought for less."

"Is he that great of a teacher that Habbernathy would fork over the extra dough?" I questioned. "I mean, he's the school's newspaper editor and an English teacher. What's the attraction for Habbernathy?"

"No one knows," said Muckleroy. "In public they're careful to avoid each other, but it's common knowledge that Habbernathy has always looked out for Skolaris, just like his father did when he was dean."

"Maybe there was some kind of directive from Habbernathy's old man," Gilley reasoned. "And that's why he pays him and puts up with him."

"You wouldn't catch me putting up with

that," I said distastefully. "Skolaris is a grumpy old curmudgeon, and he's got no business teaching children."

"So, what's next?" Gilley asked Muckleroy.

The detective reached back into his folder and pulled out a stack of papers and handed two to Gil and me. I looked at the sketch of a man with dark hair, angular features, and wide-set eyes and asked, "Who's this?"

"Hatchet Jack," Muckleroy said with a grin. "Hardly looks like himself without the hatchet and the crazy eyes, huh?"

"This is Amelia's drawing?" I asked, amazed at the difference.

"It is," said Muckleroy, glancing at his watch. "I was really hoping you two might help me by putting these up around town. The number to call in case anyone recognizes the face is right there," he said, pointing to the bold typeface at the bottom of the sketch under the words, HAVE YOU SEEN THIS MAN?

"Absolutely," I said, volunteering both Gil and me. "You heading back to the office?"

"Yep," said Muckleroy. "I've got a meeting with the captain in ten minutes. If Doris Hinnely calls me, I'll give you a shout." With that he was gone, leaving Gil to pout in my direction.

"How come we got stuck with poster duty?" he groused.

"You have someplace more pressing to be?"

Gilley gave a gigantic yawn and said, "I was really hoping to take a nap, actually. I'm not getting enough beauty sleep on this job."

"No rest for the weary," I said, standing up from the table.

"At least we'll be able to sleep tonight," Gil reasoned as he followed me out of the restaurant.

"How do you figure?" I said, giving him a backward glance.

"It's Thursday," Gilley said, like I should know what he was talking about. "Nicholas said Hatchet Jack only shows up on Mondays, Wednesdays, Fridays, and Saturdays."

"Which is exactly why we're going to head back to the school and try to reach Eric and Mark," I said. "With any luck I'll be able to cross them over without Jack attacking me again."

"Slave driver," Gilley moaned.

We decided that we would divide the posters in half and work the town separately. We started at a grocery store, where we both raced to be the first to put up the poster. (I

310

found the bulletin board first, so I won that round.) We also agreed to meet back at the store by three, which gave us about two hours to get the job done.

While I was taping one of the posters to a streetlamp my cell phone gave a jingle. Pulling it out of my pocket I saw that the good Dr. Delicious was calling. I took a deep breath and answered with a cheery, "Hey, there, Doctor. How goes the lecture circuit?"

"It goes well," Steven's smooth and silky voice replied. "How goes the ghostbust?"

"It's coming along," I said. "We've made a little bit of progress, at least." And then I filled him in on all that had transpired, minus revealing the nasty attack from Jack the night before.

He seemed to sense something had happened, because he asked, "Are you being careful with this ghost, M.J.?"

"Of course," I said a little too earnestly.

"It makes me nervous that you are engaging him," he said. "He could turn out to be more dangerous than even you can handle."

I smiled. "I'll be fine, Steven," I assured him. Then, feeling bad for having been impatient with him on this job, I asked, "Are you heading back this way to help us finish the bust?"

"You are wanting me to?" he said, and I heard the little note of surprise in his voice.

"Sure," I said, working to keep my voice light and encouraging. "But I have a feeling we're about to wrap it up, so if you're going to come back you'll need to haul some butt up here."

There was a pause on his end, and I thought maybe I could have been a little nicer with how I asked him to come back to the job. "I will see what I can do."

"Great," I said, feeling bad that the conversation had just turned awkward. "That's really great."

Steven and I made small talk for another minute or two before we said good-bye. As I put the phone back in my pocket I wondered how people ended up staying together. It seemed this whole relationship thing was going to require a lot more work than I was used to.

I met Gil about an hour later back at the grocery store. He was standing in front of the bulletin board, staring curiously at it and looking around. "What's up?" I asked.

He pointed to the board and said, "Someone ripped down your sketch."

I looked up and noticed what he was talking about. Right where we'd tacked up the image of Hatchet Jack were a few tattered

312

pieces of paper still held by the thumbtacks. It appeared someone had torn it down quickly. "That's weird," I said. I reached into my folder and pulled out another flyer and tacked that one up again. "I wonder why someone would tear down our poster."

"Maybe they recognized the guy in the sketch," Gilley said. "Maybe they took it home to call it in."

My eyebrows lifted. "Wouldn't that be awesome?" I said. "If we had a name to go with this guy it sure would help solve a lot of the mystery here."

"Let's go visit your detective and see if he's heard anything."

Gilley and I climbed into the van and made our way out of the parking lot, heading toward the police station. It was then that something caught the corner of my eye, and I turned to look at the lamppost where I'd personally taped up a poster of Jack. It too had been torn down.

"Crap," I said, feeling a cold, prickly sensation along my spine.

"What?" Gil asked.

I pointed to the lamppost. "Seems you were right about someone recognizing Jack," I said. "They're tearing our signs down."

Gilley changed directions, and we back-tracked along the route I'd taken around my half of town, and without exception every single sketch had been torn down. I was so mad by the time we'd circled back that I was seething. "That son of a bitch!" I snarled. "It took me two hours to put all those up!"

"Let's check my route," Gil offered, but at that moment my cell rang.

Pulling it out of my pocket I looked at the caller ID and said, "It's Muckleroy."

"How'd you two make out?" he asked when I answered.

"Not so well," I said. "We've got a wise guy following behind us, ripping down our sketches." I went on to explain how Gil and I had just followed my route and discovered all the posters missing.

"You're kidding," Muckleroy said with a heavy sigh.

"Wish I were, Bob," I said. "I think someone recognizes Jack and they don't want anyone else to."

There was a hint of laughter in Muckleroy's voice as he said, "It could also just be some local kids having fun at your expense."

I pouted in my seat. "It's not funny. I worked hard putting those damn things up."

"Okay, okay, M.J. I'll give a stack to my foot patrol and they can take over for you and Gilley. Besides, I just got a callback from Eric's mother. Thought you two might want to ride shotgun over to her place for an interview."

"That works for me," I said, and filled Gilley in quickly. "We'll see you in five minutes."

The ride over to Mrs. Hinnely's was much quicker than either Gilley or I would ever have made it. I suppose when you're a cop you think nothing of exceeding the speed limit and racing down side streets. I resisted the urge to get out and kiss the ground when we finally stopped in front of a well-maintained and surprisingly large home on the east side of Wheaton.

By the look of Gilley's rather green complexion as he exited the car, it was pretty clear he hadn't enjoyed the excessive speed and hairpin turns either. "Maybe we should catch a cab back," he whispered, holding his stomach.

"You can sit up front when we leave," I replied, feeling bad for him and thinking it would help with the motion sickness.

"Great," he said with a huge roll of his eyes.

We both shut up as Muckleroy came around and led us up the walkway. "Wheaton's nicer on the east side of town," he said. "You go to the west side and even I drive with the doors locked."

"We took a tour earlier," I said, referring to our visit with Vesnick.

A trim woman in her late fifties with silver blond hair, startlingly beautiful aqua blue eyes, and a bit of a forced smile greeted us at the door when we stepped onto the front porch. "I saw you pull up," she explained. "I'm Doris Hinnely, but everybody calls me Dory."

"Nice to meet you," Gilley and I said.

"Thank you for agreeing to see us," Muckleroy said, extending his hand.

"Won't you please come in?" she asked, holding the door open for us.

We trooped inside and entered her living room, which was beautifully decorated with mostly white upholstered furniture, robin's-egg blue walls, and beech-wood flooring. The interior had a very soothing quality about it, and I'll admit, knowing that Dory had been a former drug addict made the interior of her home a complete surprise.

"Please take a seat," she said, and hurried into the adjoining dining room, where she retrieved a silver tray with a pitcher of iced tea and a few glasses. "Would anyone like some refreshment?"

I glanced over at Muckleroy, willing to take his lead on whether to accept or not. He seemed a little uncomfortable in the face of so much politeness, especially when I knew he had to tell Dory about the death of her son. "That would be nice, thank you," he said, trying to put her at ease.

Gil and I each took a glass after she'd poured it for us. I took a sip and was surprised at how fabulous it tasted. "This is amazing," I said. "There's no bitter aftertaste."

Dory nodded, and her forced smile became a little more real. "I import it from Istanbul."

Gilley took a tentative sip, and he nodded too at how light the tea was. "Just the thing to settle my stomach," he whispered to me.

Dory sat down in one of the large overstuffed chairs that sat across from Gil and me on the sofa, and next to the detective in a similar chair to the right. She laced her fingers together tightly and folded them in her lap. "Now," she said, turning slightly to face Muckleroy. "I believe you said you had some information for me about my son Eric?"

Dory's posture was ramrod straight, and my heart went out to her, because I knew she was bracing herself. I'm sure she'd known all along that Eric was gone forever, and I could only imagine the range of conflicting emotions that must be going through her thirty years later.

Bob put his tea on the coaster Dory had set out for him and scooted forward a bit in the chair to rest his elbows on his knees. The look he gave her was somber. "I'm afraid we suspect that the remains we found yesterday near Hole Pond may very well be your son's, Mrs. Hinnely."

Dory's expression became blank, and I had a feeling she was suddenly far away in a past that included her son still vibrantly alive. She swayed in her chair ever so slightly, and I watched her carefully, ready to leap up if she tipped over into a faint. But a few moments later she was back with us, blinking hard and swallowing the painful truth. She gave one sharp nod of her head. "I knew years ago that he was gone," she whispered. "One night I just felt him leave me, like his soul were no longer connected to mine."

"I'm so sorry for your loss," I said gently.

Her eyes glanced over at me, as if she were seeing me for the first time. "I'm sorry," she said, placing a hand on her chest. "I'm afraid I don't know who you two are."

I felt my cheeks grow red. Why hadn't I introduced myself? "My name is M. J. Holliday, and this is my partner, Gilley Gillespie. We were the ones who located

318

your son for the detective."

Her expression seemed puzzled. "Located him for the detective?" she asked, wanting me to clarify what I meant.

I always took a deep breath before I explained what it was that I did for a living. "I'm a professional medium," I said carefully. "I specialize in helping energies that have become grounded on the earth plane cross over to the other side."

The puzzled expression on Dory's face deepened. "I'm sorry . . . you what?"

"I am someone who can talk to the deceased," I tried again. "I can communicate with people who have died almost as easily as I can communicate with you. Your son appeared to me and told me that he'd passed away. It was clear when I first communicated with him that he was what I call grounded, or a soul who has not quite made it to heaven yet. I've been trying to help him make it the rest of the way for a few days now."

"Eric is a . . . a . . . ghost?" she stammered, and the look of horror on her face made me wish I'd stuck to giving her just my name and not my profession.

"Yes," I said. "But he seems to have adjusted to that quite well, and I will do everything I can to help him find his way to heaven."

Tears welled in Dory's eyes. "My poor baby," she said, the tears leaking over onto her cheeks.

No one spoke for several long, awkward moments as Dory put her hands over her face and openly wept. I wanted to go over and give her a soothing hug, but her posture was still ramrod straight, and I knew she wouldn't welcome it. Finally she wiped her eyes and turned to the detective. "How do we make sure it's Eric that you found?"

Bob cut me a quick look before he said, "We'd like to take a sample of your DNA. The coroner thinks there might be enough usable DNA in one of the teeth to identify whether he was your son."

Dory nodded. "That's fine," she said. "Do you know how he died?"

Bob glanced at me again, and Dory seemed to catch the exchange. She swiveled back to me and said, "Eric told you, didn't he? He told you how he died?"

"He did," I said, knowing that this woman deserved the truth.

"He was murdered," she said, reading my expression. "He told you he'd been murdered."

"Yes, ma'am," I said. "I believe he was."

"Did he tell you who did it?"

Muckleroy cleared his throat and called Dory's attention back to him. "There is an ongoing investigation, Mrs. Hinnely. I can assure you we're doing everything we can to try to determine who killed your son."

And it was then that Dory seemed to wilt into the chair. Her shoulders sank and she leaned back into the cushion. "You may start by pointing that finger of blame at me, Detective," she said.

Muckleroy's eyes became wide. "Come again?" he asked.

"My son died because his mother was a drug addict who couldn't take care of her sons. They were taken from me and sent to foster care. It took me years to get off the drugs, and by then they were gone."

"I'm sorry," I said quickly. "You said 'sons,' as in *plural?*"

Dory nodded. "Eric and Ethan. They both ended up in foster care and went missing."

Muckleroy and I exchanged a look that said, *What?* "Were they sent to the same foster home?" Gilley had the sense to ask.

"Yes," Dory said. "But I didn't find that out until much later, after I got clean and off the streets. That horrible woman, the one who was fired because her records were so incomplete, told me that Eric had run away with his little brother. She said she heard they were in California. I knew she was lying, but I could never prove it because the police were all too familiar with my history and didn't want anything to do with me."

"When was this?" I asked. "I mean, when did you talk with that social worker?"

"It must have been right after I got out of rehab — nineteen eighty, I believe. Eric would have been in his late teens, and Ethan was a few years younger. Later, when the money came in, I hired a private detective, but he turned up nothing."

"When the money came in?" Bob repeated.

Dory's face turned profoundly sad as she turned again to look him straight in the eye and confess, "Yes, Detective, that is the supreme irony here. I won the lotto in 1985 by playing the numbers of my sons' birthdays."

"Whoa," Gilley said.

"Whoa is right," Dory said. "That's why I live here," she said, motioning to the room. "I had always hoped that Eric would come home."

"Eric but not Ethan?" I asked.

There was another sad smile on Dory's face. "Ethan was very young when he was taken away, and I was so into the drugs by then that he and I had barely bonded. I was in too much of a haze to pay much attention, but I doubt he'd remember much of me."

An awkward kind of silence enveloped us as each of us struggled for something to say. I looked down and noticed that I'd carried the folder of sketches with me into the house for the interview. Pulling the sketch out I took a shot and asked, "Dory, do you recognize this man?"

She studied the sketch for a long time, but as I watched her I saw no hint of recognition cross her face. "No," she said. "And if you're showing that to me, I'm assuming this is the man you think is responsible for Eric's death?"

"We're not sure," Muckleroy said carefully. "But we have labeled him a person of interest."

Dory sighed. "I really wish I could identify him for you," she said. "But I know I've never seen him before."

She handed it back to me, and I tucked it into my folder. "Thanks for looking," I said. I really felt for this woman. The kind of guilt she carried must have been unbearable at times.

Muckleroy was jotting a few notes into his notebook. After he'd finished he stood up and handed Dory a business card. "Thank you so much for your time, Mrs. Hinnely. Please call the number I circled on the card to schedule a time to go in for a DNA swab. I'll do my best to put a rush on the lab, and then we'll be able to release Eric's remains back to you."

Dory stood up and took the card. "Thank you, Detective. At least I can give Eric a proper burial. And please don't forget about my other little boy. If they're both gone it would give me closure to know when and how."

"I won't forget," Muckleroy promised.

As Gilley and Muckleroy headed out to the car, Dory reached out and touched my arm, stopping me from leaving with them. "M.J.?" she said. "Can I ask you something?"

"Yes, of course," I said.

"The next time you speak with Eric — you know, before you help him to cross over into heaven — would you please tell him I'm so sorry and that I love him?" Dory's voice cracked, ending on a whisper.

Now I didn't hesitate, and I reached out to squeeze her hand. "I absolutely will, Dory. I will tell him all that, and let him know that you still think of him and that you're doing so much better."

Dory nodded, too overcome with her emotions to speak.

We left her standing on the porch watching us pull out, and I wondered how a woman seemingly so strong now could ever have lost her way so profoundly.

"What's your feeling on her story?" Muckleroy asked me.

"What do you mean?" I asked.

"Ethan," Muckleroy said. "Your psychic sense didn't pick up on him, did it?"

"No," I said. "Which doesn't mean he wasn't also murdered. It may be that he just crossed over more easily than his brother."

"So what? This Hatchet Jack guy just swooped in and nabbed a whole horde of kids and killed them without anyone noticing?"

"Maybe he didn't take them all at the same time," I said. "He could have snatched one at a time and come back for more."

"How does a woman who's supposed to look after these kids just let three or four of them disappear like that?" Gilley asked from the backseat.

"I don't know," I said, shaking my head. "It seems pretty extraordinary, doesn't it?"

"Like something out of *The X Files*," said Muckleroy. "No offense, but I'll be glad when we get to the bottom of this and I can go back to my nice, normal petty-theft detective beat."

"I'll bet," I said with a grin.

We drove for a bit in silence, and then an idea occurred to me. "Detective?" I said.

"Bob," he corrected.

"Oh, yeah, sorry — Bob. Listen, I was wondering if maybe it might be worth it to put a few of these sketches up near the foster home where we know Eric and Mark were taken."

"That's a great idea," he said, putting his blinker on. "And as it happens, we're not far away from there."

We arrived at a large but neglected home a few minutes later. Everything about the house seemed to be rusting, from the siding to the chain-link fence around the property to the swing set in the backyard. The lawn was overgrown and filled with dandelions and crabgrass. The front steps were crumbling, and the front door to the porch hung slightly sideways.

"Someone *lives* here?" Gilley asked, with a frown of disgust.

"Looks like it," Muckleroy said, indicating a curtain in one of the side windows that had pulled back to reveal an older woman. We headed up the walkway and the front door pulled open with a loud groan. "Yeah?"

asked the elderly woman who mirrored the general feel of the house with her unkempt hair, raggedy clothing, and yellow teeth.

"Good afternoon," Muckleroy said, pulling his badge out of his suit pocket. He introduced himself and explained, "We're here looking into a person of interest who might have been seen in this neighborhood about thirty years ago."

"You cops really are behind on your paperwork," the older woman said with a snort.

Muckleroy grinned at the woman's pluck. She was sharper than she appeared. "It's a cold case that we've been given new information on," he said. "I know the former owner of this home has passed away, but are you in any way a relative of Mrs. Clayburn?"

"If you're talking about Maude, then yeah, I'm her sister."

The detective's eyebrows rose. Maybe we'd get lucky after all. He motioned to me, and I quickly took out the poster of Hatchet Jack. "Do you by any chance recognize this man?" he asked, showing her the sketch.

The woman squinted and came down the steps to take the paper out of my hand. "Yeah," she said after a moment. "I knew him."

Gil and I both gasped, the break we'd apparently just gotten taking us both by surprise. "Do you remember his name?" Muckleroy asked, and I could hear the excitement in his voice.

"That's Jack," she said, handing him back the sketch. "My sister went with him for a while back in the late seventies."

"Jack who?" Muckleroy pressed.

The woman shrugged. "I dunno," she said. "I only remember his first name."

"Do you remember if he had any family in the area?" Muckleroy asked.

This got us another shrug. "Not sure. He was a mean son of a bitch, from what I recall. He had a wicked temper. He liked to take the foster boys out on fishing trips."

"Fishing trips?"

"That's what I said," Maude's sister snapped impatiently.

"So what happened between him and your sister?" Muckleroy asked.

"They split up over it," the woman said.

"Over Jack taking the boys on fishing trips?"

Maude's sister rolled her tongue over her teeth. "Not so much taking them as not bringing 'em back. He claimed that he'd found a boarding school where the boys could learn better than the schools around here. Maude wanted 'em back 'cause she got her money by taking care of 'em."

"So what happened?" Gilley asked.

The old woman scrunched her face up into a really good pout. "They split up!" she snapped. "Ain't you been listening?"

"And Jack never returned the boys?" Muckleroy asked, taking over for Gil.

"Nope."

"Did your sister report this to her social worker?"

Maude's sister seemed to sense a trap. She folded her arms across her chest defensively and said, "Don't know. You'd have to talk to her about that."

Muckleroy pressed his lips together. He couldn't talk to Maude, and they both knew it. "How many of the boys did he take with him on these fishing trips, ma'am?"

"I dunno. A few."

"Like, three?"

"Two, three, four. Maude had so many little brats runnin' around that I can't remember."

"Do you remember the year?"

The old woman shrugged. "Nope."

Muckleroy was beginning to get annoyed. We were so damn close to finding out who Jack was, and this woman was barely helping. "How about the time of year? Do you remember the time of year?"

Maude's sister rolled her eyes, clearly out of patience with the detective. "It was August, right after Maude's birthday." With that she turned around and climbed back up the steps.

Meanwhile Muckleroy was scribbling in his notebook. Glancing up at her departing figure he said, "Uh, can I get your name?"

"Sure," she said, crossing her threshold. "I'm sure that'll be the next thing you look up." And with that she slammed the door and we were left stunned and a little bewildered, again on our own.

"She's lovely," Gilley said sarcastically. "M.J., put her on our Christmas card list!"

"Gil," I said, giving him a warning glance to chill out.

Muckleroy, however, laughed. "Yeah, she's my pick for warm and fuzzy of the year."

We turned and headed back toward the unmarked car in the driveway. "Let's put a few flyers up around here," he said. "I'll go this way," he said, pointing right. "You two go the other way."

"How many should we put up?" I asked as I took half the stack I had left and gave those to him.

"A couple blocks in each direction should do the trick," he said. "Meet you back here in an hour or so."

Gil and I hurried around the neighborhood, posting the flyers on trees and lampposts. I was glad I had him with me, as the neighborhood didn't look like it'd seen the welcome wagon in a *long* while.

We met back at Muckleroy's car and waited for him for another half an hour before we spotted him lumbering down the street. "About time," Gilley muttered, glancing at his watch.

I hid a smile, as I knew that Gil was impatient to get back to town so that he could have a nice hot meal followed by a long nap before we went back on duty at the school. "Sorry it took me so long," Muckleroy said. "I was asking a couple folks if they recognized Jack."

"Any luck?" I asked as he unlocked the doors and let us into the car.

"Yeah, actually," Muckleroy said.

"Do tell," I said.

"About two blocks down I found an old man on his porch who looked at Jack's picture and thinks he remembers him from one of the teams in his bowling league."

"Really?" I said, looking down the street.

Muckleroy nodded. "Yep. Said he didn't remember the name, but thinks it's the same guy who played on one of the opposing teams for a short time before dropping out. And the best part is that he also mentioned the teams got together on Tuesday, Thursday, and Sunday evenings."

"Whoa," said Gilley. "That explains why Jack is active only on Monday, Wednesday, Fridays, and Saturdays."

"Could he give you any more details? Like what team he might have played on?"

Muckleroy scowled as deep lines of frustration formed along his brow. "No, he says he only saw him a few times, and the bowling alley closed down years ago. I asked if anyone from the neighborhood might have played on the team and he said most everyone's died or moved away by now."

"So we're back to square one," said Gil.

"Looks like it," Muckleroy said. "But now that we know Jack was in this neighborhood and hung out with some of the locals, maybe someone with more information will come forward and give us an identification."

"The question is, Will they come forward in time? We have only one day left before we've got to exit the premises and the construction crews come in," said Gilley.

"Well, we're going to go back to the school tonight," I said. "I'll do my best to make contact with Eric and see if he can give us more info. If Eric's foster mother was going out with the man who abducted him, Eric might be able to give me a clue about a surname."

"Weird how his name is Jack, though, ain't it?" Muckleroy said with a sideways glance at me. "I figured the name Hatchet Jack was just something the kids had coined when they first started seeing and hearing about his ghost."

"It's not as weird as you might think," I said. "You'd be surprised how many homes I visit where the residents don't know anything about the ghost that's haunting their house, but they feel a need to name it, and the name ends up being right on or real close to what the ghost's name was in life."

"Well, the whole thing is creepy," Muckleroy said. "And I don't think you should go back to that school without a little backup. Maybe I should assign one of the officers to go with you."

"No way!" I said quickly. "It's really better if I work alone. Besides, Jack's not supposed to be on the school grounds tonight."

Muckleroy grunted. "I sure wish the son of a bitch were still alive. He's one piece of scum I really would have liked to have put away."

I leaned back in my seat and closed my eyes, feeling the weariness of this job settle into my bones. "Trust me, Bob, he's not going to get away with it. I'm not leaving this job until I know he's been sent where he belongs."

CHAPTER 10

That night around ten, Gilley and I drove back to the school. Gilley was wearing his protective sweatshirt and a nervous frown. I was in my usual black cargo pants with plenty of pockets, a black T-shirt, and a hooded sweatshirt.

We had tested all of the equipment before loading up the van, and I was now fiddling with the electrostatic meter as the miles melted away under our tires. "What's up?" Gil asked, sensing my jitters.

"Not sure," I lied.

"Oh, really?" Gilley said, his voice dripping with skepticism. Damn. He was onto me.

I sighed heavily, the weight of all this responsibility pulling me down. "What if Eric won't go? What if I can't convince him?" I said, and followed that quickly with, "And what if I can't find Jack's portal? We've only got tomorrow left, Gilley. What if all this effort — all this pain that we've unveiled for Eric's mother and the other boys' families — is all for nothing?"

Gilley reached over and squeezed my shoulder. In a tone holding a tiny bit of mockery he said, "It's tough being you, isn't it?"

That made me laugh. "I'm serious," I said. "What if we don't get to finish this one?"

"Then it'll be demons one, M.J. and Gilley fifty-five."

I gave him an impatient look. "That's unacceptable," I said. "The bad guys don't get one or two or any when we're up against them."

"Yeah," said Gilley. "That is exactly the spirit you'll need tonight. Do not take no for an answer, M.J. But just so you know, no matter what happens you're still a kick-ass ghostbuster, and giving only one up to the bad guys after so many successes is an amazing track record."

"I just want to give Mrs. Hinnely a sense of closure," I said. "And I want to shut that demonic piece of slime down."

Gilley turned the van into the school parking lot and came to a stop near the elementary wing. "Then go to it," he said gently.

I unbuckled my seat belt and swung into the back of the van to grab my duffel. "I'll set up in the same classroom we saw the boys in before," I said. "If I get nothing then I'll head over to Nicky's window and see if Eric is there. I might be able to coax him into talking with me."

"Gotcha," Gil said with a salute. "I'll monitor from here."

I turned to walk to the building when I heard Gil call my name. I looked over my shoulder and asked, "Yeah? Did I forget something?"

"No," Gilley said, and his expression was slightly hesitant. "If you need me, M.J., just holler, okay?"

I broke into a grin. "You gonna come to my rescue?"

"I'm wearing the supersuit," Gil said. "And I've got one of these," he added, pulling out the magnetic grenade we'd made from the lead pipe and spike. "Jack won't stand a chance."

I gave him a wave and jogged to the school. The grounds were quiet except for the sound of crickets and frogs from Hole Pond just across the field. The air was damp and chilly, perfect ghost-hunting weather, and there was something of an oppressive air in the night. I opened up my senses and couldn't tell from where, but I knew I was being watched. I wondered if maybe Nicky was off, and if Jack came whenever he damn well felt like it and not only to keep the schedule Nicky had quoted.

I opened the door to the elementary wing and stepped inside, my radar still dialed up to high alert. Pulling the night vision camera out of my duffel I turned it on and flipped it around to point down the hallway. In my ear Gilley said, "Confirmed visual from the camera."

"Cool," I said, and moved down the hallway. When I got to the classroom where we'd first encountered the boys I heard a scraping sound. Hurrying to the room I opened the door and peered inside, my heart racing a little in my chest.

"Whoa," Gilley said into my ear. "Looks like Jack's been working his interior design skills again."

The desks in the classroom had all been stacked into a pyramid, except for one lone desk at the back of the classroom. My senses told me there was an energy around it, so very slowly and carefully I set down my duffel, putting the camera on the teacher's desk at the front of the room so that it pointed at the student desk in the back, and pulled out my electrostatic meter.

"You've got activity?" Gilley asked.

"Yes," I said. "In the back of the room."

"Who is it?"

"Not sure yet," I said, watching my gauge, which was bouncing around.

"Try the thermal imager," Gil suggested. I reached back into my duffel and pulled out the gadget, but before I could turn it on I heard another scraping sound. "The chair!" Gilley hissed in my ear. "It just scooted back from the desk!"

I froze and looked at the desk in the back, waiting for something else to move. When nothing did I said calmly, "Hello, there." I could feel a slight tremor in the ether; the energy at the back of the room felt small and afraid. I knew it was one of the boys. "Eric?" I asked. "That you?"

No, I felt in my head. *Mark.*

I relaxed a little. "Hi, Mark!" I said brightly. "I am so glad you're here!"

The response I got back was mistrusting. It felt like Mark didn't believe me, something like *Yeah, right.*

"I'm serious," I said. "I really wanted to talk with you. See, we've been to your foster home and we've seen where you were living."

Hate her!

That caught me a bit by surprise. I wondered who "her" was. "You hated Maude?" I asked.

I felt something like a nod in my head and the repeated phrase, *Hate her!*

"Well, I totally don't blame you," I said easily, turning the thermal imager on and placing it next to the camera. "And that's why I'm so glad I found you. I really wanted to let you know that you never have to go back there."

Again I felt a sort of distrust echo across the ether into my mind. "I'm not joshing you, Mark. Maude's been taken away by the police, and all the foster kids get to go to really good new homes now."

Mark waffled. *I'm scared,* I felt come at me from across the room.

"Yeah, I know, guy. I'd be scared if I were you too. You go from that awful foster home to this place, and you've got Jack chasing you all over the grounds."

He hurt me! Mark said, and the energy of fear hit me like a kick in the gut.

"I know he did, sweetie. But we're going to arrest Jack now and send him to jail. And that's why I wanted to talk to you. If you can tell me where Jack goes, then I can send the police after him and make sure he gets what's coming to him."

Jack goes across the water, Mark said. *He goes to his house there.*

I felt the urge to look out the window and

glance across the lawn. I could just make out the area where Hole Pond was, and I knew that was where Mark was indicating. "That's awesome, Mark!" I said, even though his information wasn't especially clear. "I will call the police and send them to Jack's house. They'll arrest him and he'll never hurt another little boy again."

What about me? Mark said.

The plea was so clear and so needy that I felt my eyes well up. I swallowed and worked hard to pull it together. "You, my friend, get to go home now!"

Can't, said Mark. *I have no home.*

Ah, now I knew why he hadn't crossed over on his own. For someone who didn't believe he had a home to go to, the promise of it could be something like a cruel joke. "But that is the great news!" I said. "We've found you a wonderful family, Mark. They have heard all about you, and they want to adopt you and give you a home to come to."

Mark's energy hesitated. He didn't believe me. Finally he asked, *Who are they?*

I smiled. "They're the Angels, Mark. They have this really fantastic house, and it's warm all year round there. They have tons of toys, and there are other kids to play with. They're inviting you to dinner, and if you like it, you can stay." I was totally making this up, but I had to convince Mark to take the first step toward the light that wanted to carry him to a place where I knew he could be loved and nurtured like all souls should be. I waited with held breath for Mark to say something.

Okay, he said after a bit. *Will you take me there?*

I breathed a sigh of relief and sent a sort of mental hug to his energy. "You are so great!" I said to him. "Now, I won't be going with you, but I've ordered a special elevator that will take you there without stopping."

Where is it?

"If you look up, Mark, you'll see this big ball of light over your head near the ceiling. That's the special elevator."

I felt a sense of surprise at that. *I've seen that before,* he seemed to say. *But I didn't want to go into it.*

"Well, it is never too late, my friend," I encouraged. "And I know the Angels will be so happy to see you. What you'll need to do to lower the elevator is just to think about that light coming down from the ceiling. Can you do that?"

In my head I saw the light I was talking about lowering itself, and the room began to literally crackle with energy and static electricity. "That's it, Mark!" I said. "You're *so* doing it!"

The ball of light got lower and lower, and I knew it was expanding to encompass Mark. For a split second it hesitated, and I felt, *It's so pretty!* pop into my head. "Going up!" I said, and a nanosecond later there was a blue flash in the corner of the room near the desk and Mark's energy was swept away.

"Whoa!" Gilley said into my ear. "That was so cool!"

"You saw that?" I asked.

"I saw it on the thermal imager," Gil said. "This yellow ball of energy came down from the ceiling and it expanded to, like, half the room; then it just disappeared!"

"That little guy was so cute," I said, noticing that my back and brow were slick with sweat. I'd wanted to cross him over so badly, and I was really relieved that he'd gone.

"Good job, M.J.," Gil said. "Good guys fifty-six, bad guys nil."

I smiled. "Thanks, sweetheart, but we . . ." At that moment my voice faded because outside the window I clearly saw Eric standing there. Reaching back, I grabbed the night-vision camera and pointed it at him.

"Eeeek!" Gilley squealed when he saw

what the camera was recording.

I winced. "That's my ear," I hissed.

"Sorry!" Gil said. "But you gotta give me some warning!"

"You see him?" I asked of the statue-still figure in the window.

"I do," Gil said breathlessly. "Thank God I've got the monitor on record!"

For a moment no one spoke and no one moved. I looked at Eric, he looked at me, and Gilley breathed heavily in my ear. Suddenly Eric's placid face broke into a smile and he pointed across the room where Mark had been. Gilley gasped. "He saw you cross Mark over!" he whispered.

I nodded to Eric encouragingly. "Mark has gone to a really lovely home, Eric. There's room for one more, if you'd like to go too."

Eric looked back to me, his face unreadable. Then he motioned with his finger and I felt him say in my head, *Follow me.*

"He wants you to follow him," Gilley said.

"Gee, what gave it away?" I said sarcastically as Eric turned and began to walk away from the window.

"Go, M.J.!" Gilley ordered.

"I'm going!" I said, and grabbed the camera before bolting out of the classroom. Running as fast as I could I raced out the back door and looked frantically around. I didn't know how long Eric could sustain his visual form, and I knew I didn't have a lot of time. Across the lawn I saw him trotting toward the main building. "I've got a visual on him!" I said, and took off after him.

Eric stopped at the door of the building and looked back at me. He seemed to be waiting. I kicked it up a notch and put on the speed. I knew we had limited time, and there seemed to be something important Eric wanted to show me. "He's at the door of the main building!" I said. "I think he wants me to follow him inside!"

"What are you going to do?" Gilley asked. "You don't have a key to anything but the elementary wing."

The answer came when I reached the steps to the building and watched Eric reach out and touch the door handle. The door gave a *click* and then it swung slightly ajar. Eric looked back at me, gave me a smile, and vanished through the door to the interior. I raced up the steps to the door and said, "Thanks for opening that, buddy."

"Wouldn't it be great if you had him around every time you got locked out of your condo?" Gilley said into my ear.

I ignored him because at the moment I was trying to locate my little ghost. I scanned the hallway in front of me and didn't see anyone. "Damn," I swore.

"What?" Gilley asked.

"I've lost him," I growled, turning this way and that.

"He's on the stairs!" Gil said. "And stop swinging the camera around; I'm getting motion sickness."

I pivoted toward the stairs at the end of the hallway and noticed a pair of jeans and sneakers trotting up the steps. "Good catch," I said as I hurried down the hall toward him.

Eric had completely disappeared by the time I reached them, but I trotted up anyway, hoping he'd give me a hint as to what direction he wanted me to go when I got close to him again. I reached the second-story landing and had the feeling I needed to keep going. I did and hurried up to the third story. At the top of that landing I distinctly heard footsteps walking down the wood floors, which creaked under the weight of an unseen force. "Right behind you," I said, breathing hard from the run across the lawn and now up the steps.

"He moves fast," Gilley commented.

I kept following the sound of footsteps until they stopped about three yards in front of me. There was no indication which way to go for a moment, and I bit my lip in anticipation. "Where'd he go?" Gilley asked me.

"I don't know," I said. "But I really wish he'd give me a clue about where to go next." As if in answer our agreeable little ghost clicked the lock on the door just to my left. It creaked open slowly and I said, "That-aboy."

"He sure is a helpful ghostie," Gilley said. "Not at all like the typical nasties we usually deal with."

I moved forward into the room Eric had indicated and scanned the interior with the camera held up, pointing it around the room so that Gilley could see too. "It looks like the teachers' lounge," I said, seeing the comfortable couches, chairs, and tables. "What the heck are we doing in here?"

There was no reply from Eric, and I scanned the room searching out his energy.

"What do you make of it, M.J.?"

"Hell if I know," I said, and swiveled in a 360-degree turn around the room. "Damn it!"

"What?" Gilley said.

"He's gone," I said, scratching my head.

"What do you mean, he's gone?"

I stomped my foot in frustration. The room was empty of spiritual energy. Eric

347

had absolutely vanished the moment he'd unlocked the door to the lounge. "I mean he's not here," I said. "He's disappeared into the ether."

"Why?" Gilley said. "I mean, why would he go and leave you hanging about what to look for in this room?"

I sighed heavily. "I don't know, Gil," I said, scanning for anything that seemed out of place. "There isn't anything odd in here that catches my eye."

"Do a slow panorama with the camera, M.J.," Gil said. "Maybe we're not seeing what we're supposed to see right now. We can record what's in there and analyze it later."

I stepped to the middle of the room and began to record it through the lens of the camera. There wasn't much that was special about it, just some rather worn-looking furnishings and historical pictures of the school on the wall. I moved in for a close-up of the photos, thinking maybe some of the people in them were important.

There was a wall that held all of the graduating classes of Northelm since its opening over a hundred years earlier. These were all encased in frames with little brass nameplates indicating the year. I looked at the pictures with the kids lined up in different sections of the school grounds. A few were taken on the lawn, others by Hole Pond, and still others on the steps of the school.

I moved row by row, pausing slightly at each photo until I'd nearly reached the end of the line. That was when Gilley seemed to take an interest in what I was doing, and he asked, "Um, M.J.?"

"Yeah?"

"Why exactly are you recording these?"

"No idea," I said honestly, swinging the camera away from the wall after recording the last photograph. "It's just that there's really nothing in this room that's giving us a hint about what Eric might want us to notice."

"As long as you're recording pictures, how about that long one over on the other side of the room?" Gil said in my ear.

I noticed a photo of the school taken with a wide-angle camera lens. I moved closer to get a better look, and through the camera's monitor I could see it clearly. It looked like it was taken on the same dock I'd seen in some of the other graduating-class photos, as the wooden planks were in the foreground. The photo was lovely, really. It captured the essence of the character of the school, sitting stately on the green grass with the Adirondacks in the background looking so pristine and inviting.

There were no people in the photo, just a panoramic view of the school and the surrounding countryside. "Nothing suspicious about that," said Gilley, seeing the photo too.

"I was thinking the same thing," I said, circling around to give the room one last long look and see if anything caught my eye or called out to me as something of interest. "There's nothing here," I said, trying to keep the defeated tone out of my voice.

"Time to call it a night, sweetheart," Gilley said, and I could hear him yawn.

"Okay," I said, moving toward the door. That was when we both heard a scream from across the lawn that sounded so awful I nearly dropped the camera.

"What the . . . ?!" Gilley yelled in my ear.

I didn't reply. Instead I tore out of the room and dashed to the stairs. From out on the lawn we heard it again, another horrible, bloodcurdling scream that sent a shiver down my spine. "Jesus!" I said as my feet flew down the stairs. "It sounds like someone's being murdered out there!"

"I'm calling the police!" Gilley said.

I reached the second-floor landing. "Wait!" I shouted, willing my feet to move faster. "What if it's Jack?"

A third scream echoed across the lawn, this one just as terrified but stifled somehow — as if the scream had been cut off in the middle. "M.J.!" Gilley wailed. "That's a real person!"

"I'm on it!" I yelled back, dashing to the door and bursting outside.

"Stop!" Gil commanded. "You can't go out there! It could be dangerous!"

"Call nine-one-one!" I shouted, ignoring his command to stop, and running as fast as I could across the lawn. Ahead I saw a figure looming large in the darkness. As I got closer I noticed the figure was standing over a crumpled form on the ground. My intuition told me there was no ghost on the lawn — that was a real somebody standing there.

"Hey!" I yelled as I drew close. "What are you doing?!"

"I've got the police on the line!" Gilley shouted into my ear. "M.J.! Back off! Don't go there!"

The figure turned as I yelled, but it was too dark to see his face with any distinction. I could only tell that he was tall and broad shouldered and that there was something in his hand. I squinted at the thing he was holding, and at that moment it suddenly occurred to me what it was, and it sent ice through my veins. I pulled up short, slamming on my running brakes so hard that I felt my shins rattle. In the man's hands was a hatchet, the end of which was black and dripping in the dim light. "Ohmigod!" I yelped as I spun around and began running as fast as I could away from the scene. "Gilley!" I screamed. *"Gilley!"*

Behind me I could hear fast footsteps coming after me. For the second time that night I dug deep and turned up the speed, willing my legs to move faster and faster. Still the thundering noise behind me was keeping pace with me, and I was now so terrified that I was nearly blind with fear.

Ahead of me two bright lights flashed on, and the roar of an engine grew nearer and nearer. "Help me! Gilley, he's after me!"

"Hang on!" Gil shouted, and the two lights became brighter and brighter as they bounced across the lawn, heading directly for me.

The pounding of feet behind me seemed to falter as the lights became so bright I had to hold my arm up to shade my eyes. "I'm going to stop the van right next to you!" Gil said. "Jump in when I hit the brakes!"

Two more seconds passed, and the van

pulled neatly along my right side as the sound of ripping sod as Gilley applied the brakes. I was panting hard as I slammed against the side of the van and yanked open the door. I lunged for the opening, throwing the camera I still held up onto the seat, and screamed, *"Go!"*

Gilley punched the accelerator, and the van's back wheels spun dirt while it fishtailed in a circle and moved away from the figure chasing me. My legs were hanging out of the van door, and I had to hold tightly to the base of the seat so that I wasn't whipped back out from the force of our turn.

"Are you in?!" Gilley yelled as he glanced at me over his shoulder.

"Yes!" I shouted back. "Just drive!"

We made it to the parking lot, and that was when I was able to pull myself completely inside the van and close the door. In the distance we could hear police sirens making a beeline for us. Gilley didn't wait for them in the parking lot; instead he drove straight for the school's entrance. "Where are you going?" I asked as I made my way to the front seat.

"The hell outta here!" he said, his eyes wide and frightened.

"We have to stop for the police!" I shouted at him.

"Nuh-uh!" Gilley said. "We are outta here!"

"Gilley," I said, trying hard to make my voice calm. "Stop the van."

"He's coming for us!" Gilley said. "Jack is coming for us, and he's going to kill me!" And then he burst into tears.

We were almost all the way up the driveway then, and in the distance I could see the first cop car make the sharp turn onto school property. "Gilley!" I pleaded. "The police are here! *Please* stop the van!"

Tears were streaming down Gilley's cheeks, and I knew he could barely see. One cop car passed us going about ninety, and another had also just made the turn into the driveway. Gilley gave two huge gulps and pulled over to the side of the pavement. A third car turned into the drive, this one an unmarked car with a strobe light, and it stopped at the entrance not ten yards from us.

I reached out to hug my partner, knowing full well that he didn't take scares like this easily, and that was when I saw a bullhorn poke through the window of the car up ahead, and a metallic voice called out, "Come out of the van with your hands in the air!"

Gilley yelped, and his shoulders shook with emotion. "I thought you were dead!" he wailed. "I saw that man running at you with his ax and I thought I wasn't going to make it to you in time!"

"People in the van!" yelled the metallic voice again. "You have ten seconds to come out of the van with your hands in the air!"

"Gil," I said gently, rubbing his back. "We've got to go, sweetie."

"Five seconds!"

Gilley's sides shook with sobs, but he nodded and opened up his door. I did the same, and we very slowly exited the van with our hands in the air. A spotlight was flashed directly at us from the unmarked car, and I squinted hard into the brightness of it. The moment it lit on us we heard, "Gilley? M.J.? What the hell's going on?" come from the bullhorn.

"Someone was murdered back there," I called. "You may want to check it out, Bob, before your suspect gets away."

The spotlight clicked off, and I could see detective Muckleroy hurrying toward us. Gilley and I lowered our hands and waited, out of breath and tense, for him to come to us. "Mind telling me what the hell's going on?" he asked.

It was then that I noticed his disheveled look, with messy hair, a shirt half buttoned, and pants with no belt that kept sliding down his waist. He must have been self-conscious, because he pulled them up hard when he stopped hurrying to us and held the waistband with one hand. "There was a man," I began.

"And he had an ax!" Gilley said.

"He had a hatchet," I corrected.

"And he *killed* someone!"

"We're not sure if they're actually dead," I reminded him.

"There was blood everywhere!"

"I only saw it on the hatchet," I said.

"And he tried to kill M.J.!"

"He was chasing me; he never got close enough to take a whack at me."

"We left him in the dust back at the school!"

"That part is true," I said.

The detective's head was going back and forth from Gilley to me as if he were watching a tennis match. His mouth was partially open — as if he couldn't quite believe what we were saying to him — and when we finished he opened his mouth further to say something, but his radio crackled and a garbled, excited voice whipped off some numbers through the speaker. Muckleroy's eyes became even larger than when he'd been listening to us, and he pulled the walkie-talkie from his waistband and spoke into it. "Unit ten, what is your location?"

"On the school lawn next to Hole Pond. Just follow the blood, Detective; you won't be able to miss it."

Gilley and I both gulped, and he mumbled, "Aw, man! I didn't have to hear *that!*"

Muckleroy clipped the walkie-talkie back onto his waistband and pointed to the two of us. "You two," he said. "Get in the back of my car."

His tone meant business, and Gil and I shuffled quickly to his car. While we waited in the backseat we watched Muckleroy pace back and forth in front of his car, his form illuminated brightly by the headlights, which were still on. He was talking into his walkie-talkie and making large gestures with his free hand.

A moment later he came around and got into the car, but he didn't speak a word to Gilley or me. Instead he put the car in gear and punched the accelerator hard. Gil and I both jerked backward at the force of the acceleration while the car whipped down the driveway, across the parking lot, and up onto the lawn. Muckleroy stopped where the other two patrol cars were parked and looked over his shoulder at us to bark, "You two, stay here!"

He then got out of his car and moved over to the other two officers, who were setting up a perimeter of crime-scene tape using some stakes and any available tree. In the center of the perimeter was a form lying prone on the ground. From the headlights of the three patrol cars we could see a lot of red, and Gilley moaned and went slightly pale. "I hate this job, M.J.," he said as he sat back in his seat and laid his head against the headrest.

I reached out and grabbed his hand. "Sorry, Gil. I had no idea this was gonna happen."

"How is it even possible?" Gilley asked. "I mean, I understand the cut on your forehead, but for a ghost to actually kill someone . . . I've never heard of that."

I looked sharply at him. "You think that was Jack?" I asked.

"Who else would it be?"

"Gilley," I said firmly, "that was no ghost. That was a real, live human being."

Gilley's eyes became huge and he sat up. "No way!"

I pumped my head up and down vigorously. "Way," I said. "A ghost couldn't inflict that much damage. They wouldn't have the strength for that kind of attack. The cut on my forehead was the very most someone like Jack is capable of."

"Then that means there's a real, live man walking around with a hatchet, killing people?"

"I'm afraid so," I said with a shiver.

Gilley was silent for a few seconds, and then, in a voice that was high-pitched and frightened, he said, "Please tell me we can quit this job and go home."

I looked at him with sympathy. I really wanted to say, "Hell, yes!" but I had made a commitment to Mrs. Hinnely and to Karen and to Evie that I wouldn't quit the job until it was done.

"How about if you stay at the ski lodge and I work this one alone?"

Gilley grabbed me by the shoulders and shook me. "Are you *crazy?!*" he screeched. "Or just a little slow on the uptake? M.J.! There's a maniac running loose out there *killing* people with a *hatchet!* This isn't something you can fix! This is real life, and you're in real danger if you continue this job!"

I didn't get a chance to respond because Gilley's door was whipped open, and Muckleroy yelled, "What's going on here?"

Gilley let go of me instantly. "Nothing at all, Detective," he said sweetly. "Just having a little talk with my partner here."

Muckleroy glared at Gilley. I could tell he thought Gil had been manhandling me so I was quick to reassure him, "Gilley is a little overcome with emotion, Detective. It's been a tough night for us."

Muckleroy grunted and motioned to me with his finger. "You, come with me."

I scooted out of the car, leaving Gilley to sit tight. I tried to give him a reassuring look as I closed the car door, but he was busy pouting in the corner of the cab and wouldn't look at me.

I rounded the car and met up with the detective. "So tell me *exactly* what happened here," he said. "And don't leave anything out. I want to know what you did and saw from the moment you arrived here tonight."

I gave him a lengthy statement, leaving nothing out. He asked a few clarifying questions along the way about Eric's request to follow him up to the teachers' lounge. "And you didn't find anything?" he asked me. "Nothing at all that was suspicious?"

"No," I said to him. "I have no idea what he wanted to show me. He'd already gone by the time I entered the lounge."

"Why do you think that is?" Muckleroy asked.

I shrugged. "I wish I could tell you. It could be that he simply ran out of energy and had to leave, or that he felt I'd find a clue on my own."

"Could it also have been to keep you out of harm's way?" Muckleroy asked. "I mean, while you were up in the teachers' lounge, Skolaris was being murdered."

My mouth dropped open and my head whipped over to the prone figure on the ground some ten yards away. "That's *Skolaris?!*" I gasped.

Muckleroy nodded. "You didn't know?" he asked me.

"No!" I said. "I didn't get close enough to identify who it was that had been attacked."

"Well, it's Skolaris, all right," said Muckleroy. "And he's a mess, let me tell you."

"That poor man," I said.

"So how do we stop him?" Muckleroy asked me, and his expression held deep concern.

"Stop who?"

"Jack," Muckleroy said, like I should know.

And then it dawned on me. Muckleroy thought this had been the handiwork of a ghost too. "Detective," I said, "let me be clear on this. Skolaris wasn't attacked by a ghost. He was attacked by a real, live human being."

A mixture of emotions seemed to cross the detective's face. He looked almost relieved when he asked me, "Are you sure?"

"Absolutely positive," I said. "Jack was nowhere near here tonight. I would have sensed him. Hell, given that I'm responsible for taking another little boy away from him, he'd have come after me, not Skolaris, if that's what you're thinking."

"So we've got a real killer on the loose. Maybe a copycat?"

"I don't know," I said. "But that sort of makes sense, doesn't it?"

"What do you mean?"

"Well," I said, thinking out loud, "if you wanted to murder someone, and you knew this area was known for sightings of a ghost with a hatchet, wouldn't that be the perfect cover to help hide the crime?"

"Detective!" someone yelled from behind us, and we both whipped around to see one of the officers pushing Nicholas Habbernathy in front of him. Immediately I noticed that the front of Nicholas's shirt was covered in dark red smears and there were grass stains on the knees of his jeans. He was walking with his head bent and his arms secured behind his back. "I found him around back, behind one of the buildings. He had this," the officer said, and he held up a hatchet with blood on the blade.

"Oh, no," I said as the two men approached. "Not Nicky!"

The officer stopped in front of us, and I could see tears streaming down Nicholas's cheeks. "I didn't do it!" he sobbed. "I didn't do it!"

"He was hiding behind the dorm wing," said the officer. "I found him digging a hole, and the hatchet was in his possession. I figured he was going to toss the hatchet in the hole to hide it."

"Bury the hatchet!" Nicky wailed. "I've got to bury the hatchet!"

I looked sharply at Nicky. The double meaning was a little too ironic. "Who told you to bury the hatchet?" I asked him.

"Eric!" Nicholas moaned. "He told me that I should bury the hatchet. Forgive and forget."

Muckleroy looked at me. "Eric left you in the lounge to go to Nicky?"

"That makes sense why Eric left so quickly after showing me the teachers' lounge," I said.

"You think Eric made him do it?"

"Do what?"

"Kill Skolaris," Muckleroy said impatiently.

I turned to Nicholas and asked him, "Nicky, did you hurt Mr. Skolaris?"

"No!" Nicholas said. "I saw a man chasing you! I ran after him and he dropped that on the ground. Eric always tells me to bury the hatchet, so I did."

"What happened to the man you saw chasing us?"

Nicholas paused. He seemed to be thinking carefully about how to reply. "I dunno," he finally said.

"Nicky," I said earnestly, "if you have any information about who this man was or where he went, it's very important that you tell us."

Nicholas shrugged his shoulders. "I dunno," he said again.

Muckleroy sighed. "Take him in," he said to the officer. "Book him on suspicion of murder and call his brother. I'll want to have a talk with him too."

"But he just told you he didn't do it!" I protested.

Muckleroy looked at me like I was incredibly naive. "If it's all the same to you, M.J., I'd just as soon lock up the guy in possession of and with intent of burying a murder weapon."

"Detective," I said, trying like hell not to yell at him, "I know he didn't do it."

"Can you give me a description of the guy who did?" he asked me.

I hesitated. "Not really," I admitted. "It was dark, and I didn't get a good look at him, but I know he was tall."

Muckleroy looked pointedly at Nicholas. "Nicholas," he said, "how tall are you?"

"Six feet tall. I am six feet tall," Nicky said.

"The guy I saw was taller!" I insisted.

"So we're looking for an NBA player, then?" Muckleroy said sarcastically, motioning to the officer to take Nicky away.

"Bob," I pleaded, "you have to believe me. I know Nicky didn't kill Skolaris! There's not a mean bone in that man's body! He couldn't have done it!"

"And you know this because . . . ?" Muckleroy asked me skeptically.

"I've spent time with him," I said defensively. "Gil and I hung out with him one night. He's a sweet guy who wouldn't hurt a fly."

"Are we talking about the same guy who was swinging a bat at your partner the other night?" Muckleroy asked.

"That was different!" I insisted.

"Still," Muckleroy said, not backing down. "I'll go ahead and question him anyway. Just to be thorough."

By this time a large squad of police and crime-scene technicians had arrived and were crawling all over the area. One of them yelled, "Detective!" and Bob looked over his shoulder at the cop wearing blue latex gloves holding up a crumpled and bloody piece of paper.

"What's that?" he asked, moving closer to the cop, who was also moving toward him.

"We found it in the vic's hand. There are also a bunch more in his pockets."

I motioned to Gilley, who came out of the squad car, and the two of us crept closer to see what the paper was about. Muckleroy must have seen us from the corner of his eye, because he turned the paper around in our direction.

"Whoa," said Gilley when he saw what was on the paper.

"Our flyers," I said breathlessly. "Why would Skolaris have our flyers?"

"He must have been the one who pulled them down after we hung them up," said Gilley.

"Or they were planted on him by the killer," said Muckleroy.

"*Or* when Skolaris confronted someone with them, they were what drove the killer to kill," I said.

"I like your theory best," Gil said to me with a nudge.

"So, who did Skolaris confront?" Muckleroy asked thoughtfully. "You've said Jack is dead, but are you sure, M.J.? Are you sure Skolaris didn't confront the real, live Hatchet Jack?"

"I'm sure," I said immediately. Hatchet Jack was dead; there was no doubt in my mind about that.

"So who could have been upset enough by these flyers to want to kill Skolaris?" Gilley asked.

"Someone who knew the real story behind Jack," I said. "Someone who either was related to Jack or knew him well enough to know what he'd done."

"Or . . ." Muckleroy said, then let his voice trail away.

"Or what?" Gil said.

Muckleroy gave the two of us a pointed look. "Or it was someone who may have murdered Hatchet Jack, and didn't want to get pegged for *that* crime."

That thought rattled me. I had never considered that Hatchet Jack might have been murdered, because I'd been too distracted by looking at him as a murderer. "That is a really great point, Detective," I conceded.

"So you think Skolaris knew who either Jack or his murderer was, and was . . . what? Threatening to go to the police with it?"

"Blackmail is a great motive for murder," Muckleroy said. "Prosecutors love to whip that one out in court."

"Still, it could just as easily have been Skolaris who was being threatened with blackmail," Gilley said. "I mean, it's just as likely that maybe he had some sort of personal connection to Jack, and he's been trying to hide it all these years." Muckleroy and I gave Gil a curious look, and Gilley continued. "I mean, if I were going to blackmail someone, I'd go after the guy with money, and we've been to Skolaris's house, and we know he's the guy getting paid the big bucks here at the school. Maybe he tore the flyers down thinking they were put up by *his* blackmailer, and maybe *he* confronted the other guy and threatened *him,* and that's what started the hatchet hacking!"

I looked at Gil and the enthusiastic *By Jove, I've solved it!* look on his face. "You're proud of yourself, aren't you?" I said with a grin.

Gil nodded. "Kinda, yeah," he said.

"Well, a look around Skolaris's bank accounts should tell us a lot," Muckleroy said.

Just then we noticed a man running from the parking lot. We all looked up and saw Dean Habbernathy wearing a raincoat over hastily buttoned silk pajamas and with wet, disheveled hair hurrying over to us with a frightened look. "Bob!" he said when he got to us. "What's happened? I was in the shower getting ready for bed when my phone rang. It was your dispatcher; she said to come here right away, something about William having been attacked?!"

Muckleroy laid a hand on the dean's shoulder and in a calm, cool voice he said, "It's bad, Owen."

The dean looked over Muckleroy's shoulder at the blanket that had now been thrown over Skolaris's body. His hand flew to his mouth and he gasped, "Oh, God, no!"

Muckleroy looked at Gil and me as he put a soothing hand on the dean's shoulder. "Why don't you two go back to your place and get a little shut-eye? I'll call you in the morning and let you know if we find out anything else."

Gilley and I took our leave quickly. We'd both had enough drama for the evening.

A little later we'd made it back to the ski lodge and I headed to my room, exhausted and spent. When I came out of the bathroom after having changed and washed my face I noticed Gilley sitting on my bed, looking sheepish. "What's up?" I asked him.

"I'm scared of the dark," Gil said. "Can I sleep in here?"

I smiled. "Sure, babe," I said, pulling back the cover and climbing underneath. "But if you snore, your butt is gonna get tossed."

"So you can snore but I can't?" Gil said, trying to hide a grin.

I laughed. "Shut up," I said, pushing at him as he too climbed under the covers.

"Just try not to dream about that Dr. Delicious," Gil added, still giving me a hard time. "I wouldn't want you to think you were lying here with your Prince Charming."

"Oh, trust me." I giggled. "When it comes to happily ever after, we all know you're the guy with the wand and the wings trying to turn pumpkins into coaches."

"If the glass slipper fits," Gilley said, rolling over and pushing his back up against mine.

My last thought as I listened to Gilley's breathing grow slow and regular was that there was something I wasn't getting that I felt I should. Something about tonight should have tossed me a huge clue and allowed us to move forward. If I hadn't been so tired, I might even have figured out what that was.

CHAPTER 11

"They do make a cute couple," a male voice said, and my eyes snapped open. I realized immediately that I was staring right at Gilley, who had the same look of alarm I must've been wearing.

"Seems a shame to disturb them," said a female voice.

Gilley and I immediately sat up and looked to the foot of the bed. Standing there were Steven and Karen, looking smugly down at us as if they'd just caught us red-handed. "It's not what you think!" I said, pointing to Gilley and scooting away to the edge of the bed.

"We're not a couple!" Gilley added, moving in the opposite direction.

"He's gay!" I said.

"She's straight!" Gilley said, and we both hurried out of bed.

Steven and Karen began giggling, and that turned into some pointing and laughter as

Gil and I looked at each other and realized how disheveled and alarmed we both looked. Grumpy Gilley mumbled, "I gotta take a shower," and walked out of the room in a huff.

"What is his problem?" Steven asked, still grinning.

"We had a rough night, and he doesn't do well on" — I paused as I glanced at the clock on the nightstand and did the math — "four hours sleep."

Karen looked surprised. "You guys got in at four a.m.?"

I rubbed my eyes, which were dry and irritated. "Like I said, it was a rough night."

"What happened?" Steven asked, his amused look completely gone as he came over to me and ran a finger along the gash on my forehead.

"Long story," I said. "Why don't you guys go into the kitchen and let me get myself together and I'll come give you the lowdown in a minute?"

"Take your time," Karen said, coming over to give me a quick hug.

After Karen and Steven left my room I looked longingly at the rumpled bed. With a tired sigh I forced myself to turn and head into the bathroom, where I took a very quick shower and changed into some clean clothes.

When I got to the kitchen there was a fantastic aroma in the air, a mixture of coffee and something delicious cooking on the stovetop. "Whatcha making?" I asked Steven when I entered.

"Blueberry blintzes," he said. "They are, how you say, the shitzel?"

I smirked. "Shizzle," I corrected. "I don't think anything good would begin with shit."

"Good point," said Steven. "I will remember this shizzle."

Karen was standing against the counter looking her usual gorgeous self, even for eight thirty in the morning. "How was Europe?" I asked when she handed me a cup of coffee.

"It was fine," she said, which was Karenspeak for fabulous.

"You and John back together?" I asked, sticking my nose firmly into her business.

Karen waved her hand airily. "Who knows?" she said.

"I'm sure John would like to," I said. "Seems like he really missed you and would like to think maybe he's earned himself a second chance."

Karen sipped her coffee and looked at me over the brim, refusing to elaborate on her on-again/off-again relationship with *the* most eligible bachelor in New England. There was a shuffling noise behind us, and we all looked to see Gilley standing at the table looking puffy and tired. "Is that food?" he asked meekly.

Steven took a plate from the cabinet and loaded it with three blintzes and some bacon and carried it over to Gil. "Here," he said. "You look like you could use some energy. These blintzes will do the trick."

Karen brought him a cup of coffee, and I had a moment in which I was incredibly happy to have two friends who took such good care of Gil and me. "You're next," said Steven, reaching for another plate. "Go sit and I'll bring these next few to you."

I took my coffee and sat down across from Gilley, who looked like he was in heaven. "Ohmigod," he moaned. "These are incredible!"

"Old family recipe," said Steven.

Karen came over and sat next to me. "How did you two arrive here together?" I asked as she scooted her chair in and Steven set down a plate in front of me.

"Lake Placid has a small airport," she said. "I flew into New York on the red-eye and got here early. Steven's plane arrived from Boston right after mine."

"Good to have you both back," I said, making sure to look sincerely at Steven.

He noted my statement by giving me a kiss on the top of the head, and again he ran his finger along the gash on my forehead. "You were going to tell us about this rough night you two had?"

Gilley and I each told parts of the story to catch them up. We'd had a pretty exciting time since last we saw them, and their amazed expressions confirmed that Gil and I had been through a lot in a few days. "I'm so sorry," Karen said breathlessly.

That took me by surprise. "For what?"

"I had no idea this job was going to be so dangerous, M.J.," she said. "If I had known you were going to be in any kind of physical danger I never would have encouraged you to get involved."

I was quick to reassure her. "It's what I do, Teeko. Besides, if Gil and I hadn't intervened, the moment that elementary wing was turned into a dorm those kids would be in real danger."

"Well, with a teacher being murdered on the school's property, I doubt many of the parents will let their kids back in September."

As Karen finished speaking the doorbell rang. We all looked at one another to see

376

who was expecting company. None of us were, so Steven got up to answer the bell. He returned with Dean Habbernathy, looking exactly as he had just five hours earlier, if a bit more frazzled and concerned. "I'm so sorry to interrupt your breakfast," he said, noting our dirty plates and mugs of coffee. "But I'm afraid this couldn't wait."

Gilley pointed to an empty chair, and the dean gratefully took a seat. "Would you like some coffee?" Gilley asked, picking up some of the empty dishes on the table while he was at it. "I was just about to put a fresh pot on."

"That would be wonderful, thank you," said the dean. I felt for the man. The last several hours had perhaps been the hardest on him.

"How is Nicholas?" I asked gently.

His face tightened and he said, "They're keeping him for now on suspicion of murder. I've got a wonderful lawyer on retainer, and he's recommending a colleague to represent Nicky at his bail hearing on Tuesday morning. We think we'll be able to clear Nicky at the arraignment, or at the very least get him out on bond."

"Nicky's a good man," I said. "I know he would never resort to violence of this sort."

The dean seemed to wilt in his chair. His

finger made circles on the tabletop as he said, "No, Nicky really is as gentle as a lamb. I believed him when he told me he found the hatchet and merely wanted to bury it."

We all fell silent for a moment, and I searched for something to say. "I'm so sorry for the loss of your friend," I said, meaning Skolaris.

The dean winced. "I've known Bill almost my whole life," he said, still looking down at his finger on the tabletop. "It's hard to believe he's gone."

Gilley came back to the table with a steaming mug of fresh coffee, setting that down with a carton of cream before he refilled all our cups and again took his seat. We all waited in silence while the dean poured a little cream into his mug and stirred in some sugar. He seemed to be struggling with something he wanted to say. Finally he found his voice and said to me, "I'm afraid I haven't been very truthful with you about the ghost haunting our school."

"No, you haven't," I said, being careful not to sound accusing. "But in my line of work I've often encountered a skeptic or two, so there's been no offense."

"Yes, well, I am sorry for that," the dean said. I could tell an apology was difficult for such a proud man. "I've built my life trying to make Northelm the very best educational facility in the state. I couldn't really generate a reputation for excellence if I admitted to a violent poltergeist running loose around the grounds."

"How long have you known about Jack?" I asked.

"Since I was very young," said the dean. "My father told me about him. Nicholas and I were living in the same quarters Nicky still lives in today, and for some reason the ghost of Hatchet Jack never comes there. My father directed us strictly to stay inside during the summer evenings to keep us from getting the daylight scared out of us." The dean gave a small shudder.

"You had an encounter with him," I said, picking up on his body language.

Habbernathy looked sharply at me, but admitted, "Yes. Many years ago Jack chased me across the lawn. I'd never been so scared in my life, quite frankly."

"What happened?" Gilley asked.

"Eric saved me," the dean said quietly, with the tiniest hint of a smile. "When we were younger Eric was very real to us. But that faded with age. Ironic that Nicky still plays with him, but then, Nicky isn't more than a six-foot-tall child himself."

"Eric has impressed me every time I've come across his energy," I said. "He must have been one hell of a young man."

The dean nodded. "I'm sure that's true," he said.

"Say," I said, suddenly reminded of something. "Do you know why Eric wanted to show me the teachers' lounge?"

The dean looked like I'd caught him off guard. "The teachers' lounge?" he said. "That's in the main building. How did you get in there?"

I blushed. "Sorry," I said. "I know you told us to stick to the elementary wing, but Eric told me to follow him, and he unlocked the main building's door for us."

The dean's jaw dropped. "Ghosts can *do* that?"

I smiled. "You'd be amazed at their craftiness," I said. "Anyway, he led me up to the teachers' lounge and then he bolted. I never got a chance to figure out why."

The dean scratched his head. "I don't know what's of interest up there, other than some old furniture. Truth be told, the teachers have been complaining that it needs to be updated."

I frowned. "Well, I have no idea why he led me up there," I said. "And I hope I can figure it out by tonight, because it's Friday, the last chance I have to bust this ghost and I know Jack will be on the prowl."

"You're going back there?!" Steven and Teeko asked together.

"Of course," I said. "I'm here to get a job done, and that means seeing it through."

The dean was shaking his head. "I'm afraid I simply can't allow it, Miss Holliday. Now that Jack has killed one of my staff, I simply cannot allow you to engage that evil demon."

"Dean Habbernathy," I said, "Jack did not murder Bill Skolaris."

Again the dean looked quite taken aback. "What do you mean, he didn't kill him?" he said. "Nicky found a hatchet at the murder scene!"

"Yes, but it wasn't Jack who was wielding it," I said.

"Did you see who did?" asked the dean.

"Not exactly," I admitted.

"What do you mean, 'not exactly'?"

"It was really dark, and all I actually saw was someone standing over Skolaris with the hatchet. Then he came running after me and I didn't look back."

"Then how do you know it wasn't Jack?" asked the dean.

"Because no ghost moves like that, Dean Habbernathy. They may be capable of violence, but to have the energy to actually *kill* someone is quite beyond their capabilities. It doesn't happen."

The dean looked very worried. "But if the police here don't believe that it was Hatchet Jack, then Nicky could very well go to prison for the rest of his life."

"Well, then," I said, putting a soothing hand on his arm, "I suppose we'll just have to figure out who really murdered Skolaris."

Gilley spoke up with something that had obviously been on his mind. "Dean Habbernathy?"

"Yes?"

"M.J. and I believe that the real Hatchet Jack might have died in the summer of 1976. Since there is an obvious connection to the spirit of the man and the school, I was wondering if you might have any childhood memory of him. Maybe he worked on the grounds and your father might have mentioned him to you over dinner that summer?"

The dean frowned. "No, I'm sorry, Mr. Gillespie. Although the school has been in my family for many generations, my brother and I were adopted by my father, the former dean, in 1978 — which would have been two years after you believe Jack died."

"Is there anyone you can think of at the

school who might have been there during the late seventies?"

The dean's shoulders seemed to droop. "The only person who would have been there during that time was Bill Skolaris," he said. "Everyone else was hired later."

"That's telling," I said, and the dean gave me a curious look, so I elaborated. "If Skolaris was the only one who might have been able to identify who Hatchet Jack was, then that means he very well could have been killed because of it."

"How can you be certain?" the dean asked. "I mean, I liked and admired Bill, which is why I kept him on even in the face of adversity. But in general the man was not well thought of, and he tended to rub people the wrong way. It's just as likely he was killed by someone who had a completely unrelated quarrel with him."

"Well, there's one way to find out," I said, scooting back from the table. "Steven?" I asked. "Would you like to come with me into town to do some fact finding?"

"Sure," he said, getting up quickly.

"Do you need me?" Gil asked.

I looked at my tired and worn-out partner with sympathy. "You stay here, pal. Get some rest and we'll be back by this afternoon." Looking at Karen I added, "I don't want to exclude you, Teeko. You're welcome to join us if you'd like."

Karen got up and began to gather the breakfast dishes. "That's okay," she said. "You two go on ahead. I'll clean up here and get some rest myself. I'm feeling pretty jet-lagged suddenly."

The dean followed us out and gave Steven and me a tired wave as we took off in the van. "Where are we going to find these facts you are looking for?" Steven asked me from the passenger seat.

"First we have to get permission," I said.

"Permission?"

"Yep," I said with a nod. "From Detective Muckleroy."

"This is confusing," Steven said.

I waited until I'd let the desk sergeant at the police station know we were there to see Muckleroy to explain what I intended to do. "I have to get inside Skolaris's house," I said as Steven and I took a seat in the lobby.

"Why?"

"I'm going to try to connect with him," I said. "He's the key here. If I can connect with his energy then I might be able to get him to tell me who murdered him, and why. I might also be able to get some information about Jack out of him."

"Has Skolaris become a ghost?" Steven asked.

I shrugged. "I won't know that until I try to make contact."

"Wouldn't it be better to go back to the place he was murdered and connect with him there?"

"It might," I said. "But I'd rather try his house first. Ghosts are as likely to inhabit the places they're very familiar with as they are to inhabit the place where they died. Moving around in their home gives them a small sense of security in the face of so much confusion. Of course, there's the added bonus that if Skolaris *has* crossed over successfully, we'd be far more likely to connect with him from his home, surrounded by the things that still have his residual energy."

"This is why you need the detective's permission? To get inside Skolaris's home?"

"Exactly," I said, getting to my feet when I saw the detective come out the door leading to the back offices.

"This way," he said, motioning us over.

We followed him into his cluttered office, and I introduced Steven before getting down to business about what we wanted to do. The detective allowed me to speak uninterrupted, his face unreadable. When

I'd finished he said, "You really think that will work?"

"There's only one way to find out," I said. "My goal is to find something metallic that he might have touched a lot to connect with him."

"Something metallic?"

"Yes. Metal holds energy for long periods after someone touches it. If there was something that Skolaris touched a lot, like a set of keys, or a ring, or even his watch, then it will really help me to get a handle on his energy."

"Okay," said Muckleroy, scooting back from his desk. "As it happens I've already got a small team over there, looking for any clue about why he might have been murdered."

"Did you find anything in his financial records?" I asked as we followed Muckleroy again.

"Not yet," he said. "Bank records all indicate regular deposits and withdrawals. Nothing unusual catches my eye at first pass, but it's early in the investigation."

It didn't take us long to arrive at Skolaris's house. We parked at the curb and could see a small stack of brown paper bags being deposited on the front porch. Each bag was labeled EVIDENCE in black Magic Marker.

Muckleroy knocked on the door frame as he entered the house, calling out, "Hello? Jim, are you guys in here?"

"Hey, Detective," said a man in uniform wearing blue latex gloves, and booties over his shoes. "We were just wrapping up."

"Anything good?" Muckleroy asked.

Jim shook his head. "Naw, nothing much to speak of, anyway. The guy didn't even own a computer."

"There might be one he used at the school," said Muckleroy. "Do me a favor and call Dean Habbernathy. See if we can get permission to search Skolaris's office at the school. If he won't cooperate let me know, and I'll call the DA to get the search warrant."

"On it," said Jim, then looked curiously at Steven and me. "They with you?"

"Yeah," Muckleroy said, but he didn't introduce us. "We're going to have a look around ourselves."

"Sure thing," Jim said, holding out a set of house keys that looked brand-new. "We couldn't find the keys to the house on the body, so we called the locksmith out and had him put on a new dead bolt. Do me a favor and lock up after you're through?"

Muckleroy took the keys, and Jim left

along with two other similarly dressed men, each grabbing a few of the paper bags on the porch on their way out. Once they'd gone Muckleroy turned to me and asked, "This is your show, M.J. Go to it."

I smiled and faced forward into the hallway, trying to get centered and focused. "This way," I said as I turned toward the stairs and headed up.

Steven and Muckleroy followed me. "I think I've got a male energy here," I said. "Not grounded. He's indicating that he has crossed over."

"How can she tell?" I heard Muckleroy ask Steven.

"Grounded spirits feel heavier to her," Steven explained. "Spirits on the other side feel light."

"Oh," Muckleroy said, and I could tell by his tone that he still didn't quite understand.

I was too focused on trying to pull the male energy closer to me to elaborate for Muckleroy. I stopped on the landing of the second floor and waited. The energy was very light and soft, almost feminine in its touch, even though I was convinced it was a male I was tuning in to. "Come on," I said gently to the spirit. "Where do you want me to go?"

I felt the smallest of tugging sensations in

my solar plexus and was compelled to move down the hallway. I passed a bedroom and hesitated, for a moment unsure about entering it or not. The light tug came again, and I knew then that it was originating from a room at the end of the hallway.

I moved quickly to that room and stood in the doorway taking in the decor before moving inside. This was obviously the master suite, with a large mahogany bed and matching dresser. The room smelled of scented cologne and furniture polish. My attention moved to the dresser, and I walked over to it, looking down at all the objects there. There was a pipe and a tobacco pouch, a plastic lighter and some loose change. There was also a small wooden box, and curiously I removed the lid.

Inside was a silver pocket watch with a golden dial. I picked it up gently and looked at it in the sunlight streaming in from the window. "Jackpot," said Muckleroy. "That's got to be Skolaris's pocket watch."

I closed my hand around the watch and shut my eyes. Immediately the light touch of the spirit I was connecting with intensified, and I got the initial W in my head. I felt the spirit was trying to sound out his name, and in my head it sounded like Win Ton. "This didn't belong to Skolaris," I said softly. "This belonged to Winston Habbernathy."

"Is that who you're connecting with?" Steven asked.

I nodded. "Yes," I said. "And he's telling me how much he loved this house."

"Well, it was in his family for a long time before he sold it to Skolaris," said Muckleroy.

I felt my brows knit together. "That's wrong," I said, feeling out the message coming into my head. "Winston is telling me that the house was stolen from him."

"Stolen how?" asked Muckleroy.

"I can't tell," I said. "All he keeps saying is that it was stolen. He wanted to leave it to the children, but it was forced away from him."

"I am not understanding this," said Steven.

"Makes two of us," I said, still focused on Winston. "He says it served him right in the end."

"Served who right? Skolaris?" asked the detective.

"Hold on," I said, growing impatient at the nagging questions from Steven and Muckleroy while I tried to make sense of what Winston was trying to tell me. "He's saying he had to strike a deal, and that the deal was a crime. But it was to cover up a crime as well."

"Is she making sense to you?" I heard Muckleroy ask Steven.

"No more than usual," said Steven. "With M.J. I've learned to stay quiet and let her work it out."

"I'm trying to get him to tell me about what happened with these crimes he's talking about, but he's not elaborating. I also asked if he'd seen Skolaris on the other side, and he's saying Bill is still in shock, but they're working on him."

"Huh," said Muckleroy. "Almost sounds like he's at a hospital for the dead."

I opened my eyes and looked at the detective. "That's exactly where he is," I said. "Sometimes a spirit can cross over willingly, but be in a state of panic or shock about what's just happened to them. They are assisted by friends and family until they calm down and feel better about having to leave the earth plane."

"Wow," said Muckleroy. "Being dead sure gets complicated."

"Tell me about it," I said, closing my eyes again. In my head I said, *Talk to me about Hatchet Jack.*

The reaction I got was so intense I was unprepared for it. An emotion so heavy it felt crippling hit me like a ton of bricks, and I immediately started to cry. "M.J.?" Steven said, his voice alarmed. "Are you all right?"

"Oh, my God!" I said, reaching back behind me to steady myself against the dresser. "He's saying he's to blame! He's saying it was all his fault. The boys died because of him!"

Steven pulled me into his arms, and I sobbed and sobbed. "Shhh," Steven whispered. "It's all right."

Winston must have realized that he was emoting right through me, because he pulled his energy back and I felt immediately better. I gave one last hiccuplike sob and I was fine again. "I'm better," I said, wiping my eyes. "Jesus, that was intense."

"What made you cry?" Muckleroy asked me as I stepped back from Steven.

"It wasn't me crying," I said. "It was Winston. He feels that he's to blame for the boys being murdered."

"So *he* was Hatchet Jack?" Muckleroy asked, scratching his head. He was as confused as we were.

"No, but I think he knew what was going on and he didn't stop it," I said. "The poor man feels terrible about it. All that sobbing was him through me."

"Can you ask him if he knows who murdered Skolaris?" Muckleroy said.

I shook my head. "He pulled away. I think he realized he was really upsetting me and he zipped off."

We all looked at one another, more confused than ever, when Steven said, "Now what?"

Before I had a chance to answer, my cell rang. I answered it and was greeted with Gilley's excited voice. "Ohmigod! M.J., you have *got* to come back to the ski lodge *immediately!*"

"What's happened?" I demanded. The intensity of his rapid speech was making my heart race.

"Something you have to see to believe," he said. "But I will tell you that I think I just cracked this case *wide* open!"

"We're on our way," I said. "See you in fifteen."

CHAPTER 12

"What exactly am I looking at?" I asked Gilley as we all crowded around his laptop and squinted at the screen, which held three separate frames of still images, all of them photos of Northelm's graduating classes.

"You really don't see that?" Gilley said, pointing to the group of smiling children standing at the edge of a dock.

"Gil," I said evenly, as my patience began to wear thin.

"Here's a clue," Gilley said, ignoring the warning in my tone. "What's the difference between these two photos?"

"There's a dock in one and not in the other," said Steven.

"Exactly," said Gilley smugly. He then rooted around in some papers to his right and said, "When I was researching sightings of Hatchet Jack I stumbled across this one call to the police dispatcher in late fall of 1976."

"A burning dock," I said, looking at the paper he handed me. "Yeah, so?"

"*So,*" Gilley said, handing me another paper from the police blotter. It was the second report called in about a sighting involving Hatchet Jack running over water. My brows knit together as I tried to piece all this together, but before I could Gilley pointed to the computer screen again and moved the scroll bar to the third photo in the group he had selected. "This photo was taken in 1975. What does *that* look like?" he asked, hovering the cursor near an outcropping of trees on the scrubby island in the center of Hole Pond.

I squinted hard and moved my head closer to the screen. When I realized what I was looking at I gasped. "What?" Steven and Muckleroy said together.

"It's a cabin," I said. There was what appeared to be a small cottage on the island in the middle of Hole Pond.

Steven and Muckleroy looked at each other to see if either understood why I was so excited. Neither did, so I explained, "*That's* where Jack lived!"

Jaws dropped, and the two men stared at me in stunned silence. "He lives in that old cottage?" Muckleroy said.

"You've been there?" I asked.

"No," he said. "But my senior year of high school my dad and I went fishing at Hole Pond. I remember some sort of construction happening on the opposite side of the island. And a little while later I think I vaguely remember someone saying that Owen's father, Winston, was putting a small cottage in the middle of the island, which we all thought was nuts, because for such a small island the ground was probably really marshy. When I came back to Lake Placid after college the whole island was so overgrown and scrubby that I'd completely forgotten about it."

I hugged Gilley. "You are a freaking *genius!*" I said.

Gilley blushed. "I blame it on all the coffee I've had today," he said humbly.

I clapped my hands excitedly. "Okay, gentlemen. Tonight is the night we put that evil son of a bitch away forever. Gilley, take some notes; I've got a plan."

Gilley grabbed a legal pad and hovered his pen over the bright white page. "What's first?" he asked.

"First we need to find a local pool-supply store, and we need to find it fast."

"Come on, you guys!" I said, looking anxiously at my watch. "We're coming up short on time here!"

Gilley, Steven, and Muckleroy were all puffing heavily as they carried the last of the flotation-dock squares along the row that we'd tied together and dropped it in the water. I was hurrying along behind them with a piece of rope that would secure it in place with the others. The flotations were called Instadock, and they were commonly used in large swimming pools, where coaches liked to walk beside their swimmers as they swam down the lanes. As I'd spent many years in high school looking at the bottom of a pool through my swimming goggles, I was very aware of them and their handiness.

"Do we have time to get another one?" Steven panted over my shoulder. I looked at my watch, then at the distance between the last square and the small beach of the island. "I don't think so," I said. "It's quarter to six, and I need you rested as much as possible before we start this thing. Please tell me you can jump that?" I asked, pointing to the five-foot leap Steven would have to make to hit the beach.

He nodded. "I can make that," he said.

Standing up and wiping off my wet hands I turned to Gilley, who was looking around nervously. "Gil, you can head back to the van now and monitor from there. I'll need you to track Steven's every step, okay? I've got to know when he's made it to the dock."

"On it!" Gilley said, and dashed down the Instadock, heading for the van in the parking lot.

"Where do you need me?" Muckleroy said, still puffing hard from all the labor I'd put him through.

"You're in the van too," I said. "I don't want Jack distracted by too many bodies." Then I glanced to the edge of the pond at Dean Habbernathy, who was pacing back and forth and looking extremely upset about our whole production. "And, Bob, make sure the dean doesn't get in the way."

Muckleroy frowned as he looked over at Habbernathy. When we'd briefed the dean on our plans he'd vehemently protested, insisting that we not go onto the island, and he hadn't piped down until Muckleroy threatened to get a warrant for the entire school grounds. "On it," Muckleroy said, and he walked quickly down the Instadock, waving at the dean to follow him to our van.

"I should go then and get into position?" Steven said.

"Yeah," I said, turning to him with a grateful smile. "And listen, about snapping at you the other day . . ."

The corner of Steven's mouth curled up. "I am beginning to understand how focused you need to be on these jobs," he said before I had a chance to explain. "I will try not to be such a distraction to you in the future."

I gave him a wide grin. "Thanks for understanding," I said, and glanced at my watch. "Oh, crap! You only have ten minutes! Do you have the map?"

"I do."

"And the magnetic grenade in case things get dicey?"

"Right here," he said, reaching into his pocket to pat the lead pipe he carried.

"Okay," I said, blowing out a breath. "Just remember it's important that you work to feel scared. You're a big target for Jack, and he might not chase you, but I'm hoping that if you can give off a sense of fear he'll be too tempted to pass you up and give chase. And if he does, you really need to be careful, okay? This son of a bitch is dangerous, and I need you to make it here in one piece."

Steven stroked my cheek and gave me a gentle kiss before he said, "And I need you to make it in one piece as well. Be careful yourself." With that he turned and jogged away.

I watched him for a moment before I turned to the island. Backing up a few yards

I ran to the edge and leaped off, landing easily on the beach. From here there was the trail that I'd cleared out while the boys were laying the dock. It wound all the way to the deserted and boarded-up cabin in the heart of the island.

The place must have been well made, because it had held up well for thirty years. The windows and door were boarded up, and there hadn't been time to get inside yet. This was my last task before Jack appeared, as I knew he would, because Lance had told me he'd been chased along the trails leading near the island by Hatchet Jack thirty years ago on a Friday evening around six p.m. I just hoped that in re-creating this little scenario, everything went as planned. That Jack didn't actually catch up to Steven and knock him out, and that Steven made it here to me without Jack giving up the chase.

I knew Jack's portal was nearby, but I hadn't had a chance to search for it, and I had to get the planked-up door removed before Steven and Jack showed up, so my plan was simply to have Jack lead me directly to it.

I reached down and quickly unzipped my duffel bag. Putting on my wireless headphones I said into the microphone, "Gilley, do you copy? Over."

"I gotcha, M.J.," Gil said. "We're all in position except for Steven."

"Is he close?" I asked anxiously, glancing again at my watch.

"I'm here," Steven said, slightly out of breath.

I relaxed only a little. "Great. Steven, you'll need to start jogging slowly right at six p.m. If you hear footsteps behind you then increase your speed, but head directly here, okay?"

"Robert," Steven said.

I was walking over to the cabin's front door with a crowbar in my hand when he said that, and it made me pause. "Who's Robert?" I asked.

"The man you say when you are understanding something, correct?"

I grinned. "That's roger," I said.

"Oh."

"How're you coming on the front door, M.J.?" Gilley said.

I raised the crowbar and jammed it into the tight crevice between the plank and the front door. "I'm workin' on it." I grunted, pulling back on the crowbar with a groan.

"Better hurry it up," Gilley said anxiously. "We are three minutes to go time."

I moved the crowbar down a few inches

and pulled back again. The old wood came away much easier than I'd expected, and in another minute I had the wood plank almost completely off. "Two minutes!" Gilley called excitedly. "Steven? How you doing?"

"Nervous," said Steven. "But ready to run."

"Shit!" I said into the microphone.

"What's happening?" Gilley said. "M.J.? You okay?"

"I'm fine," I said, throwing the wood plank away to the side of the cabin. "But there's a solid wood door behind this plank and it's locked up tight."

"Can you get in?" Gilley asked.

"I'm running now," said Steven, and I looked down at my watch. It was six on the dot.

"I'm gonna have to," I said, raising the crowbar again and jamming it into the frame of the door. "Steven, what's your position?"

"I'm on the trail over at the dorm area," Steven said, breathing a little hard.

"Remember to keep it slow but work up some fear," I said, jamming the crowbar into the door again.

"How's the door coming, M.J.?" Gilley asked.

"Grah!" I said, pulling back with all my might on the crowbar. "You damned piece of wood! *Move!*"

"That answers that question," Gilley said.

"Son of a bitch!" I snapped as I pulled the crowbar out and regarded the door. "This thing isn't budging!"

"How about one of the windows?" Gilley suggested, and I could sense the tension building in his voice as Steven moved along the trails, waiting for Jack to show.

"Good idea!" I said, and quickly moved to one of the windows.

"Wait!" I heard Steven say, and I held my crowbar in the air, alarmed by his tone.

"What's the matter?" I asked.

"I think I heard footsteps," Steven said, and I knew he had automatically increased his speed.

With adrenaline now coursing through my veins I thrust the crowbar into the crevice between the board and the outside wall as hard as I could. The old wood splintered and cracked and a small piece of it broke off. "Steven, are you sure you have Jack in sight?" Gilley said into my ear.

"I am not sure," Steven said, his voice holding a bit of fear. "I thought I did, but now I am not sure."

I moved closer to the wood plank over the

window and examined it. If the wood gave way in small chunks instead of one big piece it would take me longer to remove it. "M.J.?"

"I'm here," I said, moving the crowbar up along the other side of the window and gently easing it away from the wood of the cabin.

"How's it coming?" he asked anxiously.

"Focus on Steven," I commanded. I didn't want to add any more tension to the moment by revealing that I was having a hard time getting inside the cabin.

"Steven?" Gilley asked. "What's your status?"

There was puffing through the airwaves, and I knew Steven was still jogging along on the trail. "No sign of him yet," Steven said; then a moment later we all heard Steven's voice spike. "What was that?!"

"You heard something?" Gilley said.

"Ahhhhhhhhhhhhhhhh!" Steven screamed, and it was so piercing that I dropped the crowbar and yanked at my earpiece.

When I'd collected myself I shoved it back in my ear, and I could hear Gilley's voice shaking over the airwaves. "Just run, Steven! Run!"

"He's right behind me!"

"M.J.! I am tracking Steven along the trail.

He is T minus thirty seconds from the dock! What is your status with getting into the cabin?"

My knuckles were white as they gripped along the crowbar and pulled at the wood, tearing it away from the window frame inch by inch. "Almost . . . there . . ." I puffed.

"Ahhhhhh!" Steven screamed again, and I winced but kept going.

"Steven?!" Gilley squealed. "What's happening?"

"I see him! I see him! He's right behind me!" Steven shouted.

"Run!" I shouted to Steven. "Get to the dock, Steven, and run for your life!"

"He's on top of me!" Steven yelled. "I'm going for the grenade!"

"No!" I commanded as the plank finally came completely away from the wall and fell to the ground. "You're almost here! Run to me!"

In my other ear I could faintly hear the pounding of footsteps and splashing water. Steven was at the Instadock, and I still had a glass window to break. Holding the crowbar like a bat I swung with all my might and smashed the window into dozens of shards.

"M.J.!" Steven yelled, and I could hear him both in my ear and in the distance.

"I'm . . . almost . . . there!"

My heart thundered in my chest as I pulled the crowbar out of the window and smashed at the remaining glass. "Keep coming!" I shouted.

"He's cleared the dock!" Gilley shouted. "M.J., he's almost to you!"

I grabbed at the sides of the window and pulled myself quickly inside. There was a stabbing sensation in my leg, but a nanosecond later I'd hit the floor and I rolled away.

"I can see the cabin!" Steven yelled. *"M.J.! Open the door!"*

I bolted to my feet and took two lunging steps to the door. Snatching at the dead bolt I flipped it back and hauled at the handle. The door stuck fast, and I stumbled backward. "Shit!" I swore.

"Open the door, M.J.! Open it!" Gilley now.

I flew at the door and firmly gripped the handle. Gritting my teeth I set my foot against the doorjamb and gave a tremendous heave. I felt the door giving way and shouted, "Steven! Use the grenade! *Now!*"

The door released its tight seal on the jamb and opened wide. Through the opening I could see Steven running for me just yards away, and Hatchet Jack in full horrific human form was chasing him down with a bloody hatchet waving wildly about his head. Steven had the magnetic grenade out of his pocket, and he pulled at the top before tipping it and pulling out the magnetic spike.

The air seemed to ripple around him, and I watched Jack's form waver and spin away from Steven, who had suddenly stumbled and was going down. "Hold on to the spike!" I yelled at him, and somehow he did and rolled to the side of the path leading to the front door.

Jack's face was a mixture of hatred and confusion as he skirted away from Steven and the painful reaction of the magnetic spike. "Yo!" I shouted at him. "Ugly! Over here!"

Jack's face jerked up and he looked at me with his soulless eyes. There was something like a growl that emanated from him, and I knew he recognized me as the one who had stolen Hernando away from him. "That's right," I called, and moved backward into the cabin. "Come to Mama!"

Jack's figure disappeared, but there was a pounding of footsteps dashing to the cabin, and quickly I retrieved my own grenade from my coat pocket. I could feel him when he entered the cabin, a sort of smoldering electrical current oozing with hatred and malice. A dusty old chair by a stone fireplace toppled over, and a picture on the wall fell to the floor with a loud crash.

"Here I am!" I goaded. "Come and get me, hatchet man!"

I had moved behind the kitchen table, and without warning it slammed into me. I fell forward onto the top of the table with a loud, "Ugh!" as I felt it pushing me backward against the wall.

The lead pipe holding my spike had dropped from my grasp, and I watched in horror as it rolled across the tabletop and onto the floor with a thud. "The spike!" I yelled the moment before my back was slammed into the wall.

The table came up and smashed me against the wall with an incredible force. I couldn't get air into my lungs, and my arms were pinned next to me.

"M.J.?!" Gilley squealed. "M.J.! Come in, M.J!"

I couldn't respond; my head was pressed sideways, and my chest couldn't move to speak or take in air.

"He's got her wedged behind a table!" I heard Steven shout. And suddenly the table dropped and I was free.

I took a deep breath and looked at Steven in the doorway, still holding his spike in his hand. Jack's energy had retreated away into one corner by the fireplace, and as I fought for air I waved Steven back away from the door. "I got it from here," I said, quickly retrieving my lead pipe from the floor.

Steven looked concerned, but he complied.

"What's happening?" Gilley shouted, and Steven brought him up to speed while I inched forward to the repellent nastiness in the corner of the room. "So, you like to murder little boys?" I said with loathing. "And you like to scare people around here as well, huh, Hatchet Jack?"

There was an awful laughing sound that came from the corner of the room. "Tag," I heard him say. "You're it!" And with that he charged me.

I stood my ground until he was almost directly on top of me, and that was when I released my own grenade. The room rippled and the ether shook, and I could feel the impact of Jack's energy as it hit the magnetic force field my spike had created. He bounced away from me, and I charged at him with my spike held high over my head, and his energy shifted from predator to prey. I could feel him become panicked, and he ducked around me and dashed to the other side of the cabin through a closed door.

I chased after him and said, "I've got him cornered!" into my microphone. With my adrenaline fueling new strength I kicked the door open violently, and as I entered the doorway I came up short.

The room had been a bedroom. It smelled of dust, mold, and something else too nasty to describe. There was a rotten old bed in the center of the room, and on it a skeleton lay fully clothed with a hatchet sticking up out of the center of its chest. Above the headboard was a vapory, round ball of energy. Jack's portal.

Recovering myself I moved quickly forward to the bed and pulled a chair close to the edge. Standing on it I heaved the spike into the very center of the portal, and I saw the ether around it shiver and become unsteady.

"I've got him!" I shouted. "Steven, if you're outside, please bring me my duffel bag with my drill and the other spikes."

"Coming!" Steven called.

"M.J.?" Gilley said. "What's your status?"

I wiped my brow and stepped off the chair, bending over to catch my breath. "Jack's trapped," I said. "It's safe to come here, Gil. And please bring Muckleroy. He'll want to see this to believe it."

CHAPTER 13

"Jesus, Mary, and Joseph!" Muckleroy said when he entered the doorway to Jack's bedroom.

I was back on the chair with a hammer and my spikes, pounding them into the wall and sealing up the spirit of Hatchet Jack forever.

"Whoa," said Gilley. "That is freaky!"

I stepped off the chair, panting for breath. Steven handed me a bottle of water from my duffel, and I took it gratefully. "At least now we know what happened to Jack," Muckleroy said, indicating the hatchet sticking out of his skeleton.

"Not quite," I said, and looked at the dean standing directly behind Muckleroy. "What we need to put all these pieces into place is to hear from one of the boys Jack brought here to play his sick and twisted games with." With that I took a long swig of the water before pointing to the opposite wall, where four sets of shackles were screwed into the wood.

Everyone turned to look where I was pointing. Everyone, that is, but the dean. I smiled, because then I knew for certain I was right on the money. "He offered to take you boys fishing, didn't he, Dean?"

Muckleroy and Gilley snapped their heads back to me; then they both turned and stepped away from Dean Habbernathy. "I don't know what you're talking about," the dean said.

"Ah, but I'm afraid you do," I said. "You and Nicky both know."

The dean blanched, and his face drained of color. We all watched him carefully as he put a steadying hand out to the door frame. "You don't understand," he said.

"I think I do. It didn't make sense until I saw the shackles," I said. "There's a set for Eric and Mark, but the two extras threw me until I thought it through. At first I thought that one of the sets might have been for Hernando, but then I remember Maude's sister telling us that Jack took a group of boys from the foster home to go fishing in August. That means he'd already killed Hernando. So the two other sets of shackles could only belong to two other previously unidentified boys. And then I started thinking about how you told us Jack had chased after you when you were young, and how Eric had saved you. That wasn't the ghost of Eric and Jack, was it? That was the real, live boy and the man."

The dean stared at me with large, unblinking eyes, as if I were recalling memories that were terrifying to him. Finally, and almost imperceptibly, he nodded. "Nicky and Eric were brothers," he said. "We all lived with Maude up until Jack took us and brought us here. After that night Winston Habbernathy took us in, and from that point forward I became Owen Habbernathy."

"Tell us what happened, Owen," I said.

The dean let out a long breath and sagged against the wall. "Jack took the four of us here one weekend to fish on the pond and have a sleepover."

"The four of you?" Muckleroy asked.

The dean nodded. "Yes. It was me, Eric, Mark, and Nicky, but back then his name was Ethan, and my name was John."

Muckleroy had taken a small pad and a pen out of his pocket and was scribbling notes on the pad. He looked up and asked, "John who?"

The dean smiled sadly. "Smith," he said. "As mundane and ordinary a name as they come."

Muckleroy looked at him with sympathy and waved his hand. "Please continue, Dean."

"When we arrived on the school grounds Jack gave us a tour. He said that he was the groundskeeper here, that he knew the property like the back of his hand. He added that there were no hiding places that he hadn't already discovered, and the only area that was off-limits to him was the dean's private suite — where Nicky now lives."

"That's why Jack's ghost never goes there," I said, clicking that piece of the puzzle into place.

Owen nodded. "Yes, which is exactly why, when Nicky got older and wanted some independence, I felt it was a good place for him to stay. My father, the former dean, had used it as his private suite during those nights he worked late here at the school. When Nicky wanted a chance to live on his own, I felt it was the safest spot for him."

"And it was," I said. "A safe place for him to live and be close to his real brother, Eric."

The dean's shoulders slumped and he continued with his story. "As I was saying, initially Jack appeared to be true to his word; the weekend began as planned. We took the tour of the school, fished on the pond, and cooked dinner here in the cabin. Jack seemed to be perfectly normal, and there was nothing in his manner or behavior that alarmed or frightened us. Then, as dusk settled, things changed."

"How so?" I asked.

The dean drew a deep breath and let it out slowly. "I couldn't really put my finger on it. One minute he was telling us stories of his time in Vietnam — he had served a tour of duty there — and the next he was fidgety and anxious. Almost nervous."

"When did you know you were in trouble?" Gilley wanted to know.

The dean's mouth pulled down into a deep frown. "When he got up from the table and walked to his bedroom door. He told us that he wanted to play a game of tag with us, but first he had something to show us in his bedroom. We followed after him like trusting fools, and a moment later he'd grabbed Nicky and had him shackled to the wall. Eric went crazy and jumped on his back to kick and punch him, but Jack knocked him out cold with a solid punch to the face."

"That's awful." I gasped.

"It gets worse," said the dean. "Mark and I were terrified, and we ran for the front door, but it was locked tight and we couldn't

416

get out. Jack then shackled me up next to Nicky and secured Eric's unconscious body before taking Mark by the scruff of the neck, and he left the cabin."

Muckleroy stopped scribbling. "Where'd he go?"

The dean closed his eyes as a wave of emotion seemed to overwhelm him. After a moment and in a hoarse whisper he said, "Somewhere out on the grounds. It was quiet for a long time. Nicky and I were straining to hear anything at all, and then the silence was broken by screams — Mark's screams. Eric woke up just as the last of them died out, and I suppose that's when Mark died as well."

Everyone in the room was silent for a long moment, but finally Steven said, "Then what happened?"

"We heard digging," said the dean. "I learned later that it was Jack digging Mark's grave behind the cabin. After that Jack came back into the cabin. He was covered in mud, sweat, and blood. He was wearing this crazy smile and holding this bloody hatchet. He pointed to me and Eric and said, 'Normally I like to play this game with just one of you, but I think I'm up for something more challenging.' And that's when he unshackled the two of us and dragged us out onto the school grounds. The sun had completely set by then, but the moon was full, and Jack pointed to a tree on the other side of the pond. He told us that was home base, and if we got there we were free, but if we didn't we were dead. He then turned his back on us and began to count."

"Sick son of a bitch," Muckleroy spat.

"How did you survive?" I asked.

The dean pushed away from the wall and began to pace the room as he spoke. "Eric ran and pulled me along. He said that Jack would expect us to go right for the tree, and that he probably didn't mean it when he said the tree would give us our freedom. He said we'd have to hide out for a while; then we could try to make it off the school grounds and go for help."

"So you ran to the elementary wing," I said, sliding in another piece of the puzzle.

The dean nodded. "Yes. We hid there for a while, lying low, and we were beginning to think we had outsmarted that lunatic when we heard Jack calling for us out on the grounds. He said that if we didn't show ourselves he was going to play his game of tag with Ethan."

"Nicky," I said as I felt the color drain from my face. "That bastard!"

"Eric couldn't let that happen," said the

dean. "He came up with a plan. He said that he was going to make a run for the tree. While he led Jack away from me he wanted me to go back to the cabin, free Ethan, and run for help."

"And did you?" Muckleroy said.

"Yes," said the dean. "And we almost made it. To this day I don't know if Eric ever made it to the tree, but I managed to get back to the cabin, and I found a screwdriver in Jack's toolbox. I had just gotten to work on the last screw holding Nicky's shackles when the cabin door flew open and Jack came in. He saw us, and something terrible let loose in him. He grabbed Nicky's hair and slammed his head so hard against the wall that Nicky was knocked out. I tried to dodge around Jack and get to the open door, but he grabbed my arm so hard that my shoulder became dislocated. I remember screaming, and the horrible pain, but not much else for many moments. I only remember Jack putting my good arm back in the shackles, and that's when Eric appeared in the bedroom doorway."

"Eric was still *alive?*" Steven and Gilley said in unison.

The dean nodded. "I don't know how, from the looks of his wounds. He was bleeding from his chest and his head, and he was so pale and weak he could barely stand. Jack was too busy trying to restrain me to notice, and I made sure to keep up the fight while Eric picked up the bloody hatchet Jack had used on his victims and he hit Jack in the back of the head with it."

"Jesus, Mary, and Joseph," said Muckleroy as he crossed himself. "It's like a scene out of a horror movie."

The dean sank down to the floor and stared blankly at the wall where the shackles hung rusty and old against the rotting wood. "You would have thought that the blow Eric gave him would have finished Jack off, but that monster just got up and staggered around the room."

"How did he end up over there, then?" asked Gilley, pointing to the skeleton on the bed.

"I shouted at Eric to hit him again, and he did. I think he used up every last bit of life he had left in him, because he drove that damn hatchet right into Jack's heart, and the bastard fell back on the bed and died."

The room fell silent again as we all gazed at Jack's skeleton. Finally Muckleroy said, "How long after that did Eric die?"

The dean closed his eyes, and a tear slid down his cheek. "It wasn't long," he whispered. "Eric crawled over to where Nicky was lying on the floor by the door and wrapped himself around his little brother. I heard him breathe maybe two or three more times, and then he was still."

"Who found you?" I asked.

"My father, or rather, Winston Habbernathy. I started screaming for help at first light, and the dean had come to check up on his brother. He found me here."

"Who's his brother?" Gilley said.

"Why, Jack, of course," said the dean distastefully.

"Hatchet Jack was the dean's *brother?*" Muckleroy exclaimed.

"Yes, Bob, I'm afraid so. You see, Jack was Winston's older brother, and my adopted grandfather, Morton Habbernathy, planned to leave the school to both Jack and Winston. But as Winston explained, when Jack came back from Vietnam he was a different man. Winston described him as angry and given to violent mood swings. According to Winston, Jack even punched his father out when Morton wouldn't let Jack drive the family car. Things eventually got so bad between Jack and his father that the old man disinherited Jack and left the school solely to Winston. Jack disappeared shortly thereafter. Winston believed he became a drifter, one of the thousands of vets who felt disenfranchised with their homeland on their return from war."

"Then how did he end up here again?" Muckleroy said.

"Winston said that at the end of the school year Jack simply appeared in the doorway of his office. He'd been living off what he could earn on the bowling circuit and he said he was tired of traveling and just needed a place to stay and a good job. Winston felt pity for his older brother, but was still a bit nervous about Jack's mood swings, especially around the children. He made a deal with Jack, and that was that he could build this cabin and maintain the grounds during the summer, and if Jack behaved himself, then Winston would consider keeping him on once the school year began again."

"But something happened, didn't it?" I asked, sensing there was a little more to the story.

The dean nodded. "Yes. My father said that one night he found Jack drunk, soaking wet, and covered in scratches and bruises. When Winston demanded to know what had happened, Jack said he couldn't remember, but that he had found a wallet somewhere in town, and it didn't belong to him."

"Whose wallet?" I asked.

"A boy named Richard Crosby. Winston always felt like something terrible had happened that night. That Jack and this Richard Crosby had had some sort of altercation, and that Richard had come out on the losing end."

Immediately I felt a presence bump hard up against my energy, and when I directed my attention toward it I gave an audible gasp. I recognized the energy. "Ohmigod!" I said, staring at Gilley with wide eyes.

"What?" Gilley said, giving me a puzzled look.

"It's *Richard!*" I said. Gilley shook his head; he didn't make the connection.

"The ghost from the View Restaurant?" Steven asked, and I blinked at him, amazed that he'd caught on so quickly.

I pumped my head vigorously. "Yes!" I said. "Jack killed him!"

"Freaky," Gil said.

"Would someone please explain to me what's going on?" said Muckleroy.

I turned to him and explained that Gil, Steven, and I had all eaten at the posh restaurant on Mirror Lake, where we'd met a waiter named Andrew whose brother had disappeared some thirty years earlier. I explained that the spirit of Andrew's brother had come through to me and said that he'd been murdered, drowned at the hands of someone else.

"That *is* freaky," said Muckleroy. "So this Richard Crosby was Jack's first victim?"

"Probably," I said. "And also might have been the catalyst for his deciding to choose younger and more manageable victims. Thirteen-year-olds are easier to tackle than sixteen-year-olds."

"Didn't Winston think about going to the police?"

"Yes," said the dean. "I suspect he did. But my father was a fiercely loyal man, and because he didn't know for certain he made the grave mistake of waiting and watching. He decided to keep a *very* close eye on Jack, which is why he would come to check on Jack early every morning. And, as it turned out, that's why Nicky is alive today. A few more hours with the brain injury he sustained and he wouldn't be with us."

"So, let me get this straight," said Muckleroy. "Winston Habbernathy shows up here and sees two dead bodies and two seriously hurt little boys, and he doesn't go to the police about it?"

The dean nodded sadly. "Yes, I'm afraid he felt that if it ever got out what horrible things his brother had done, people would hold Winston accountable. After all, Winston knew how unstable his brother was, and I don't think he was strong enough to handle the ridicule and shame that would have followed.

"For a while I was the only person who knew the truth. Nicky was in a coma, and when he regained consciousness he had no memory of what had happened, and he had serious developmental issues, so my father knew he would never tell. And to keep me quiet Winston promised me the thing that I'd always wanted: a family and a home and a good education. I never blamed him for caring about his brother. I knew Winston was a good man, and to his credit he treated me like his own flesh and blood from day one."

"But didn't the doctors question him when he showed up at the hospital with two children with severe wounds?" I asked.

The dean sighed. "Nicky was the only one in need of their attention. Winston had done three years of medical school before his father died, and he'd had to quit to take over as dean of the school. He reset my shoulder and tucked me away in his house while he took Nicky to the local hospital. There he claimed that Nicky was his nephew, and that his brother had left him in his care while on a fishing trip. He explained Nicky's injury by saying that Nicky had fallen out of a tree and hit his head. Later he told people that his brother had drowned on the fishing trip and that he planned on adopting his nephews. Winston managed to obtain some forged birth certificates for Nicky and me, changing our names in the process, and within two years the State of New York granted his request for adoption of his two nephews, Nicholas and Owen Habbernathy."

"I can't believe anyone bought that!" Gilley said.

The dean gave him a patient look. "It was the seventies," he said. "People around town weren't as suspicious as they are now. Besides, my father was a very upstanding member of this community. No one suspected that he wasn't telling the truth, because he would have no reason they could think of to lie."

"So he covered up the murders, buried Eric by the big tree, and burned down the dock?" I asked.

"Yes. He wanted Eric to be laid to rest away from this island. Since the tree had been symbolic of escaping Jack, it seemed a natural place to bury him. As for the burning of the dock, well that wasn't the real target. My father wanted to burn down the cabin, but he started the fire on the dock, and the accelerant leading from the dock to the cabin didn't catch. The fire department arrived and there wasn't time to remedy the situation. After that my father couldn't very well attempt to burn down the cabin again; that would have drawn serious attention. So he took out the charred remains of the dock and hoped that no one ever ventured onto the scrubby island again. He didn't really have reason to worry, because within a few months the scrub had become so overgrown here that it completely hid the cabin anyway."

"So no one else knew about any of this?" said Muckleroy. "Just you and Winston?"

"And Skolaris," I said, sliding one more piece of the puzzle into place. "I'm betting he knew."

Owen looked sharply at me, but as the hard stares from the rest of us bore into him, he knew it was time to give up the ghost. "Yes," he said after a long moment. "Bill Skolaris knew."

"How'd he find out?" Muckleroy asked quietly.

"My father needed to trust someone to watch over me while he tended to Nicky at the hospital. He and Bill were the best of friends, and so he let Bill in on what had happened. At first Bill was very supportive of keeping things quiet, but then the greed must have set in, and the blackmail followed."

"That's how Skolaris got your dad's house," I said. "Skolaris forced him to give the deed over."

"That and a hefty pay increase," said Owen.

"And everything was quiet until we started putting up those posters, and Skolaris got greedy again," I said.

Muckleroy lifted an eyebrow as he too made the connection. Turning to the dean he said, "Why'd you do it, Owen? Why'd you kill Bill?"

The dean shook his head. "He was going to ruin *everything*," he said, and for the second time that day the dean's eyes welled with tears. "Skolaris said that if I didn't give him more money he was going to take those posters to the police and tell them all of it. I begged him not to, and I told him that I'd already sunk all of our extra cash back into the school's renovation. I couldn't possibly come up with more money. But that didn't satisfy him — oh, no. He decided to use the trauma of what happened to me to his advantage. He told me to meet him on the grounds that night, and he pushed one of the posters in my face. I tried to back away, but that's when he pulled out a hatchet and began waving it around. Something in my head just went off. It was like I couldn't control the impulse. I grabbed that hatchet and I struck him until he fell to the ground."

"So that was you who came after me?" I said. "You were chasing me across the lawn after murdering Skolaris?"

"No," the dean said wearily. "I was running away from what I'd done. My car was parked behind the main hall, in the administrative lot. I thought for sure that you had clearly seen me and you were on your way to the police. I was trying to get to my car and get away when Nicky found me, and in a moment of panic I told him to bury the hatchet while I went to his apartment and came up with a plan. It was there that I received the call from the dispatcher on my cell phone. She said that something terrible had happened at the school, and that I needed to get right over there. I realized then that you hadn't gotten a good look at me, and the police might be looking for Hatchet Jack, not me."

"So you showered, changed into Nicky's pajamas, and looked like you'd just gotten out of bed," I said.

The dean looked down at the ground. "Yes," he mumbled. "But at the time I had no idea that Nicky was going to end up accused of the crime. I hadn't realized he'd get caught with the hatchet."

Muckleroy tucked his small notepad away into his pocket and reached behind him to pull out a pair of handcuffs. "Dean Habbernathy, you have the right to remain silent . . ."

As the detective led Dean Habbernathy away, I found it interesting that Muckleroy read Owen his rights *after* the dean had made a full confession — in other words, any lawyer worth his salt could get the confession bounced out on its ear. Something told me Muckleroy was very aware of that too.

Gilley and Steven helped me clean up the equipment, and after closing the bedroom door to shut away the horror inside until the police could deal with it, the three of us headed to the front door of the cabin, wanting to be as far away from this awful place as possible.

Gilley and Steven stepped outside first, but I paused in the doorway when I felt a little tug that called me to look back at the bedroom door. Standing there against it was the beautiful smiling face of Eric. The vision of him caught me a little off guard, and I stood staring at him dumbly. *I'll be okay now,* he said, and I watched as he looked up above him and a ball of light came down to engulf him. Before I even had time to react he was gone.

"M.J.?" Gilley said from outside. "You ready to go home?"

I glanced over my shoulder, making a mental note to contact Dory with a full update on her sons. "Yeah," I said, feeling a smile spread to my lips. "I sure am."

Hours later we were sitting in front of a fire at Karen's place, sipping the wine I'd bought from Lance and feeling good about ourselves. "I can't believe how involved this thing was," said Karen as we finished telling her the story. "And I can't believe you guys left me here to sleep while you all chased down the bad guys."

"What were you gonna do?" I asked her with a smirk. "Flirt the truth out of the dean?"

"Hey," Karen said, grinning back. "Don't knock flirting; it's gotten me through some pretty tough spots before."

"Trust me," I said, "the thing that's gotten you through those tough spots was the fact that you're a knockout, not the fact that you can flirt."

From outside there came a now familiar thumping sound. Gilley's head snapped to attention. "Ohmigod!" he squealed with delight. "Could that be Mr. John Dodge returning for his ladylove?" Gilley *loved* romance.

Karen stood and set down her wineglass. "Actually," she said with a hint of mischief, "I believe *that* ride is for the three of *you*."

We all got up and followed her curiously to the front door, where Charlie, the pilot who had whisked her away earlier, stood with his hat tucked under one arm. "I'm here to pick up the passengers, Miss O'Neal," he said.

Turning back to the three curious folks behind her, she said, "All aboard for Cabo San Lucas!"

Gilley squealed so loud I thought he punctured my eardrum. That was quickly followed by his mad dash to his room to pack his belongings. "Really?" I said to her as Steven and I stood dumbly looking at Charlie and the waiting chopper on the front lawn.

"Really," she said. "You guys deserve a vacation, especially after all you've been through. John owns a lovely all-inclusive time-share there. He's asked that you be his personal guests for the next ten days."

"I'll get my things," Steven said, and hurried after Gilley.

"But what about Doc?" I said, stunned that she seemed to be serious.

"Take him," Teeko said. "Something tells me he'll feel right at home in the tropics."

I leaned in and gave her a giant hug. "Thanks, girlfriend."

"Just do me one favor," she said as I was about to turn away and do my own packing.

"What's that?"

"Don't come back without having figured things out between you and Steven."

"Kind of a tall order," I said to her.

"Well, you have ten days to work it out, M.J. I believe that should be plenty of time."

"Okay," I said, narrowing my eyes at her. "I'll figure it out with the good doctor if you figure it out with the good billionaire."

Charlie cleared his throat and turned away from the door.

Karen looked over her shoulder at him and gave a small sigh. Looking back to me she held out her hand and said, "Deal," and I knew then that I was in deep doo-doo.

ABOUT THE AUTHOR

Real-life psychic **Victoria Laurie** has used her unique understanding of intuition and the business of being a professional psychic to create her series characters M.J. Holliday and Abby Cooper. She lives in Austin, Texas, with her two spoiled dachshunds, Lilly and Toby, and a talkative African Grey parrot named Doc. Find out more about her psychic abilities at www.VictoriaLaurie .com.

The employees of Thorndike Press hope you have enjoyed this Large Print book. All our Thorndike and Wheeler Large Print titles are designed for easy reading, and all our books are made to last. Other Thorndike Press Large Print books are available at your library, through selected bookstores, or directly from us.

For information about titles, please call:
(800) 223-1244

or visit our Web site at:
http://gale.cengage.com/thorndike

To share your comments, please write:
Publisher
Thorndike Press
295 Kennedy Memorial Drive
Waterville, ME 04901